No Skylarks Sing

Millie Vigor

ROBERT HALE · LONDON

First published in Great Britain 2013

ISBN 978-0-7198-0957-6

Robert Hale Limited
Clerkenwell House
Clerkenwell Green
London EC1R 0HT

www.halebooks.com

2 4 6 8 10 9 7 5 3 1

Typeset in 10.75/15pt Palatino
Printed by MPG Printgroup, UK

Dedication

This book is for Slim because he whispered in my ear and said, 'Get on with it,' for Lizzie too because she believed in me.

Acknowledgements

I wish to thank all those people who have put me right where I tended to go wrong. Jennifer and Maurice Sutherland for crofting procedures, John Whitehead who explained fighting moves. Paul Rutherford of D-S-R for legal advice. Mary Blance for being brave enough to read the un-polished typescript. Martin and Sue Platt, Leslie Watts, Laura Friedlander and Betty Riddell of the Rebel Writers for good natured comments and criticism. Last, but by no means least, all at Robert Hale Ltd without whom this book would not have materialised.

ONE

1961

THE ROOM WAS warm. On the mantelpiece an old American clock ticked gently. On top of the stove, fired by peat, a kettle quirked and grunted as it made up its mind to come to the boil. Catherine was mixing pastry and from time to time, as her hands dipped in and out of the bowl, the chink of a gold ring against china joined the other lazy sounds. Her eldest child Robbie, born after his father's death and named after him, sat at the end of the table studying his books.

'What are you working on now?' asked Catherine.

'Seamanship and navigation.'

'*What? No,*' shouted Catherine. '*No.*'

'But I want to be a fisherman.'

'*No. No.*' She thumped the table with her fist. 'I will *not let you.*'

'But, Mam, I've made up my mind. Grandpa was a fisherman, so was my da and I want to be one.' Robbie's determination showed in the jut of his jaw.

Catherine looked at him. When his father said he was going to fish for a living she had had a premonition of disaster, and what had happened? He had an accident, went overboard and drowned. 'No,' she said. 'I won't let you. There's plenty of time yet to decide what you want to do.'

'I don't think so, Mother. I have to start learning now.'

'Have you forgotten how your father died?' she said. 'Your grandma said it was my fault and blamed me. You *can't* know what she put me through. Would you want that for me again?'

Robbie sat opposite her. 'It's not going to happen, Mam. I'd be on a bigger boat with a skipper and more crew. Dad was fishing single-handed. I wouldn't be.'

Catherine shook her head. 'No, Robbie. There's no need for you to go to sea. I worked to build the business your father wanted; now the sheep flock's getting bigger. There'll always be a job for you here.'

Unblinking, Robbie stared at her. 'But I don't want to be a crofter.'

Catherine had seen that look before; he'd made up his mind and she knew how stubborn he could be. 'Don't you ever listen to the news?' she said. 'Another fishing boat lost and most, if not all of the crew, drowned. Fishing's very dangerous no matter what size the boat or how many there are on board.'

'There's danger in everything, Mother.'

He was right, of course, but who wants a child to remind them? 'I need you here, Robbie. You promised to help with the sheep, remember?'

'I can still do that. I'll be at school for some time yet and anything can happen. I might not pass the exams.' Robbie came to stand beside her. He put an arm round her waist and hugged her. 'Dinna fret, Mam. It's no happened yet.'

He had looked her straight in the eye and, unable to out-stare him, she had had to look away. He called her 'Mother' and dropped the accent with which he usually spoke, only resorting to it when he felt he had made his point and was winning.

'You needn't try to use your charm and soft-soap me, Robbie Jameson,' she said. 'I am not going to give in. We'll talk about this later. Now take your books away and leave me to get on with this.' She poured water into the pastry mix, stirred it together then lifted it out and slapped it on the table. Alone again she looked at the lump of pastry and, innocent though it was, with a roar of rage she thumped it with her rolling pin. The boy had stubbornly set his heart on going to sea. What was she going to do? For the moment there was nothing, so she went to work on the pastry. It would be heavy today for anger transmitted itself to her hands.

As she rolled and turned the pastry, rolled and turned again, Catherine let her thoughts wander back to that cold December day in 1952 when, mother of a five-year-old son, she had married Norrie Williams. No longer did she have to care alone for little Robbie, a flock of sheep and a croft; she had a partner to help her, a lover to share her bed and a father for her son. Norrie had filled her days with love and laughter and a year later she had given birth to their daughter, Judith. Another year and there were the twins, Peter and Allen.

Deepdale, the valley to which Robbie's father had brought her, was still her home, for she had moved into Norrie's house leaving her own to stand empty. The valley was isolated, a closed community containing only four dwelling-houses. Robbie's grandparents, John Jameson, more affectionately known as Daa, and Jannie, his wife, lived in one of them. Daa was a kind, gentle man, but Jannie, who had not hesitated to show her dislike of her son's English wife, was at times still inclined to sting with waspish words. Jannie's younger sister, Laura, living alone in the valley now since Mina, eldest of the three sisters had died, was a sweet old lady and Catherine was very fond of her. As she worked, filling a dish with rhubarb then putting on a pastry lid, Catherine smiled. The bad days were behind her; she had a family now, she was happy, and she wanted it to stay that way.

The pie was in the oven when she heard Norrie's van pull up.

'You're late,' she said, when he walked in. 'I thought I heard you come down the track a while ago. Where have you been?'

'Daa stopped me. He wants to give up the croft and asked if I would take it on. His rheumatism's bad. Have you seen the way his hands are knotted up? It's a wonder he can still milk the cow.'

'And you said you would.'

'What else could I do?'

'Nothing, I suppose. How was the rest of your day?'

Norrie took off his work boots and hung up his jacket. He soaped his hands to wash them. 'I was in the town,' he said, 'and I saw somebody I thought I knew. But it couldn't have been.' He rinsed his hands and reached for a towel. 'I thought it looked like my cousin Magnie, but … no. I haven't seen him for … oh, must be twenty years or more. It had better not be him.'

'Why?'

'The family emigrated, went to Australia. They were a quarrelsome lot. I wasn't the only one glad to see them go. If it was him, you can bet he's up to no good.' As if wiping his cousin away Norrie dried his hands then threw the towel into a laundry basket.

'I've been going through the books today,' said Catherine. 'Money's going out as fast as it's coming in. We've got to do something about it and I was wondering if we could do up my old house and let it. The rent would help.' Her house, the one that she and Robbie's father had lived in had been left to stand empty since her marriage to Norrie. 'My house needs to be lived in; it will fall apart if it's not. Do you think we could do it up and let it?'

'It'll cost money,' said Norrie. He had extended his house to accommodate his growing family and the coming of electricity and piped water had brought it up to date. The work had taken time and money. The bank balance was at low ebb and with Catherine fully occupied at home there were only Norrie's wages and the sparse income from the crofts to feed it. 'And do you want to bring strangers in?' he went on.

'I was a stranger once. We need to do something. The house should be put to use instead of being left to rot. It's either that or I go back to work.'

'We're not that bad off, are we? And you've got enough to do here without another job.' Norrie had no time for paperwork. Catherine was the book-keeper. 'Doing up the house will cost money,' he repeated.

'I know. But surely we only need to add a bathroom and a new cooker?'

Norrie was silent for a moment. 'We ought to have a look, estimate what it's going to cost.'

Change and more change, thought Catherine as she followed Norrie, not only with people, but with the land. When the first tractors had arrived from America – lease-lend they called it – old pastures had been ploughed and new varieties of grass sown. With government grants providing money to buy seed and pay for the work, reseeding was now gaining momentum; larger areas were turning green and, with the growing prowess of tractor drivers, creeping up the hillsides. She thought back to the enthusiasm with which Robbie Jameson had talked of his plans. 'The hills will go green,' he had said.

'Anyway, I've decided to give it a go,' said Norrie.

'What?'

'You haven't you been listening, have you?'

'Sorry, I was miles away,' said Catherine. 'What did you say?'

'Never mind, it'll keep for later. Come on. Let's see what I might be letting myself in for.'

Catherine had opened windows and doors from time to time to let the air blow through her house, but otherwise hadn't spent any time there. It always tugged at her heart and brought back memories, but memories could not be allowed to intrude today. As Norrie took measurements and calculated materials, she followed him and wrote it all down in a notebook.

'With a bit of luck and somebody to help I reckon I could get it done in a month,' said Norrie. 'I don't know about the stove, but maybe this one will do.'

'So you think we can do it, then?'

'Probably. Look, I'm playing tonight so I'll have to have a bath. Let's go.'

Norrie was an excellent fiddle player and much in demand to play at dances and other social gatherings. Catherine sighed. It would be another lonely evening for her.

TWO

'TAKE THESE BANNOCKS and go along to your grandma, Judith, and you, Robbie, look after the boys. Don't let them get into any mischief.'

Robbie watched his mother put on her coat and pick up a shopping bag. 'Where are you going?' he asked.

'I'm going to Lerwick with Laura. She has to take her knitting to sell.'

'Can't she do that herself?'

'She probably could, but she asked if I would go with her. I've got some things to get anyway so I said I would.'

'Mam,' Judith tugged at her mother's sleeve. 'Will you get me some more knitting needles? I sat on mine and they're bent.'

'All right, but take more care.' To Robbie's query of, 'When will you be back?' Catherine said, 'I should be home about one.'

Laura, carrying an ancient handbag and a large shopping bag full to bursting was waiting on her doorstep. 'I hope I do right,' she said. 'Mina always said I wouldn't bargain a good price. I hope I do.'

Mina had recently, suddenly and without warning, died. A martinet, she had ruled Laura with a rod of iron. Now she was gone and Laura was left to manage best she could.

'Of course you will,' said Catherine. 'Stop worrying. Now come on, or we'll miss the bus.'

The track was in a better state now that Norrie had quarried stone and repaired it, but it was still steep and the two women puffed their way to the top.

'How long is it since you were in Lerwick last?' asked Catherine when at last they stood waiting for the bus.

'Last year,' said Laura. 'There was nothing to go for.'

'But Mina could have taken you with her. It would have been good for you to get out of the house for a while.' Laura just made a face and shrugged her shoulders. 'Don't you get fed up being stuck at home all day?'

'Not really. I never did go far. I was always the stay-at-home wife. There was always plenty to do.'

They didn't have long to wait and were soon on the bus and being carried to Lerwick. Laura was greeted by old friends. She smiled and warmed to their comments. With only a limited amount of time in the town she had said they would sell the knitwear first. Catherine thought that meant they would go to a wool merchant, but when Laura led her into an outfitter's she said, 'I thought you were going to get your shopping afterwards?'

'No, this is right,' said Laura and to an assistant, 'I've brought me work.'

'I'll get Mr Sinclair,' said the girl.

While they waited, Catherine looked around. She was always amazed when she entered the shops in the town. Small shop fronts seemed to promise nothing but one, or at most, two rooms, but once through the door, goods were displayed on a floor that went back and back and then up a flight of stairs to another floor. There was often a third. It was the same here.

A door behind the counter opened and a man came through. He walked to where Laura was sitting. Catherine stood beside her. 'Now, ladies,' he said, 'what have you brought me?' He smiled at Catherine then turned to Laura. When he did his mouth dropped open and stayed open as he stared at her. 'Laura,' he said at last. 'Laura, what on earth brings you here? Oh … but of course.'

'Willie Sinclair,' gasped Laura. 'I never thought to see you again.'

'Nor I you,' said Willie. 'I'm sorry to hear of your loss, but how've you been? Mina never said ought about you and I didn't like to ask, ken?'

'Ay, we ken what Mina was like, do we not?' said Laura. She smiled. 'And now I know why she would never let me come in with the work. It wasn't that I wouldn't bargain right, but that she knew that I would meet you again.'

'Ay,' said Willie. 'That sounds like Mina. But how've you been keeping?'

'Well enough,' said Laura.

'You never married, did you?'

'No,' said Laura. 'I didna get the chance, Mina saw to that.'

'She was always against me, wasn't she?' Willie chuckled. 'But time moves on. Now then....'

Not wishing to intrude on further private conversation, Catherine moved away and began to make purchases for herself.

On the journey home, Laura was quiet. She hugged the basket containing her groceries and more yarn to knit, and stared out of the window. They were almost home when she turned to Catherine and said, 'You'll not know that he was the lad I was going with all those years ago. His wife died ... and now he wants to call on me.'

'The way you greeted each other did make me wonder, but how lovely for you. Are you going to let him?' asked Catherine.

'I'm not sure. I'll likely tell him next time I see him.'

Laura would say no more and Catherine's mind, when she left her, raced with what the future might hold for her. The sweetheart that Mina had drummed out of the house had come back into her life. Willie Sinclair was a free man. Was Laura going to get a second chance?

Catherine put her purchases away then began to prepare vegetables for the evening meal. She tipped potatoes into a bowl, ran water on them, picked up a knife and began to peel, then stopped. It was quiet, too quiet. Silence usually meant trouble. It was Saturday. Judith was with Jannie, her grandmother. The old lady was helping her with her knitting. Robbie had been left to look after the twins. Where were they? Catherine dried her hands then went to look in the boys' bedrooms. She wasn't surprised to find that they were not there. It was highly unlikely they would be at Jannie's, and Laura had only just got home so they couldn't be with her. Perhaps they were on the beach or in her old house. They sometimes played there.

As she walked along the path she heard their laughter. But they were not at the house. The door was closed. They must be on the beach. She walked on. The dinghy had been hauled up from the shore and should have been lying beside the house. It was not, and the tarpaulin that had covered it was left lying in a crumpled heap. A shiver went down her spine. She started to run, then saw them. Robbie and the twins were in the dinghy on the bay. Fear for their safety, anger at what Robbie had done sent a chill through her. Heart thumping, she raced on to the beach and straight into the water. As she ran she screamed, 'Robbie Jameson, when I get my hands on you I'll-I'll *kill* you. Come back at once!'

Robbie heard her scream. He had already turned the little boat and was rowing towards the shore. When he reached it he ran it on to the sand, but before he could ship the oars Catherine seized him by the shoulders and shook him violently. 'How could you, how *could* you? I left you to look after the little ones and this is what you do. You *know* how I feel about the water. How could you be so irresponsible? They could have fallen in and drowned.'

Robbie succumbed to her attack, rolled his eyes and said, 'Stop panicking, Mam. We *weren't* in any danger.'

'*Don't* tell me not to panic, of *course* you were,' shouted Catherine, shaking him so hard that he begged for mercy. 'What would you have done if one of the boys had fallen in?'

'Well, they couldn't, because … stop it, Mam, let me go. We're all right. Nobody's come to any harm.'

'Mam,' called Allen. 'Will you let us out?'

Still holding Robbie, Catherine turned to the little boys. 'Let you out?'

'They're tied in,' said Robbie. 'I wasn't going to let them fall in the water. They can't swim.'

'NO!' cried Catherine. 'No, you should not have done that. Suppose the boat had capsized. Aargh!' Still grasping the scruff of Robbie's jacket with one hand, to vent her anger she delivered a stinging slap to his face. 'You could *all* have drowned.'

'Oh please, Mam,' said Robbie as he tried to prise her hands off him, 'let me go. I'm sorry.' And when she finally relaxed, 'I would never have taken them out if the water was rough, so it wouldn't have happened.'

'You don't know that. If they weren't tied and they'd fallen in you might have been able to save them and you might not. You'll never get the chance to find out now, though, because the dinghy's off limits from now on.'

'We got fish, Mam,' said Allen. He pointed to a bucket in the boat where several fish squirmed.

'Big ones for our tea,' said Peter.

Catherine had let go of Robbie and stood beside the boat. Her heart was racing; she held a hand to her chest and, breathing deeply, willed it to slow down. The little boys were still in the boat. They smiled up at their mother. They seemed to be so delighted that they'd caught some fish that it was all they were concerned with. 'Haven't we been clever?' said Peter.

'Yes, you have and thank you. That's lovely,' said Catherine. She was calmer now. 'You've been fishing. But I thought….' She turned abruptly to Robbie and, her voice sharp, said, 'You've done this before, haven't you? And you let me think you were fishing with a rod and line.'

'We were,' said Robbie.

'But in the boat.'

'Yes.' Robbie was out of the dinghy and untying the rope with which he had fastened the two little ones. 'We learn about boats at school. Lots of boys have their own already. I know what to do.'

'Whether you know what to do or not is not the point. You're grounded … for a month.' Catherine was angry and anger mixed with relief that the boys had come to no harm made her shout. 'You'll go to school, come straight home, do your homework and go to bed.'

'Oh, Mam,' pleaded Robbie. 'We were quite safe.'

'I have no intention of arguing with you. Pull up the boat, leave it and come home *now*.' Catherine left her boys and marched away. Tears had not been her lot for some time, but the tumult of her emotions, anger at what Robbie had done and disgust with herself at having struck him, along with relief that they had come to no harm, brought them to her eyes. She dashed them away with the back of her hand.

She had told Norrie that Robbie wanted to go to sea and that she didn't want him to and was going to stop him. But he had shaken his head and said that the fishermen on Burra believed if a boy was born on an ebb tide he'd go to sea no matter what. She had laughed and said that that was a load of old codswallop. It was an old wives' tale and she didn't believe it. But now she wasn't so sure.

THREE

NORRIE HAD BUILT a sheep pen on the hill behind the Deepdale houses and Catherine herded her sheep into it to tend them. She had been busy all morning. It was a warm day and close contact with the animals made her clothes smell of them. Her work finished, she let them out and went home. A young woman was waiting there. 'Would you be Mrs Williams?' she asked.

'That's me,' said Catherine.

'I heard there was a house to let here and I've come to ask for it.'

The grapevine, that form of communication that spread news faster than any other could, was at work. From the way she spoke, the girl, for she was no more than in her early twenties, was a Shetlander. Catherine had to smile. 'It's not ready yet,' she said.

'Oh, but … could I just see it?'

'If you like,' said Catherine. 'But I'll have to change out of these smelly trousers first. Come in a moment.'

'I'm June Tulloch, that was,' said Catherine's visitor when Catherine had changed and they were on their way to look at the house. 'I married an American. My name is Thomson now. We're living with my parents in Lerwick.'

'I'm afraid it will be a few weeks yet before the house is ready,' said Catherine. 'It needs a bathroom and a new stove. Is it just for the two of you or do you have children?'

'Just the two of us,' said June as Catherine led her through the house. 'You have no idea how difficult it is to find somewhere to live.' She was looking around her with interest. 'I like this place. I would take it just as it is. Please say I can. Living with your own folk isn't easy.'

Don't I just know it? thought Catherine. 'I'm sure you must have been used to something much better than this,' she said. 'You would be taking a step back if you moved in without a bathroom. It's a hassle to drag a tub indoors before you can have a bath. I should know. I did it for many years. And anyway, I've no idea yet what the rent might be.'

'I work for an accountant so I don't foresee any trouble paying what you ask and I grew up in a croft house,' said June. 'I know what it's like. It would be like old times. And a house of our own is more important than a bathroom.'

'You really are desperate, aren't you?' said Catherine.

June nodded. 'We are.'

'Nevertheless,' said Catherine, 'I think you should bring your husband to look at it first. He might think differently to you.'

'He'd agree with me. I know.'

As they walked back along the path Catherine was silent. June's desperation to be away from her family meant there was a problem and she wondered what it was. Overcrowding was probably the reason, but perhaps a clash of personalities played a part. She could sympathize if that was the case and was glad she had said that June's husband should see the house before an agreement could be made. It would give her and Norrie the opportunity to judge whether the couple would fit into the little world of Deepdale.

'Mam, I've dropped a stitch, can you help?' said Judith.

'You know I'm no good at knitting,' said Catherine. 'But I'll have a look.' Her hands weren't used to craft work and, making a poor job of it, she bundled up the piece of work and handed it back to her daughter. 'Take it to your grandma,' she said. 'She'll know what to do, but don't stay long. Be back in time for tea.'

'Oh, Mam,' huffed Judith.

Robbie, labouring over his homework, listened to the exchange between Judith and their mother. The twins were playing not far from the house; the door was open and he could hear their laughter. He could also hear the whisper of the sea, beseeching him to go to it. He sniffed the air and, breathing in, smelt the tang of seaweed. He imagined sitting in the dinghy, rising and falling on the gentle swell of the water, oars shipped, a rod and line in his hands. To wait for the bobbing of the float required patience and he had lots of that. He'd found nothing to compare with the pleasure he derived from being on the water. He would go to sea one day, of that he was sure.

'How long are you going to keep me cooped up indoors, Mam?' he said.

'Are you complaining? If you are, you've only got yourself to blame. At least it will give you time to think and if I ask you to look after the boys again you'll be more responsible.'

'But Mam—'

'I've told you once. I'm not going to tell you again. Finish your homework then set the table for tea.'

She was still mad at him and there was no way he was going to get her to change her mind. He'd have to wait. He scowled at his mother's back then packed up his school books and put them away. He had just finished setting the table when Norrie walked in.

'Busy are you?' said Norrie. 'Never mind, you won't be under petticoat rule for ever.' He grinned at the boy and patted him on the shoulder.

'Are you encouraging him to defy me?' said Catherine as she put a pile of plates on the table. She went to the door and called the twins. 'Come on, boys.'

'We're going to have to build a bigger house,' said Norrie when the six of them were sitting down. 'Just look at them, Catherine. They're little now, but they'll grow and get big and the house doesn't have elastic sides. What are we going to do? Build a byre and tie them up to feed them like Daa does the cow?'

'You are funny, Dad,' said Judith.

'You'll be like little sardines in a tin,' said Norrie. 'Judith and

Allen and Peter, packed tight. Your mother will have to winkle you out of bed with a fork.'

A knock on the door interrupted the children's laughter. 'Now who's that?' said Catherine. She opened the door and stepped back.

'Who is it?' said Norrie when he heard no exchange of greetings.

'Um-um it's —'

'Hullo,' said June Thomson and, 'Hi there,' said the man beside her.

It was the man with June that had temporarily robbed Catherine of speech. 'I … oh, I'm so sorry,' she stuttered. 'How rude of me, it's just—'

'No need to apologize,' said June. 'It happens all the time. This is Joe.'

'You'd better come in,' said Catherine. As she led the way she said, 'Norrie, Mrs Thomson has brought her husband to look at the house.'

The visitors followed her and when they stood beside Catherine a shocked silence settled on the room. Then the man smiled and showed a row of teeth that were whiter than white in a face the colour of coffee with just a dash of cream. He looked at the children, 'Hi guys,' he said.

Allen and Peter were under the table. They had slid off their chairs to hide and now, gripping the edge of it with their fingers they raised up to peer over it. Judith sat open-mouthed. Robbie just smiled. Norrie looked at his children, threw back his head and laughed. 'I think this man's been out in the sun too long, bairns. You'd better be glad you live in Shetland.' He stood up and held out a hand to his visitors. 'Sorry about that. They've never seen anyone like you before. You'll have a cup of tea, won't you? We're just going to have one.'

Uppermost in Catherine's mind, as she fetched extra cups from the kitchen, was what Jannie was going to say if this man came to live in the valley. The fact that he was married to a white woman would have her quoting the Bible morning noon and night. Now she could understand June's need to get away from her family. They probably did not approve of Joe, and she wondered what he might have had to endure.

'I don't have a job yet,' said Joe. 'But I do intend to get one. At the moment,' and here he laughed, 'I'm a kept man. My wife is the breadwinner.'

'There'll be no trouble with the rent,' said June. 'I get good money so there's no problem there … that is, if you decide to let the house to us.'

'That is, if your husband agrees to it,' said Norrie.

Leaving the children with orders to behave, Norrie and Catherine took June and her husband to look at Catherine's house. Joe made no comment as they went from room to room. Catherine, watching him, could not decide whether he was for or against, but could see that June was apprehensive. Norrie explained that it would take several weeks to add a bathroom and new stove. They were standing in the living room. Norrie looked at Joe. 'So,' he said, 'that's it.'

'You said you'd be doing most of the work yourself,' said Joe. 'What would you say to some help?'

'Well, two pairs of hands are better than one, any day,' said Norrie.

Joe gave his wife a smile then turned to Norrie. 'I like the house. June told your wife she liked it, too, and would move in as it is. Can I say something?'

'I'm listening,' said Norrie.

'If you were to let us move in as it is,' said Joe, 'seeing as I've no job to go to, I'd be glad to work for you for nothing.'

'But you wouldn't have a bathroom.'

'I told your wife it was the way I grew up,' said June. 'Lack of a bathroom, and if all went well it would only be temporary, wouldn't be a problem.'

'You seem very desperate,' said Norrie. 'And you're falling over backward trying to persuade us to let it to you. There's got to be a reason for that. Would you tell us what it is?'

June looked at her husband. She took his hand in hers and said, 'This is my Joe. He's a good man … but his skin is black and some people think it's wrong for a white woman to marry a black man. My parents are like that. They're very religious – well – if you think that a belief in the hell and damnation that's preached in the chapel is religion….'

'Don't say any more,' said Catherine.

'But I must,' said June. 'They couldn't turn us out when we came home, but they might as well have. They ignore Joe, won't even look at him and I can't stand it any more. That's why we're here.'

Catherine and Norrie exchanged looks. 'Sounds like a good enough reason to me,' said Norrie. 'But I think we'll have to talk it over and let you know.'

'Fair enough,' said Joe.

'We don't have any furniture,' said June. 'I see you have a few pieces here. If you let us rent the house could we buy them from you?'

Catherine bit her lip. My bed, she wants to buy my bed, she thought. Propped against the wall in the bedroom was her wonderful, proper, bed, the bed she had insisted on having because she had hated the box bed that, as a new bride, she had had to sleep in at Jannie's house. Now, devoid of bedding, it was a skeleton of what it had been. But I don't need it; it belongs to the past and the past can never return, she reasoned. She looked at June and smiled. 'I think we might work something out,' she said. 'Give me a day or two to think it over.'

'Does that mean you're going to let us live in your house?'

'Maybe,' said Norrie.

FOUR

WILLIE SINCLAIR HAD become a regular visitor to Deepdale. Very few Sundays went by when his car was not parked outside Laura's house. Jannie tut-tutted at first and called her sister an old fool, but as the weeks went by and Willie treated her with respect, driving her and Laura to the meeting house at Norravoe on a Sunday, she relented and declared him to be a braaly fine man.

In the early afternoon of a summer day he bowled down into the valley, bundled Laura into the car and took her out for a drive. Now, as they were home for tea before going to the kirk, Jannie and Catherine had been invited to join them. They sat at Laura's table and listened while she told them where Willie had taken her, of people she had met and gossip she had heard. So much had changed, she said. People had gone away and others moved in. How was it she hadn't known?

That's an easy one to answer, thought Catherine. Mina had kept her sister well away from distractions – men in particular. And now it was clear why. Mina, stern and frigid, had been afraid that Laura would be lured away. And where would that have left her? Living alone with not even a cat to keep her company?

'But there's something more I want to tell you,' Laura was saying. For a moment or two she hesitated, but then, with a broad smile on her face she looked at Willie and said, 'Willie has asked me to marry him.'

Jannie stared at her, her mouth hanging open. 'Hast du lost thy senses?' she said at last. 'Du's an old wife. Getting married is for the young.'

'No, no,' said Catherine. 'Everyone has a right to some happiness and Laura has waited a long time.'

'But … what will folk say?' said Jannie.

'They can say what they like,' said Laura.

'I totally agree,' said Catherine. She got up and hugged the old lady. 'I'm so pleased for you. I'm sure you'll be very happy.' She looked at Willie. 'You'll take good care of her won't you?'

'I will. I've waited long enough to do that,' said Willie.

'You'll be taking her back to the town,' said Jannie. 'What am I going to do without her?'

'The rest of us aren't likely to be going anywhere,' said Catherine.

But Jannie was in shock. 'What will you do with your house, Laura?'

'Time to think of that later,' said Catherine. 'When are you to be married?'

'As soon as it can be arranged,' said Willie. 'There's no point in waiting.'

Life was now dealing Laura a full house. She was to be married to a man who, evidently, had never forgotten her, even though his path through life had led him away. He would take her to live in Lerwick and another person would leave the valley. The winds of change were certainly blowing.

It was a wet day when June and her husband moved in. They came with a van and a few more items of furniture to add to the ones Catherine had agreed to sell them. She had left a pile of kindling wood and a bucket of peat for them to make a fire and not long after they were there, a plume of smoke rose from their chimney. Catherine smiled and left them to it.

When they had been asked, yet again, if they still wouldn't rather wait till the bathroom was done, June had said, 'I'm sure we'll manage. In fact I'm quite looking forward to a tub in front of the fire.' Norrie and Joe had done a deal and Norrie would now have help with the building work.

Catherine had just settled down to start writing a letter to her mother when Jannie opened the door and marched in. She wore no coat or hat and neither did she carry an umbrella. Her hair was wet and rain had soaked in and made dark patches on her shoulders.

'You're wet,' said Catherine. 'What on earth are you doing out in the rain like that?'

Ignoring Catherine's question, Jannie took up a belligerent stance and demanded, 'Is yon black man going to bide in your house?'

'Yes. We thought it would be better if the house was lived in. His wife asked for it and we agreed to rent it to them.'

'You should not have done that,' snapped Jannie. 'She's a Shetland lass. She should have married one of her own, not a coloured man. I don't know what her da was thinking of; he should have stopped her. It's not right.'

Jannie's outburst was no more than Catherine had expected. 'Why isn't it right?' she asked

'Well … well …' Jannie appeared confused. 'Think about the bairns, should they have some. They won't know where they belong. What colour will they be? It's not right, it's not right.'

Catherine had not been surprised at her children's reaction to Joe and she was not surprised now that Jannie was objecting to his presence, but there was no point in arguing with her. Better to change the subject. 'Sit down, Jannie,' she said. 'I'll make us some tea.' She put down her pen and went into the kitchen.

Jannie followed her. 'You'll have to keep the bairns safe. Mind you look after them. Dinna let them go out alone.'

'You're not saying they're in any danger, are you?' Catherine was annoyed at what Jannie implied. 'My heavens, it's only the colour of the man's skin that's dark. I'm sure his heart is not. He's human, just like us.'

'Ay well, I wouldn't be too sure.'

A surge of anger at the old Jannie coming to the surface made Catherine want to fight back, but she bit her lip and kept her anger to herself.

Jannie went on, 'I don't know what Daa's up to, but he'll not go to his work. He hides in the barn.'

'But he doesn't have to go to work, he's retired,' said Catherine.

'No, no, he should,' muttered Jannie. 'But he'll not listen. I canna tell what he's up to.' She shook her head. 'And he's not lookin' to the sheep either.'

'But....' Catherine hesitated. She had been going to correct Jannie again. Instead, she sighed and said, 'Will you have a bannock? They're fresh made.'

'Oh ay,' said Jannie, brightening up. 'Du makes awful good ones. I didna think du would, coming fae south, like.'

Catherine poured tea then watched Jannie spread a bannock with a thick layer of butter. Once her tormentor, now that the old lady was suffering the onset of dementia she felt sorry for her. There was nothing she could do but keep an eye on her and help when needed. It was Daa that her heart went out to. She would have to look out for him, too.

Jannie's change of mood made her relaxed and happy. 'Does du remember what an old besom Mina was?' she said. 'I wouldn't like to see her come back.'

'She can hardly do that,' said Catherine.

About to bite into her bannock Jannie, a puzzled look on her face, stared at Catherine. 'Why?' she said.

Unable to answer Jannie's question Catherine turned away and said, 'It's very kind of you to teach Judith to knit. How do you think she's getting on?'

'She's a bonnie wee soul,' Jannie smiled. 'Ken ... du knows ... no.' She shook her head. 'No, du wouldn't and I can't say.' She put her half-eaten bannock down on her plate and stood up. 'I'd better be away home. Daa'll be wanting his tea when he comes in.'

FIVE

IT WAS SHEARING time and Norrie and Catherine were making use of a hot day to gather the wool crop. Catherine rolled and packed each individual fleece Norrie clipped. Shetland sheep shed their wool naturally, the old wool rising up and parting from the new growth. They were easy to shear, but the fleece of cross-bred and pedigree kept on growing. It was also thick and heavy and to shear them was hard work. Constantly bending over the animals made for sore backs and when it was almost time for Catherine to fetch the children from school, she called for a break before they came home. While she made a pot of tea, Norrie stretched to relieve his aching back then sat down on a wooden chair, the sort that, hard and uncomfortable though they may be, were very sensible pieces of furniture. The work she and Norrie had to do was often dirty, clothes tended to get mucky and that muck was liable to transfer itself to the furniture. Plain wood could be taken outside and scrubbed; upholstery could not.

'I'm a bit worried about Jannie,' said Catherine as she poured tea. 'She's confused. Sometimes she makes sense, but she often talks a lot of nonsense.'

'Why, what's she been saying?'

'She says Daa won't go to work, but hides in the barn. I told her he had no work to go to and then she went off on something else. She told me to keep the children way from Joe. I don't know what she thought he was going to do.'

'You'll have to keep an eye on her,' said Norrie. 'If she gets worse ask Doc Lumsden.' He stopped and looked towards the window. 'What was that?'

A car had drawn up outside. There were men's voices, car doors being slammed, then footsteps on flagstones and a knock on the door.

'Nobody round here knocks. Must be strangers,' said Catherine as she went to answer it.

The man who stood on the doorstep was tall. His clothes were not those of a working man, but were well cut casuals. He smiled at Catherine. 'Does Norrie Williams live here?' he asked.

'He does. Who's asking?' From the look of him, thought Catherine, he was there in some official capacity. From his accent he was not a Shetlander and not from England either. Norrie was behind her. He put a hand on her shoulder and in a shocked voice, said, 'So I wasn't mistaken. It was you I saw, Magnie.'

'Sure thing, cobber. No worries, it's me.' Magnie inclined his head to include the man who stood behind him, 'And Jamie too.'

'What the hell are you doing here? You've never come halfway round the world just to see me. Couldn't you have let us *know*?' Norrie was shaking his head in disbelief. 'Well, don't stand there; I suppose you'd better come in.'

Catherine had stepped back out of the way. She looked from one to the other. Norrie caught the look on her face and laughed. 'They're my cousins from Australia,' he said. 'Magnie, Jamie, meet Catherine, my wife.'

'I'll make some more tea,' said Catherine. What on earth did they want to turn up for, and right now when she and Norrie were in the middle of clipping a couple of hundred sheep. If they were Shetland born they should have known better, known that visitors weren't really welcome when they were so busy. She fetched more cups, poured tea and put out bannocks and then, while Norrie plied his cousins with questions, went to change her clothes. Leaving the men arguing the merits of various breeds of sheep she excused herself and set off to fetch the children from school. Robbie was at the Anderson High in Lerwick and would come home on the bus, but the twins and Judith went to the local school in Broonieswick.

'There's a surprise waiting for you when you get home,' she told them once she'd gathered up their bits and pieces, lunch bags, exercise books and homework, and they were on their way. 'You have two brand new uncles.'

'Where did they come from?' asked Judith.

'Why are they new?' said Allen.

'Because your da hasn't seen them for lots of years and you haven't seen them at all. They've come all the way from Australia. They're your da's cousins.' Nosing her car onto the track she looked down at her house, the cousins' car was still there. Why hadn't they written to say they were coming? Silly question, they might not have known where Norrie was living, or even if he'd survived the war. But they were here; someone must have told them. And if they were staying in Shetland, were there other relations Norrie didn't know about?

The twins, eager for the sight of their new relatives tumbled out of the car to rush indoors. 'Where are they?' they shouted and, 'I want to see them.' Judith followed at a more leisurely pace.

'Did you come on a boat?' asked Peter as he studied the men.

'No, we came on an aeroplane.'

Allen stood next his father. 'You talk funny,' he said.

'So do you.'

'Go and change your clothes, boys. You too Judith.'

'But I want —'

'Go,' said Norrie. 'Do as you're told.'

'But —'

'Go,' said Norrie, his voice stern, and the boys disappeared like shadows. When Norrie raised his voice he had to be obeyed. Judith said nothing, glanced at her mother, looked at her father, then slid quietly by him and went to her room.

'What's wrong?' asked Catherine when the children had gone.

'I don't know yet,' said Norrie. 'That's what I'm trying to find out. But Magnie said I had to wait till you were home.'

'Well, I'm here,' said Catherine.

Magnie looked at Catherine, at Norrie and back to Catherine. 'Norrie says Auntie Kay left him her croft, her house, and everything in it,' he said. 'This one, in fact, but that can't be right because Uncle Callum left it all to me.'

'*What?*' Norrie thumped the table with his fists. 'It's the first I've heard of it. And if you're right, why have you waited so long to come and claim it?'

'Well, cobber, it's like this. The nature of my work keeps me moving about and things tend to take a long time to catch up with me.'

'But it's nigh on twenty years since Uncle Callum died.'

'I know.'

For a moment or two Norrie was silent, then, 'Oh, I see,' he said. 'It wasn't worth claiming before, but now something's happened to make it worth your while. Why else would you have come all this way?'

'That would be right.'

'You'll have to prove your right to it before I'd hand it over.'

'I intend to. I'm seeing a solicitor tomorrow.'

'Much good may that do you,' laughed Norrie. 'He'll cost you more than the house and bit of land's worth.'

Catherine watched the faces of both cousins. Magnie was obviously the dominant one for Jamie, sitting on a chair near the door, said nothing.

'I can't believe you've travelled all this way to try to take a few acres of scrub land off me,' went on Norrie. 'The fare must have cost you a pretty packet; you'd be out of pocket if you succeeded.'

'That's where you're wrong,' said Magnie. 'You have no idea what the few acres you have are worth. I've already had a good offer for it and I know I can get more. . .'

Norrie jumped to his feet, tipping his chair to the floor as he did. 'Get out,' he shouted.

'Now don't take on,' began Magnie as he pushed back his chair and stood up. 'You'd get your share.'

Watching Norrie, Catherine could see that he was grinding his teeth. Not a good sign. Anxiously she stood twisting her hands together. Tense as two dogs spoiling for a fight the men faced each other, each anticipating the other making the first move.

'And precious little that might be coming from you,' snarled Norrie.

'You don't know that.'

'Oh yes I do. You always were a twisted, conniving bastard. I've a good mind to —'

Magnie made to step back out of harm's way, but he was too slow and before he could do anything about it, with one big hand Norrie grabbed him by his shirt front and, jerking him forward, he slammed his head into Magnie's face. There came the sound of crunching bone. Then he drove his knee into his cousin's crotch and as Magnie fell, crashed his fist into the side of the man's face. Catherine cringed at the sight of blood spurting from Magnie's nose and the obvious pain of the second assault.

Norrie stood over the fallen man, his face pale, his body shaking with anger at what Magnie wanted to do and at himself for losing control. Magnie lay on the floor. He couldn't stay there. Taking hold of his jacket Norrie dragged him out through the doorway. Jamie had fled long since and was sitting in the car, the engine running. Dropping his cousin on the flagstones Norrie shouted to Jamie to take him away. Dusting his hands of them both he turned back indoors.

'The bastards,' he muttered. 'All smiles, weren't they. Lovely to see you, but you've no right to the house or the croft, so we're going to throw you out.'

Catherine stared at Norrie. She had never seen him so angry, didn't know he could be so violent. It was not like him. 'Come,' she said. 'You need to calm down. I'll make a pot of tea.'

Norrie's hand was on the cupboard door and bringing out the whisky bottle. 'You can have *tea* if you like,' he said. He unscrewed the top of the bottle and splashed a generous measure into a glass. Lifting it to his mouth he tossed off the contents and poured another.

To Catherine it was obvious that he was set on a drinking spree and who could blame him. It wasn't every day someone knocked on the door and said you weren't entitled to what you thought was your property. It was obvious that no more sheep would be shorn that day and there were several animals still penned and waiting. When Robbie came home she would get him to set them free.

Judith had been standing unnoticed in the doorway at the bottom of the stairs and had watched all that had gone on. Carrying her knitting she looked first at her father then at her mother. She shrugged her shoulders, made a face and said, 'I'm going to Granny's. What time's tea?'

'Have you been there all the time?' asked Catherine.

'Yes,' said Judith. 'I wasn't able to get by, so I had to wait.'

The answer was so matter of fact that Catherine looked at her child and shook her head. 'I don't know about you,' she said. 'Go on with you. I'll send the boys along for you later,' and, 'Come on you two,' to the twins who were peeping out from behind their sister. 'Go outside and play.'

Norrie was filling his glass again. Catherine watched as he frowned and ground his teeth. 'You're planning something, aren't you?' she said.

He looked at her. 'They will never take my property from me. They have no right. There's nothing for you to look so worried about; they won't be back.' He chuckled. 'Magnie'll have a job to blow his nose for a while.'

'But they'll report you,' gasped Catherine.

'So what? It's their word against ours. What did you expect me to do? Say yes, all right, you can have it? Damn it, they always were a thieving lot. I wasn't the only one glad to see the back of them.'

'But they can have you for assault.'

'And who's to prove it?

SIX

DRESSED AS NO one in Deepdale had ever seen her before, Laura was escorted up the aisle of Broonieswick church by Daa. Gone the long black skirt, the shawl, the subservient manner, and in their place a happy, confident woman stepped out wearing a suit, a pretty hat on her head. True, the hair was still unruly, but the dancing tendrils only enhanced her smiling face.

The little church had filled to overflowing. Second, third and distant cousins had crawled out of the woodwork to see Laura wed her girlhood sweetheart. Many others were there out of curiosity; many more to wish Laura happiness, but whatever the reason, the sound of their voices as they sang rose to the rafters and filled the little church with a glorious noise. A smaller celebration was held at Laura's house afterwards; she had only wanted close family there.

The new ferry between the islands and Aberdeen, the *St Clair*, had made her maiden voyage and docked for the first time at Lerwick a few weeks before. Willie Sinclair had lost no time in booking a passage on it for him and his bride to sail away for a holiday on the mainland. Laura, apart from the jaunts round Shetland that Willie had taken her on, had never ventured further than the few miles into Lerwick and she was nervous.

'Will I have to wear a lifebelt?' she asked Catherine.

Catherine smiled. 'No,' she said. 'You will sleep in a bunk with a pillow and bed clothes. You'll love it.' Mentally she added, as long as the sea is calm. She had driven the couple into Lerwick to board the ferry, and now, a teary-eyed Laura hugged her as they said goodbye.

'Have a safe journey,' said Catherine. 'Enjoy your holiday and don't forget to tell me all about it when you come home.'

'Oh, I will,' said Laura. 'Mind now, the builders will be starting soon. Keep an eye on them, won't you.' Laura had instructed builders to extend her house and update it so that it could be let. Soon more strangers would come in to Deepdale.

'I will, don't worry. Now off you go.' Catherine watched as Laura and Willie boarded the boat. First Mina had been carried away, now Laura was leaving. The day was not so far off when Jannie and Daa would be gone too. It was not a prospect she found pleasing.

'I see you have a letter from the solicitor.' The postman gave a toothy grin. 'Have you come into money?'

'I won't know till I open it, will I?' Catherine took the proffered letter and read the address. 'It's not mine, it's for Norrie. It'll have to wait till he's home.'

'Solicitors' letters is usually bad news,' said the postie, shaking his head. 'I hope it's nothing serious. What's wrong wi' Jannie?'

'Why? What's she done?'

'She didna ken who I was. She telled me she got bread off the van yesterday and didna want any.'

'Her eyesight's failing, but she won't be persuaded to get glasses. She must have mistaken you for the baker.'

'Mmm, ay, well, maybe.' The postie nodded his head, not in agreement, but as in, 'Well, if you say so'.

When he was gone Catherine stood holding the letter. It was from a firm of solicitors in Lerwick. She had been expecting it. Now that it was here she wanted desperately to open it, but it was addressed to Norrie and it would have to wait. With a sigh she tucked it behind the clock on the mantelpiece. She would give it to Norrie after he had had his meal. If its contents were what she thought they might be, the evening was not going to be one of joy.

For the rest of the day the letter was uppermost in her mind. In the house her eyes constantly strayed to it. When she came in from outside it was the first thing she looked for. The day dragged on till at last the children were home, the evening meal was ready, the table laid and all that was needed was Norrie.

And then he was there, hot, tired, hungry and ready for his tea. He was not in the best of moods so the meal was not the jolly affair it usually was. It would be better to get the children out of the way before she gave him the letter. As she began to clear the dishes she said, 'Take the boys along to Daa, Robbie. He said he was going to teach you how to make a straw basket and Judith, would you go and sit with Grandma? She was asking for you.'

Norrie laughed and reached out to take hold of his wife. 'You're getting rid o' the kids,' he said. 'What have you got in mind?' He pulled her towards him, made to sit her on his lap, but she pulled away.

'Your overalls are covered in grease, Norrie,' she said. 'I wish you'd take them off before you sit down.'

'Oh, hoity toity. You never used to complain.'

'Perhaps I should have.'

'Huh.' Norrie let her go, crossed his arms, leaned back in his chair and yawned. 'What have you been doing today?'

'The usual,' said Catherine. 'The postman asked me what was wrong with Jannie – she was confused. I said her eyes were getting bad and I think she must have mistaken him for the baker. We'll have to do something about her, but I don't know what. What do you think?' Why am I burbling? she thought. I've got to give Norrie the letter. She finished clearing the table and made tea. Norrie still sat slumped in his chair, his eyes were closed and he was beginning to snore. He hadn't heard a word she'd said. She set a mug of tea in front of him. 'Has it been a bad day?' she asked.

'Not the best,' said Norrie. 'In fact it's been a bugger.'

And it's probably going to get worse, thought Catherine as she reached for the letter. 'This came for you today,' she said and watched Norrie's face set into grim lines when he saw who it was from.

'Bastards,' he muttered as he ripped the envelope open and,

'bastards, bastards,' again as he read the typewritten page he pulled out.

'What is it?' asked Catherine.

Norrie jumped up and began to walk back and forth. 'They want me to prove ownership. How can I do that? I never got it in writing.'

'Oh, Norrie. Didn't Kay leave a will?'

'I don't know.'

'What did you do with her stuff then? Do you still have it?' Heaven help us, why don't men think?

'I put some up under the roof,' said Norrie. 'And the rest went in the barn.'

'But the house has been ripped apart since then. Oh God! Didn't you go through any of her things? Didn't you even *think* to look for a will?'

'Why should I? She said it was all to be mine. What more did I need? There wasn't anybody else.'

Catherine, elbows on the table, put her head in her hands. Norrie was reaching for the whisky bottle. Did he not care that the cousins might ruin them? It was no use telling him that alcohol never held the answers to life's problems. All too often these days he nursed the whisky bottle as a comforter. The trouble was that it was usually empty before he went to his bed.

Catherine jumped up. 'No. You're *not* going to hide behind a bottle. You're not a baby.' She snatched at it but he held it at arm's length, away from her.

'I'll drink when I want to,' said Norrie. 'Not you or anyone else is going to stop me.'

'Norrie Williams,' shouted Catherine. 'I am *not* going to let you become a soak because you won't face up to it. DO SOMETHING.'

With a roar Norrie lunged at her. 'What *can* I do?'

'Look for Kay's will for a start, and,' Catherine put a hand up in front of her, the flat of the palm towards Norrie, 'don't even think of hitting me.'

Norrie aborted the instinct to lash out. 'I haven't got a clue where to start looking,' he said. 'I wish I did.' He looked away from her as he muttered, 'I'm sorry, Catherine, you know I would never hit you.' But he quite possibly would have and if he had she would have made him regret it.

'Put the bottle away, Norrie, please,' she said. 'It's too late to start looking now, but I will tomorrow.'

SEVEN

FROM EARLY TILL late Deepdale rang to the sound of the hammers and saws of the men working on Laura's house. Catherine went to mark their progress as she'd promised. She watched the little house expand, its roof raised and more rooms added. Mina would surely turn in her grave if she knew what was going on.

But this morning Catherine did not visit. As soon as Norrie was away to work and the children at school she hurried through her household tasks and, praying that she would find what she sought, went out to the barn. Not a big building; its walls were of stone and its roof of galvanized steel sheets. It was Norrie's domain. At one end he had built a workbench and on it were boxes of nails, hammers and other small tools. By the side of it were stacked fence posts and a fencing hammer, a large and very heavy one. The centre of the barn had been cleared and swept ready to store the hay, yet to be made, that would be winter feed for their sheep. At the opposite end of the barn, pushed up against the wall, was an old sea chest.

Catherine remembered seeing the chest in Kay's bedroom. She would start her search there. She pulled it away from the wall and lifted the lid. 'Oh, Kay,' she said as she looked at the jumble of papers, unfinished knitting, books and framed photographs that were in an untidy heap inside it. 'Where do I start?' Kay would never have left it like this, what was Norrie thinking of? Going down on her knees she began to lift out and sort the contents. The knitting had been attacked by moths that had added their own lace pattern to a piece of plain work. Damp had buckled and warped photographs and papers. One by one she peeled sheets of paper off one another. When she found teaching certificates belonging to Kay her excitement mounted; surely she would find Kay's will now. But as the pile of stuff outside the chest grew bigger and that inside, smaller, hope faded. At last it was empty and had not given up the will. Catherine sat back on her heels and looked at it. It was a sea chest, a sailor's treasure chest. No it wasn't, it was just a box. Disappointed, she stretched, put her hands behind her head and rotated it to ease her neck. Round and round and up and down, up again, and there it stopped.

There was no upper floor to the barn, but Norrie had tacked a few planks of wood across some of the rafters and on them were several boxes. Boxes! He said he had put some up under the roof. Was it this roof? And if they were the boxes that held the stuff he had cleared out of Kay's house, they were what she was looking for. But how was she going to get at them? The platform was small; no room to stand and no stairs to get up to it if there had been. And even if she could get to them, the boxes might be heavy so how was she going to get them down?

But first she had to put the things she'd taken out of the chest, back into it. That done and the lid closed she shoved it back against the wall. She stood up, rubbed sore knees then looked up at the boxes again. She needed a ladder. Norrie's was hung on some hooks on the wall. She took it down and propped it against the rafters. It stood at a dauntingly steep angle. Hesitantly she stood on the bottom rung and tested it with her weight. She looked up. It was very steep. But she had to get up there. Taking a deep breath she began to climb. She was nearly at the top when— 'My heavens, lass, what are you doing up there?' It was one of the builders' men. She hadn't heard him come in and, surprised, she clung to the ladder like a limpet.

'Oh my God, what a shock you gave me. What do you want?'

'One of the lads cut his hand and we were hoping you could clean him up. The boss said he saw you come in here and for me to come and find you. What are you doing up there?'

'I need to look in these boxes. But I suppose I'd better come down.'

Catherine looked over her shoulder as she began to descend and as she did, leaned too far to the side. Her shifting weight caused the ladder to slide sideways. She screamed. The builder shouted, 'Jump!' and, trusting that he would catch her, she did. The ladder clattered to the floor, but a pair of strong arms caught her. She thudded into the man, and he, staggering under her weight, collapsed and fell, Catherine with him. He was middle-aged and portly, had landed on his back with Catherine lying on his stomach. His arms tightly round her he began to laugh. 'If my wife could see me now,' he chuckled, 'she'd have grounds for divorce.'

'What the hell's going on here?' It was the foreman, the injured man standing behind him. 'Is this what you get up to when I send you to get help? I heard the scream, but I didn't expect to see you playing roly-poly.'

Catherine pulled herself up off her rescuer and put her crumpled clothes to rights. 'He's my hero,' she said as her saviour scrambled to his feet. 'If it hadn't been for him, I might have broken my neck.'

'She was trying to get at those boxes.' The workman pointed at the boxes sitting on the rafters. 'She was up the ladder and it wasn't safe. We ought to get them down for her.'

'All right, we will. But can we get this man seen to first?'

'Come with me,' said Catherine and led the injured man to her house where she bathed, disinfected and bound the cut. 'You should wear a glove on that hand while you're working,' she said. 'At least until it heals enough for just a plaster.'

When the man returned to work Catherine went back to the barn. All the boxes had been taken down and set on the floor. She opened the first one. As she began to sort out the jumble of stuff she wondered why Norrie had thrown everything together without sorting it out first. Surely the respect he had for his aunt would have made him take more care? But perhaps he cared too much and his emotions had got the better of him. To have thrown away or burnt things would have destroyed memories.

On her knees again Catherine sorted through letters, newspaper cuttings, knitting patterns, pieces of jewellery, scarves and a shawl that had also been attacked by moths. The more she turned over the more a sense of Kay's presence hovered over her. She began to feel like an intruder. 'I'm sorry, Kay,' she whispered, 'but I have to find the will.' *It's not here.* What put that into her head? Box after box she opened and searched without result. With a heavy heart she closed the lid on the last one. She would have to go through them again another time.

EIGHT

WITH NO FOXES on Shetland to raid the hen houses the birds were free to rise with the sun and wander where they pleased. They fed mostly on what they could scavenge, which was added to by scraps from the Deepdale house tables and sometimes a handful of corn. Jannie had wandered out to feed the chickens Laura had left and that were now hers, then stood in front of Laura's house and stared at it. The renovation was finished, the inside painted and decorated and the builders long gone. Now it stood empty.

'I never thought to see this day,' she said to Catherine, who had joined her.

'Neither did I, but everything changes.'

'Ay. The Jamesons and my folk lived in this valley for longer than I know,' said Jannie. 'My granda and my da were born here and now folk are leaving, first Kay, then Mina … now Laura.'

'Be happy for Laura,' said Catherine. 'She's going to spend her days with a man who cares for her. She won't have to knit all day to make a few pennies.'

Abruptly Jannie turned to Catherine, 'And what will I have with my sisters both gone?' she snapped.

'You have Daa and we're still here and you know Judith loves you.'

'Ha. I think Daa's….' Jannie tapped her head. 'Du canna know where he is or what he's doing. He'll not work and if he doesn't he'll not get any wages. Who's going to pay for our meat then?'

'He doesn't have to go to work. He's retired.'

Like a sudden burst of sunshine the expression on Jannie's face changed and a broad smile spread across her face. 'The old lady Queen of England is coming here. Are you going to see her? You could ask her to come to tea wi' us.' As quickly as it had come the smile faded. 'But you'll not go, you think too much of the sheep.' Abruptly her attitude changed again. 'We canna stand here talking. Are you going to make me a cup of tea?'

How quickly Jannie changed the subject. 'Yes, of course,' said Catherine.

'And have you made bannocks?'

'I have.'

'So will we go and have some?'

'We will.'

The new Gilbert Bain hospital had been built on a hillside overlooking Bressay Sound. Many of its windows overlooked the waters of Breiwick. The Queen Mother was to declare the hospital officially opened. Catherine had no plans to go and watch; neither had she made the journey to see the Queen and Duke of Edinburgh at the official opening of the Lerwick Harbour Works. Once she would have jumped at the chance, but that would have been when she could go with a friend and criticize the clothes and jewels that were being worn. No, she would not go; she had other things to do.

Jannie didn't stay long at Catherine's. It was only mid-morning but she said she had to go and make Daa's tea for he would soon be home from work. Catherine stood at her door and watched her mother-in-law stomp her way home. Jannie's condition was getting worse. How would Daa cope if Jannie had to be put in a home? Neil Lumsden would have to be consulted. It was all very unsettling. But good things were happening, too. Joe and June had moved in and maybe a young family with children would take Laura's house. She sighed. She should be happy to have others of her own age round her. Why, then, did she feel so lonely?

The work on her house was taking much longer than that on Laura's. Norrie was obliged to do his contract work during the day and able only to work on the house at weekends. Joe Thomson, who so far had tried and failed to get a job, worked by himself and there was usually the sound of a hammer or some other implement being used. But today the sounds coming from the house were not of building work. The first thought that came to Catherine's mind was that Joe had turned the radio up very loud, for she could hear jazz being played on a piano. Well, at least he was happy. She smiled as she turned to go indoors then stopped, for a crashing chord had been played and someone was laughing heartily. That was never a radio programme. Curious to know what was going on she went to investigate.

As she approached the house the playing began again and after a few bars a voice began to sing, a rich warm voice. Catherine stood to listen. The music was fast and furious and the singing interrupted at intervals by laughter. There was no way this was coming from a radio. When the last chord had been played, she heard Joe's laughter and his voice saying, 'Oh *man,* that was good. *Great* day I found *you,* baby.'

Catherine knocked on the door. 'Well, hi there,' said a beaming Joe. 'What can I do for you?'

'You can tell me what's going on for a start,' said Catherine.

The smile dropped from Joe's face. 'I'm sorry, have I been making too much noise? Have I annoyed you?'

'No. But was that you I heard playing and singing? I didn't know you had a piano.'

'Only just got it. Come and have a look.'

The piano was an old upright. Brass candle holders adorned its front. A row of discoloured keys, like an old man's teeth, were exposed by the open lid. There was no sheet music on the stand. Catherine looked at it.

'Don't you need...?' She indicated the empty music stand.

'I guess not,' said Joe. A wicked grin spread across his face. He widened his eyes till the pupils appeared as black lozenges in the whites. 'Ah is a black man,' he mocked, 'and ah've got rhythm.' He laughed. 'No, I've grown up with jazz; all my family play somethin'. I was in a band back in the States. I miss it, so when I got the chance of this....' He patted the top of the piano. 'Well, I took it. June got a friend of hers to fetch it for us. It was a real hassle.'

'It hasn't left you much room.'

'We don't need much.'

'Perhaps you'll play for us some time.'

'I'll play somethin' for you now.' Without hesitation Joe's fingers began to fly over the keys and from the old piano came the exciting rhythm of one of Scott Joplin's piano rags. He finished on a flourish and both he and Catherine dissolved into laughter.

'That was great,' said Catherine. 'I loved it!'

At that moment there was a pounding on the door. It was thrown open and Jannie stood there. 'What is this wickedness I hear? Music playing when there's work to be done. And what are you doing alone with this man? It's a good job I came by.' She reached out and took Catherine by the arm. 'Come, you, with me.'

There was no point in resisting and as she was pulled away Catherine rolled her eyes at Joe. He smiled and raised his eyebrows.

'You should not be there with that man,' said Jannie as she hurried Catherine away. 'I don't know what my Robbie would say. I'll not tell him, but you should not go there again.'

'All right, I won't,' said Catherine. A visit to Neil Lumsden was definitely needed. 'I have to go to the shop when I fetch the children. Is there anything you'd like me to get for you?'

'Na, I dinna think so.'

At Catherine's house Jannie pushed her through the door, refused to go in and stay for tea and bannocks, but again warned Catherine of being alone with a man, that one in particular. The warning brought a smile to Catherine's face.

As she settled to work again her thoughts turned time and again to Kay's will. She must have made one. Kay was too intelligent a person not to have known it was an important document to leave. Why did she not tell Norrie where to look for it? Or did she think that it wasn't necessary? Finding some written evidence that

Norrie was the rightful owner of the house and croft was vitally important, but where else was there to look? She had exhausted all the places left and all she could hope for now was a miracle.

But miracles don't happen.

NINE

A STEADY INCOME from Norrie's contract work hadn't made for security; hanging over his head was the fear that his cousins might yet turn him out of his house. His sense of humour failed him, meal times were no longer the happy gatherings they had been and in the evenings he all too often turned to the bottle for comfort. Catherine watched and worried as he drank more and more while Norrie, slurring his words, demanded that she look yet again for proof of ownership. Time was running short and there were only a few days left before it had to be produced. Catherine shook her head, sure that there was nowhere else to look.

'I've looked everywhere, Norrie,' she said. 'I've turned Kay's stuff out of the boxes you put it in twice. I've opened every envelope, looked between the pages of every book and it still hasn't turned up. There's nowhere else to look.'

'Blasted – Aussie – bastards,' spat Norrie. He got up and began to pace the floor. 'I don't know what to do, Catherine, short of murdering them both. And that would be too good for them.' He stopped pacing and looked at her. 'You might as well start clearing out the house, then, because there's nothing I can do. We'd better make ready to leave.'

He went to bed in a bad humour and beside him, Catherine had a restless night. In the morning she was reluctant to rise. It was not going to be a good day. But the sun was shining. Though it was none too warm, there was not much wind and it was the ideal day to spend on the hill, still her favourite place to go to chill out. She looked up at it, then closed the door on home and work and set off.

Passing Laura's house with its bright new windows and door, she wondered when it would be occupied. From Jannie's house she heard the rattle of pots and pans then saw the brief wave Daa gave her as he disappeared behind the barn.

She climbed up out of the valley then on up the hill. When she reached the top she turned to look back. Nothing of Deepdale was in sight, nothing except the beginning of the track leading to it; nothing else except the far end of the rigs, the bay and the sheltering headlands. She looked down on the road from Sumburgh to Lerwick. It snaked round the hill and dipped down towards Broonieswick. Snaked was the right word to describe it, she thought, for she could follow its sinuous journey past the village, see the way it slithered down into valleys and round hillsides on its way to the town.

When she first stood on the hill with Robbie there had not been many cars on the road, but now there were quite a few. She was about to turn away and walk on when a bright blue lorry caught her eye. She watched as it came through Broonieswick then crawled up the hill out of it. It was a removal lorry and must be fully laden to be so slow. It was a lorry she hadn't seen before and she wondered where it was going. As it came near the entrance to Deepdale it moved even slower and then stopped. She felt compelled now to wait and see what its next move was. To her surprise, when it started again it turned on to the track into the valley. Surely that meant someone was moving into Laura's house. She hoped it was someone nice, but wasn't about to go back to see.

Peat banks had all been cut, slabs dried and carried home and today there was no one else on the hill. She smiled as she remembered how she'd been warned not to go there alone then foolishly, late in the day, without thinking, she had and had been caught in a blizzard. There was no danger of that today and as she walked on, curlews warbled and skylarks rose up to charm her. The turf was springy beneath her feet and, somewhere hidden under a mat of heather, a little stream gurgled secretly.

But this was not where she wanted to be and she walked further.

The land sloped gently now, heather had given way and the ground was drier. At a spot not too far from the cliff edge where grass was green, favoured by sheep and cropped short, she sat down. The sea beneath the cliff rumbled against the rocks. Gulls and fulmars soared and danced in the currents of air rising up the cliff face.

Legs drawn up, arms clasped round them, Catherine rested her chin on her knees and gazed out to sea. Somewhere out there boats were sailing, little boats, big boats, fishing boats, steamers, cargo boats, and all with people on board. The boats were cockleshells tossed on an endless mass of water, water that was never still, even on days when it lay with a surface like glass. For who could tell what was going on underneath?

There were whirlpools in the sea, she'd been told, tides and currents that had to be learnt about and known, for to ignore them could lead to disaster. Sometimes killer whales were sighted round the islands. They came at the time the seal pups were born. Though she had watched for them Catherine hadn't seen any, but had caught sight of the rounded backs and fins of porpoise.

She had come to the hill for the peace she found there, for the wind that whispered through the grass, the birdsong that sweetened her day and for the sound of the sea that spoke to her of the man she had loved and lost. She lay back on the turf and gazed up at the blue void of the sky. Only when the immensity of it and the sounds around her made her troubles fade into insignificance did she get up and make for home. It was time to start clearing out the house and make ready for what surely was to come.

In her bedroom Catherine opened the wardrobe door. Norrie's best suit and one or two items of casual clothing hung beside her coat and some dresses. She took the dresses out and looked at them, considered throwing one or two away, but the material in them was still good and though they were not in the height of fashion – though who cared about fashion here – she might get more wear out of them yet. She put them back on the rail. In the bottom of the wardrobe were their shoes, among them the going-away pair she'd had when she married Robbie, her first husband. She had never worn them again. They were still in good condition and she hadn't the heart to throw them away. A busy outdoor life left her and Norrie very little time to socialize so best clothes lasted a long time.

The chest of drawers that stood beside the wardrobe had once belonged to Kay. It was big and old and had seen better days, but it was capacious and Catherine had been loath to get rid of it when Norrie asked if she wouldn't prefer to have a new one. She polished it regularly as she knew Kay had done and the wood glowed rich, warm and dark.

Starting with the bottom drawer she pulled it out. It was filled with Fair Isle jumpers that had been knitted by Kay. Too warm for the summer months – and it had been unusually hot and dry this year – they were essential garments for winter. There was nothing to throw away so she slid the drawer back into place. From the next drawer she threw out some shirts of Norrie's that she had intended to mend, but hadn't, also some of her blouses that were too small and which she had failed to lose weight to get into. Only a few items were removed from the last long drawer, which held underclothes, vests and pants which, though past their best, no one but she and Norrie were going to see.

The two small top drawers, filled to bursting, promised to yield more. Catherine pulled one open. Socks, thick ones, thin ones, old ones, new ones, crammed in and imprisoned when the drawer was shut, sprang to life when it was opened. When she had thinned them out, the drawer shut with ease.

The last drawer in the chest contained an assortment of objects. It was the drawer into which trivia from Norrie's pockets and hers were emptied. It was an overflow for socks, handkerchiefs, scarves and gloves, too. Nestling in amongst it all were two small boxes; one held a bottle of perfume that had been a Christmas present from her mother and in the other were what few items of jewellery she possessed. The drawer was full.

When she had thrown out what she considered rubbish she

pushed the drawer back in, but it would not go all the way. She pulled it out and tried to shut it again. Once more it refused to close completely. Now she pulled it right out to see what was jamming up the works. She put it down on the floor and looked into its vacant space, and there at the back was a wodge of paper. So that was it.

She reached in and took it out … looked at an envelope … containing … what? The paper was old and had yellowed round the edges. It was something she had never seen before and was nothing she had thrown in the drawer. There was no writing on it, no address to indicate who it was intended for. She hesitated, but then eased up the corner of the flap and opened the envelope. She spread out the folded papers that were inside and looked at the typewritten sheet that was on top. Her heart began to pound when she realized what it was. She reached for the bed and sat down, closed her eyes and took a few deep breaths before she started to read.

In trembling hands she held Kay's husband's will. It wasn't what she had been looking for, but was another step on the way. She began to read.

I, JOSEPH CALLUM BURNETT, husband of Kay Margaret Burnett, residing at Sinclair's Croft, Deepdale, hereby leave to my wife …

Where is the date?

… the whole Means and Estate, heritable and moveable, wherever situated, belonging to me …

Quickly Catherine scanned the page …

… I revoke all previous wills by me …

Ah, at last …

… the sixth day of February, nineteen hundred and thirty-one….

This was the Holy Grail – or nearly. Everything depended now on whether he had written this will after the one the cousins had. Folding the sheet of paper Catherine laid it aside and began to look at the larger, thicker sheets fastened together with pink string. They were deeds of servitude. In legal terms they rambled on and were of no interest to her, but she unfolded each one, scanned their contents then refolded them. The last one held a loose sheet, folded into four; she spread it out and laid it on her lap. One glance told her that it was what she had searched so diligently for, the paper containing the few words that would save her family from being evicted. This was Kay's will. Dashing away the tears of relief and joy that persisted in filling her eyes she was about to read it when there was a loud knock on her door. She got up and, putting the paper on the bed with the others, went to see who was there. It could only be Jannie.

But it wasn't. Catherine took one look at the young man standing on the doorstep, felt the blood drain from her face and her knees buckle. She held tight to the door thinking she was going to faint. And then she burst into tears.

'Ah me,' said the young man. 'First a frightened woman slams a door in my face, and now I've scared another.' He stepped forward. 'Please sit down.' Taking Catherine by the arm he led her to a chair. 'Can I get you some water?'

Catherine shook her head. 'No, no, it's all right. It's just ... it's just....' She was breathing fast. 'It's just that one shock at a time I can deal with, but one right after another is a bit much.' She pulled a handkerchief from her pocket and began to dry her eyes. 'Where have you come from and what do you want?'

'I am here to help my uncle, Lars Johansson, move in, and I've come to see if you can let us have some milk; we have none.'

Catherine had walked past the lorry on her way home but had seen only the removal men. 'You need to see Jannie for that, though I may have some to spare.'

'Does she live at the end house?'

Catherine nodded.

'I saw the cow and went to ask. She looked at me and slammed the door. Why would she do that?'

Why wouldn't she? To see the double of your dead son, standing on the doorstep, was surely enough to make any woman react in that way. Now, that same young man – a carbon copy of her first husband, Robbie – stood before her. This young man was Robbie's double. Same build, same dark hair, same face, same grin … but not the same eyes. Where Robbie's had been brown and bottomless this man's were the deep blue of the sea on a summer day. 'You're a vision, the exact likeness of someone we both loved and lost. It's no wonder Jannie freaked out.'

'Or you.'

'Or me. Let me get you some milk.'

TEN

WITH JOY IN her heart at the discovery of Kay's will and her mind going back to it again and again, Catherine struggled to concentrate on what she was doing. She ached to tell Norrie, couldn't wait for him to come home, and time seemed to stretch for ever. At last the children were home, the evening meal ready and Norrie would soon be there. Catherine dished up their food and put the dishes in the oven to keep hot. There was nothing more to do but wait. But I can't, she thought, I can't sit and twiddle my thumbs. She jumped up. Robbie was reading a comic. 'Look after the boys, Robbie, and don't get into mischief.'

'Why, where are you going?'

'I've some important news for your father. I'm going to meet him.'

Hurrying, half running, Catherine sped through the valley and up the hill. She had been overwhelmed with relief to find the will and couldn't wait to tell her husband. A great weight had been lifted from her, had been replaced with joy, a lightness and a feeling of walking on air. The excitement she had felt when she held that piece of paper had stayed with her, and she was bathed in happiness.

She was on the road, looking toward Broonieswick and for sight of Norrie's van. Where was he? He should be in sight by now. She took a few hesitant steps, stopped and twisted her hands together. This was stupid. She was nervous, acting like a child. Come on, Norrie, hurry up. She began to walk back and forth hoping that every time she turned around he would be there. He wasn't. But then there he was and she was running to meet him. Before he could bring the vehicle to a stop she had grabbed the handle of the door, pulled it open and was on the seat beside him, her arms round his neck. 'Oh, Norrie, Norrie,' she gabbled through a sudden rush of tears. 'It's all right, we won't have to move, I-I …' and burying her face in his neck she sobbed while he held her.

'Come on,' he said, relaxing his hold on her. 'What's happened?'

She lifted her head and her tear-streaked face broke into a smile. 'I found Kay's will … and her husband's. It's all there.'

Norrie gasped and his mouth dropped open. He sat speechless, then he roared and, grabbing Catherine in a bone-crushing hug, cried, 'You little beauty!' as he showered her with kisses.

'Let go, you're breaking my ribs,' laughed Catherine.

'Where did you find it? I thought you said you'd looked everywhere.'

'It was stuck behind one of the drawers in the chest in our bedroom. I think Kay hid it for safety and then forgot to tell you where to find it.'

'She probably thought there wasn't any hurry.'

'Never mind that,' said Catherine. 'I want you to see it for yourself. Our supper is in the oven and it'll dry out while we sit here. Let's go.'

The absence of children when they got home was not noted; of more importance was the will.

'I hope you put it somewhere safe,' said Norrie.

Catherine fetched the precious piece of paper from their bedroom. She put it, along with Kay's husband's will, on the table. Heads together, she and Norrie read every word. When they had finished Norrie took Catherine in his arms, not so fiercely this time, but with love.

'There's not much doubt about it, is there?' he said. 'In fact there's none at all. They can do nothing to us now, my darling. They can sue me for assault if they like; they won't get away with it. I'm starving. Where's the bairns?'

'They must be outside. Go and call them, will you?'

Norrie went to the door and stepped out. But he didn't call and he didn't come back. When Catherine had put all the dishes on the table and no Norrie or children had appeared she went to look for them. From the beach she could hear shouts and laughter and saw Norrie heading that way. He was as bad as the boys; she would have to fetch them all and, closing the door against thieving cats, she followed him.

Added to the sound of raised voices, shouts and laughter, she heard the snock of a ball on wood. They were never playing cricket; they didn't have a bat or ball. As she got closer Joe's curly head came into view, a lean brown arm was raised and a ball thrown, curving in an arc towards an out-of-sight batsman. She smiled. She might have known it would be him. Norrie had stopped at the end of the path to the beach. Catherine joined him.

'They're playing rounders,' said Norrie.

'It's baseball, it has to be. Joe's in charge.'

Robbie saw them. 'Hi, Mam, come and have a go,' he called. 'We need more fielders. The boys can't catch.'

'Not true,' said Allen. 'Come on, Mam, it's fun.'

'Another time. Your tea's on the table. It'll be getting cold.'

'No, not yet,' cried the twins in unison.

'Yes, I say. Come now.'

Judith had been sitting on a rock watching play. She had refused to join in. 'Stupid game,' she muttered as she got up. 'What a waste of time.'

'Pick up the cushions, boys,' said Joe. 'We can play again another day.' To mark the bases – Joe called them cushions – they had taken off and put down their jumpers. He had whittled a baseball bat from an offcut of timber. It was the right size for small hands.

'I hope you don't mind, ma'am,' said Joe as they trooped up the path.

'Not a bit,' said Catherine. 'It's nice for them to learn something new. Maybe you'll tell them about America. I'm sure they'd like to know.'

'Mam,' said Judith when they were sitting down to eat, 'Joe said he was brown all over.'

Knives and forks and jaws stopped moving. Catherine slapped her hand on to the table. 'Judith!' she exclaimed. 'Tell me you didn't ask him.'

'Yes. I did. I wanted to know. But how could—'

'I don't *believe* it,' said Catherine. 'Be quiet and don't let me hear that you've ever said anything like that to him again. That was very rude of you. Anything you want to know you must ask me.'

Judith put food in her mouth, chewed a little, then said, 'But we only go brown where we don't wear any clothes—'

'That will do.'

'But if he's brown all over how does he—?'

'Judith.'

Norrie chuckled. 'You've got your work cut out there,' he said. 'And I don't think you're going to win.' The chuckle grew and became laughter. At first, the children stopped eating and looked at him, then as they realized the situation was out of their mother's control they joined in and, laughter being infectious, Catherine, despite herself, laughed too.

'I'll talk to you later, young lady,' she said to Judith. 'Now get on with your tea, all of you.'

The meal over, the table cleared and dishes washed up and put away, the children, who had helped, went out to play again. Though the summer was on the wane the evenings were still long and light and no one wanted to go to bed. They were still at school, though, and on school days Catherine insisted they were all in bed by nine o'clock. Robbie protested that as he was older he should be allowed to stay up later. 'You can always read for a while,' said Catherine and sent him on his way.

When the children were in bed, the house quiet and Norrie reading the paper, Catherine fetched her sewing basket and prepared to embark on yet another pile of mending. Norrie said, 'Put that away. We have to celebrate. You'll take a dram with me now, won't you? Just one?'

'As long as it's only one. You've been taking rather too much lately.'

'Yes, I know, but I was worried. What would I have done if you hadn't found the wills? We would have been out of here and I didn't have anywhere for us to go. I would have failed you.'

He looked so dejected that Catherine hated what she was going to have to say next. 'We're not exactly out of the woods yet, are we?' she said. 'We still have to find out if Kay's man's will was written later than anything your cousins have got. If it is, we shall be all right.'

'Magnie's mam and da emigrated in twenty-eight. I remember because Magnie was just leaving school. But Uncle Callum's will was dated 1931.' Norrie grinned. 'They're trying to pull a fast one, because I don't think Auntie Kay would have told me I'd inherit if she knew different. She wasn't an old croft wife; she was a teacher and too clever to make a mistake like that.'

'We've just got to hope everything's going to be all right, then,' said Catherine. 'There's no point worrying about it. Sit there – I'll get the glasses.' She poured their drinks. Grouse for her; she wouldn't drink his malt.

Norrie said, 'To the future.'

'To the future,' echoed Catherine.

'You're a good wife,' said Norrie when their drinks were done. He took her hand in his. 'You're better than I deserve. I haven't loved you properly for some time. Come to bed and I'll see if I can make amends.'

She went with him, but when Norrie held her, caressed her and kissed her, despite herself her thoughts persisted in turning to the handsome young man with eyes that reminded her of the drifting, shifting, sea.

ELEVEN

DETERMINED THAT NOTHING should stand in the way of Kay and Callum's wills being put into the hands of the solicitor, Catherine took the bundle of papers to Lerwick herself. She had not made an appointment and, though she was told that Mr Smith was too busy to see her, she insisted on waiting. 'Please let him know I'm here and that it's very important,' she said. When told that he would spare her a few minutes, she sat down to wait. And for the best part of an hour, until the client he had with him left, wait she did.

'I won't take up too much of your time, Mr Smith,' she said when she was finally shown into his office, 'but I would like you to look at this.' She handed him the precious envelope.

The solicitor quickly read the wills. 'Mmm,' he said as he nodded his head. 'They will have to be proved, of course, but that shouldn't take too long.'

'My husband's cousins were threatening to take his property from him. One said that it had been willed to him, but we found Norrie's auntie's will. Won't that cancel out any other ones?' asked Catherine.

'Well, I couldn't say until I've read them, but leave them with me and I'll be in touch with you just as soon as I have.'

'I'll have a receipt for them, if you don't mind,' said Catherine.

John Smith looked over the top of his glasses at her and smiled. 'You certainly shall,' he said.

Catherine ran down the steps from the solicitor's office. While she was in the town, she thought, she would do some shopping.

There was work waiting at home and she didn't have much time, but as she sped along the street, her head in the clouds, she felt like singing. If all went well, life would soon be back on an even keel again. Her Commercial Street shopping done she headed towards the harbour. Maybe there was a fishing boat in and she would be able to buy some fresh fish.

As she walked along the harbour wall she looked down into the boats that were tied up alongside. It would be a boat like this that Robbie wanted to go on. She didn't think they looked very nice. There were coils of rope and stuff on the decks and not much room to walk about. But he would be in the galley and not helping to haul nets. All the same, it didn't seem a very savoury place to work.

She didn't see anybody on the boats and there were no fish to be had. She walked on then, but as she was about to turn away, something caught her eye. It was the blue of a coat and the same colour as one that Robbie wore. It was worn by a boy on one of the boats. She thought he looked about the same age as Robbie. For a moment her heart missed a beat. No, it couldn't be. Her Robbie was in school. Wasn't he?

The boat's engine was throbbing and it was about to cast off. As it did, the boy turned and looked up. Catherine caught and held her breath: she was looking straight into the eyes of her son. 'Robbie!' she shouted. 'Robbie, come back at once!' Even as the words left her mouth she knew he probably couldn't hear her, and even if he could it was too late. Unable to stop him, she stood and watched as the little boat headed out into the sound, carrying Robbie with it.

Born on an ebb tide. How many times was that going to come back to haunt her? The feeling of euphoria that had buoyed her up and carried her along since she had spoken to the solicitor evaporated rapidly. She stared after the boat, at its wake bubbling and churning the water behind it, then fanning out to dissipate in smaller and smaller ripples. It was heading away from her and she feared that that was what Robbie was doing, too. Was she going to have to give in and let him go his own way? She couldn't stand there thinking about it. It was time to go home and if she didn't hurry she would miss the bus.

With the approach of autumn, lambs had to be separated from their mothers. The best ewe lambs would be kept for breeding and as replacements for older sheep that would be culled. The whethers – castrated males – had to be graded for sale. With Norrie still working long hours away from home, separating and grading was Catherine's job.

She toiled up the hill to the sheep pens, her dog at her heels. Her thoughts turned again and again to the sight of Robbie on the boat, but now she concentrated on the job at hand. The dog at her side, trained to the whistle and spoken commands, was off like a shot when she said, 'Fetch.'

Fly had a keen eye and, having already seen where the sheep were, set off on a wide outrun and came up behind them. Catherine, using the whistle, slowed the dog down then brought him on behind them to bring the sheep to the pens. Using her voice now to command the dog, the flock was herded into the pen and the gate secured. 'Good dog, Fly,' said Catherine as she patted its head. 'Go lie down.' The dog, red tongue lolling, sank to the ground.

For the next hour Fly watched her every move as Catherine selected lambs for the market and pushed them out of the pen and into the field. Later, she and the dog would drive them down to better pasture where they would graze till market day. The ewe lambs would have to wait for another time.

When she had selected all she thought fit to go she shut the gate on the pen, stretched to ease her aching back then sat down with her dog. The summer weather was still holding; the day was hot and working with sheep was tiring. She sometimes compared it with her job at the hospital. That was a tiring job, too, but in a very different way to what she was doing now. How naïve she had been to think that life on a farm, or a croft, was idyllic. Nothing could be further from the truth. When she had been a nurse she had had days off when she was able to do just as she liked. What wouldn't she give for days off now? How many times had she planned to go somewhere only for a sheep to get entangled in some old fence wire, or the rams to start fighting? Outings had to be abandoned till the problem was solved. If she was lucky she might get away, but if not, she stayed at home.

For several nights she hadn't slept well. Norrie's drinking bothered her, but asking him to ease off only made him drink more. And then there was the worry of what the cousins threatened to do. It was no good thinking that now she had delivered the wills to the solicitor it was all over. They had to wait for what he had to say. If only it would all go away.

She yawned, closed her eyes and relaxed. There was no wind and other than the guttural bleating of the ewes and lighter answering ones of the lambs that were outside the pen, all was peace. Her tiredness mixed with the warmth of the sun was balm and she sat there peacefully, her eyes shut.

The young man with the ocean-blue eyes had been walking on the hill, enjoying the view and the freedom of the island. From a distance he had watched Catherine and her dog working. The path he chose to walk led her way. He looked at Catherine. 'I hate to wake you,' he began, his voice loud. Fly gave a low growl. Startled, Catherine opened her eyes and said, 'What? I wasn't asleep. Oh, it's you.' She shivered. Not from cold, but from the tremor that ran through her at sight of him.

'I've frightened you again. I'm sorry.'

'Yes, you have. Please don't make a habit of it.' Catherine was still sitting; her dog pressed close to her side. She put her arm round it. 'It's all right,' she said. 'Quiet now, Fly.' She looked at the young man. He smiled and Catherine felt her heart leap. She chided herself for being silly. 'Is your uncle settling in?'

'Getting there. May I sit and talk a while?'

No, go away, thought Catherine, but instead said, 'Be my guest.'

'Have you lived here all your life?'

She couldn't look at him, not at those wonderfully blue eyes. 'No, I came here from the south of England many years ago.'

'Then you must have thought it a lovely place to want to stay.'

It could have been, but it wasn't. It had been a determination to fight the odds that had made her dig in her heels and refuse to be pushed out. She shook her head and gave a little chuckle. 'It is a lovely place,' she said. 'In fact,' she threw her arm out in a wide arc, taking in the hill, the land down to the top of the cliff and the expanse of ocean, beyond which, as the sun was shining was a clear and sparkling blue, 'it's beautiful.' She sighed then, a deep sigh. 'But I don't like the way things are going and I can't hear the skylarks anymore.'

'You can't?' Bjorg looked up as a skylark winged its way up into the blue.

Catherine followed his gaze. 'Oh that,' she said. 'I can hear that one. No, to me skylarks mean happiness and I don't like what's happening in the valley, and I'm not going to talk about that, Mr-what is your name?'

'I'm Bjorg, Bjorg Larsen.'

'Well, Mr Larsen, if our paths should happen to cross again we'll have to continue this conversation then,' said Catherine as she got up. 'I have to get these lambs down the hill and then fetch my children from school.'

Bjorg had scrambled to his feet, too, and now stood looking down at her. To her embarrassment she felt her cheeks grow hot. Quickly, she turned away. 'When I've got the lambs through this gate would you be kind and let the ewes out? Just open up the pen; they can stay in this field.'

On Catherine's command, Fly brought the lambs to her and together they herded them through the gate and down the hill. After a few minutes Bjorg caught up with her. 'I am here for a holiday only,' he said. 'I hope we shall have time to talk again.'

'We probably will,' said Catherine, wondering how she was going to avoid him. The last thing she wanted was a man who set her thoughts in turmoil, who played havoc with her emotions, who she wouldn't trust herself to be alone with.

'I think you are working very hard,' said Bjorg. 'Do you have to?'

'I don't think I have any other option,' said Catherine. 'It's the lot of every croft wife, unless her man is a secret millionaire. But then if he was he wouldn't be a crofter and his wife would live in luxury.'

They were at the bottom of the hill now. The lambs had bunched together and when Catherine stopped walking and called Fly to her side, they stopped too.

'Would you stand here?' she said to Bjorg. 'And stop the lambs going back up the hill while I open that gate.' She pointed to a gate that she wanted to drive the lambs through and into a park. She wasn't going to tell him that if he hadn't been there her dog was quite capable of holding the sheep where they were till she told him to bring them on. 'Fly will stay beside you.'

She left Bjorg standing there. The gate opened she whistled to the dog. Fly sent the lambs towards her and he and Catherine directed them into the park.

'Thank you, Mr Larsen,' said Catherine as she shut the gate and Bjorg joined her. 'I have to go now. Goodbye.'

TWELVE

'YOU'RE QUIET,' SAID Norrie. 'Is anything wrong?'

'I saw Robbie in Lerwick this morning. He was on a fishing boat. I shouted at him to stop, but of course it was too late and the boat was leaving the harbour. I've sent him to bed without any supper.'

'I wondered where he was.'

Catherine turned her woebegone face to her husband. 'What am I going to do? Is nothing going to stop him?'

Norrie didn't reply. He put up a hand to stroke his beard. 'Well,' he said, 'put yourself in his shoes. He's got it into his head that it's what he wants. What would you do if you'd set your heart on something? You don't need me to tell you, do you? You'd let nothing stand in your way so what else do you expect from your boy?'

'I know one thing, and that is that he's as stubborn as a mule,' Catherine laughed. 'I remember when I wanted to take him to school on the back of my bike. "I'm not going to ride on yon," he said. And he wouldn't. He fought me when I wanted to put him on it. So I suppose you're right, but I still don't want him to go to sea.'

'You'll have a hard job to talk him out of it. Why were you in Lerwick, anyway?'

'I took Kay's will and all the rest of the papers in to the solicitors. I had to wait for ages. Mr Smith said the wills would have to be proved, but though he wouldn't say for certain, it looks as though we shall be all right.'

'Thank God for that,' said Norrie.

With Robbie banished to his bedroom, the twins outside and Judith once again with her grandmother, the brief spell alone was a welcome oasis in a busy day. It was a time to catch up on the day's doings and plan for the next. Never one to waste time, Catherine darned socks as she told Norrie how she had selected sheep for the market and asked if he would take time off work to help her get them there. She didn't tell him about Bjorg, but when he asked if she had been along to welcome the newcomers she said she hadn't and he asked her why.

'I've been busy,' she said. But not that busy, she thought.

'Go now,' said Norrie. 'They'll think they're not welcome otherwise.'

There was really no excuse. Catherine put down her work and got up, but as she was about to leave Judith came in.

'Mam,' said Judith, 'you are my mother, aren't you?'

'Good heavens, whatever makes you say that?' said a shocked Catherine.

'Grandma keeps calling me Jeanie. She says that's my name and that I'm her little girl. I'm not, am I?'

Catherine put her hands on Judith's shoulders. 'No, darling, you're her grand-daughter. You *know* I'm your mother, don't you? Grandma gets confused. It happens to old folk sometimes.'

'But she says I ought to live with her and Aald Daa. I don't want to.'

'You don't have to. Your place is here with us.' Catherine wrapped her arms round Judith. 'Don't bother your head about it. Grandma's getting old, that's all. Now,' she said, 'show me how you're getting on with your knitting.'

From the bag in which she carried it, Judith pulled out a piece of work in two colours. Catherine enthused over it. 'I don't know how you do this. I can't even knit with one strand of wool. But this is lovely.'

'Mam,' said Judith. 'What's wrong with Grandma?'

'Why?'

'Sometimes I don't know what she's saying. She talks about

people I don't know and she gets cross when I tell her I don't know who she's talking about.'

How do you make a child understand? 'Sit down, Judith. I'm going to ask you to do something. You'll have to be very grown up to do it, so listen to me.'

In the simplest way she could, Catherine explained how sometimes old people's minds got confused and some of the things they said didn't make sense. 'As we go through life we store up memories and by the time we get old we have lots. But sometimes they get jumbled up, and when people like Granny try to tell them to others they come out wrong. But we have to be kind and humour them,' she said. 'And you will have to as well. Go along with whatever Granny says. Don't contradict her, if you do it might worry her and may make things worse. Play a game of pretend while you're there; let her think you know what she's talking about and hopefully it will keep her happy.'

Judith clasped her hands together and brought them up to her mouth while she thought about what her mother had said. Then she put her hands down and smiled. 'So you want me to *pretend* to be Jeanie when I'm with Grandma? And *pretend* I know all the people she talks about?'

'Yes, that's it.'

'All right,' said Judith. 'That'll be fun. I can be two people; Jeanie when I'm there and Judith when I'm home. It'll be like being in a play. I shall have to be an actor,' she laughed. 'Can I go now?'

Though the days were getting shorter, evenings were still light. But there was a nip in the air so Catherine put on a light jacket before she stepped out to visit her new neighbours. She had seen the wife briefly in passing, but, knowing that the first few days in a new house were usually spent finding homes for things, then trying to remember where they had been put, had hesitated to call.

She knocked on the door and when it was opened, smiled and said to the woman standing there, 'Hello, I'm Catherine. Welcome to Deepdale.' She held out a freshly baked pie, one she'd made that morning. 'I haven't any flowers, so I'd like to give you this to welcome you.'

'How kind of you, thank you. I'm Gerda. Come in and meet my husband.'

Lars Johansson was a tall, scholarly-looking man with greying hair going thin on top, and kind blue eyes behind gilt-framed glasses. The hand that clasped Catherine's was soft, not as soft as a woman's, but Catherine guessed it was not a manual job he did. 'How very nice to meet you,' he said. And then Bjorg was there. 'This is my nephew, Bjorg,' said Lars. 'I think you've met.'

'Yes, we have,' said Catherine. She looked at Bjorg and was unprepared for the frisson of excitement that flared between them. This wouldn't do. She turned to Gerda. 'Are you finding everything to your liking? If there's anything I can help you with you have only to ask.'

'Thank you,' said Gerda. 'Lars will be taking the car to work, but I shall have to use the bus, so if you have a timetable that would be a help.'

'I'll write it out for you and let you have it tomorrow,' said Catherine. 'It's very quiet here. I hope you'll be happy.'

'I'm sure I will find plenty to do to occupy my time,' said Gerda. 'You will come and have coffee with me some time, yes?'

Catherine was about to open her mouth and reply when Bjorg butted in. 'This lady is a very busy person,' he said. 'She looks after a large flock of sheep while her husband is away working. I don't think —'

'Oh, hush, Bjorg,' said Gerda. She turned to Catherine. 'You don't work all the time, do you? Surely your evenings are free?'

'Well, it's summer, you see. We have to make good use of the long days. It's better in winter … that is if the weather isn't too bad. And, of course, the children take up a lot of my time.'

'We shall have to wait for winter, then,' said Gerda. 'You will come and spend an evening with us then.'

'That would be nice,' said Catherine. 'I must go; it's time to get the children to bed.' She couldn't look at Bjorg. Her face felt as though it were on fire. She had to get out of there before the others noticed. 'Bye.'

Norrie was nursing a glass of whisky when she got home. 'What are they like?' he asked.

'They're nice. Their name is Johansson – Gerda and Lars. I think I'm going to like her. She asked me to go along and have coffee with her. I didn't ask where they come from, but I think it's Norway.'

'Good.' Norrie was refilling his glass. 'It'll be good for you to have someone your own age here besides June. I take it the wife is around your age?'

'I think so, but he seems a lot older. He's rather quiet.' And then there was Bjorg, of course. Why didn't she tell Norrie about him? She hadn't even told him how he'd given her such a shock when he came to her door. There was nothing to hide, so what was stopping her?

Norrie sat slouched in a chair by the stove, his whisky in his hand. Did he have to drink? His hair needed to be cut, his beard too. Looking at him Catherine could see the sprinkling of grey in both. She hadn't noticed that before. He was forty-five, middle-aged, so perhaps the arrival of a few grey hairs was to be expected. She would have a look later to see if she had any.

'Where are the children? Is Judith in her room?' said Catherine.

'She went out.'

'She'll be with the boys, then; I'll go and fetch them.'

THIRTEEN

'TROUBLE CERTAINLY DOES find you, my girl, doesn't it?' Neil Lumsden sat back in his chair and looked at Catherine. 'But we all get our share. I've no doubt you've heard that my wife left me. She never settled here.'

'I was told,' said Catherine.

'It was my fault for insisting on staying. Coming from the city she never did fit in, but I love the place.' I came from a city too, thought Catherine, but I'm still here. 'Anyway you didn't come here to listen to me,' Lumsden went on. 'But to tell me what Jannie's been up to. ' He gave Catherine a twitch of a smile.

'She's getting confused and seems to think that Judith is her little girl. Sometimes she's perfectly lucid and you'd think there's nothing wrong with her. Then she goes off about something that happened long ago and about people I don't know. Time means nothing and she rails at Daa for not going to work.'

'Is she aggressive?'

'Not to me,' said Catherine. 'I don't know about Daa, but then he wouldn't tell me if she was.'

'Does she wander out of the house at night?'

'I wouldn't know about that. If she does Daa hasn't said.'

'Mmm.' Lumsden tapped the top of his desk with the butt end of a pencil. 'She doesn't live alone, she isn't aggressive and she doesn't wander … as far as we know.' He was speaking his thoughts aloud. 'There's nothing to be done at the moment, my dear,' he said. 'Keep an eye on her the best you can and get her husband to keep you informed of any changes. I'll drop in when I'm that way.'

'Thank you,' said Catherine.

As she started to get up Lumsden stopped her. 'Don't be in such a hurry to go. Wait a moment.' Catherine sat down again. 'You're looking peaky. Are you all right or is something wrong?'

Wrong? Oh nothing's wrong. My son wants to go to sea. The valley's turning upside down. Laura has moved out and new people moved in. Jannie's senile. Norrie's turned to drink and his cousins want to throw us out. Oh … and a virile young man who reminds me of my first husband attracts me so much that I lust after him and I'm afraid of losing control. Oh no, nothing's wrong. Catherine's lips lifted into a smile.

'Nothing more than might trouble any family, you might say,' she said.

'There's more to it than that, isn't there.' It wasn't a question. 'Come on, tell me.'

Catherine hesitated then blurted out, 'It's possible we might get thrown out of our house. Norrie's cousin has come home from Australia and claims it was left to him. Everything's upside down. Norrie's drinking too much and telling him to stop doesn't help.'

'Is that all?'

'I've already told you about Jannie. Isn't that enough?'

Neil Lumsden had taken a liking to Catherine the day he first met her. He remembered how she had asked for a job at his surgery. He still hoped she would come back to work for him but knew that with four children and all the work that went with them, not to mention a flock of sheep and the croft, she had more than enough to do, so it wasn't likely to happen.

'Now listen to me, young lady,' he said. 'I'm sure your man doesn't realize how hard you work. You've taken on a lot more than many others your age. When did you last have a holiday?'

Catherine shrugged. 'Can't remember, six or seven years ago now, I think.'

'Well, it's high time you had another.'

'But I … but—'

'No,' Lumsden shook his head. 'You need one.'

Abruptly, Catherine stood up. 'I'm sorry, but there's no way I can go on holiday. I've got too much to do. It's a busy time of year, you should know that. I have the children to see to then there are the sheep sales and now Jannie.'

'All right, all right, sit down.' When Catherine had seated herself again, Lumsden said, 'You've got to try to get some time to yourself. You're a bundle of nerves. You need to relax. You'll cope better if you do. If you can't get away, the best I can do is give you a tonic. Will you take it?'

'If you insist.'

Armed with a bottle of some evil-looking green liquid Catherine got on her bicycle and rode home. As she pedalled along she thought about what Neil Lumsden had said. 'Try to get some time to yourself.' Well, that's just what she would do. It was only mid-morning; the children wouldn't be home from school till later in the afternoon. What did it matter if socks weren't darned, sheets washed, or shirts ironed? The doctor was right. She *deserved* some free time and by golly she was going to get it.

Where once she would have got off and walked, today, now that the track down into the valley had been upgraded, she rode down it. At home she propped her bike against the wall, went inside and made a flask of tea, buttered a bannock, put them both in a bag and, shutting the door, set off to climb the hill.

'Don't go there alone,' they had said, but she didn't care, today she would. It was unlikely there would be anyone else on the moor for the peat had all been dried and carried home and there was no Billie these days to come leaping across the tussocks to greet her. She would have the place to herself.

How hot the summer had been, but it would soon be September and the rain would come, rain and gales, and then winter would be upon them. There would be no more chance to sneak away to find the peace she needed. For months to come when she wasn't fighting the weather to work with the sheep, she would be closeted with her children, doing her best to entertain them and pouring oil on the troubled waters of quarrels. She would pray for Norrie to pick up his fiddle again and take himself off to the dances instead of sitting at home drinking.

A cool breeze met her when she reached the top of the hill, but the sun was warm. Which way was she to go? Not up the hill, for the higher she went the cooler it would be. She turned south and hoped to find some sheltered spot in which to have her picnic. She found one, for many were the undulations in the hill, and throwing down the rug she had brought, she sat down. Letting her breath go long and slow she put her hands behind her head, closed her eyes and lay back. Lying there she realized how tired she was and how her body ached with it. Never mind, nothing could be better now than an uninterrupted hour or two.

Above her, lazy clouds drifted, changed shape, melded into one another. The busyness of summer birds, mating, nesting and rearing a brood, had given way to the making ready for migration and birdsong was very little, nothing more than the occasional squawk of a crow or the 'ka-ka' of a gull. Catherine's thoughts drifted with the breeze that crept across the hill to tease her hair and cool her face. She sighed over Jannie, once the thorn in her side, but now an old woman of changeable moods. She groaned at thoughts of Robbie and knew she had to let him have his way, smiled, thinking of Joe and the way he pounded the keys of his old piano. She wondered how much of a friend Gerda would be. The woman's lifestyle was so different to her own – that much was obvious from the way she had furnished her house. Would it be a barrier? And then there was Norrie. What was she going to do about him? If he kept on drinking the way he was he was going to make himself ill. But I'm here to get away from all that, she thought, and resolved to dismiss them all from her mind for the afternoon. Gradually, she relaxed and let the seductive whisper of the wind lead her away into the land of illusion. She dozed, drifted and slumbered.

'Halloo.'

Catherine stirred in her sleep. Was that a voice? Or was she dreaming? No, there it was again. 'Halloo.' It wasn't a dream. She opened her eyes. And there, outlined against the sun, was the figure of a man. She shaded her eyes with her hand and he, realizing she couldn't see him properly, stepped aside.

'Oh, it's you,' said Catherine when she recognized Bjorg. 'What are you doing here?'

'Lars and Gerda are both out and it is very boring to sit indoors alone. I thought I would go for a walk, but I did not expect to see you. I thought you would be working with your sheep.'

'Well I'm not. I'm taking some time off and I would much prefer to be alone.' No I wouldn't. Don't listen to me, please stay.

'I would rather stay and talk with you. May I?'

Catherine sat up. If he wasn't going to go away she couldn't remain lying down. 'I'd rather you didn't.' That was another lie, but what else could she say?

Bjorg sat; then, stretching out his legs, lay back, turned and, elbow on the ground, rested his face on his upturned hand. He didn't talk but gazed at her. She had daydreamed about him and secretly longed for another meeting, but now that it was happening she was nervous. She chided herself for behaving like a teenager on a first date. But, try as she might to bring her emotions under control, there was nothing she could do to stop every nerve in her body tingling with excitement. Did he know what he was doing to her?

'Do you realize how beautiful you are?' said Bjorg at last.

'You flatter me,' said Catherine.

'No, I do not. I am very attracted to you and I wonder why your husband expects you to work so hard. I would not treat you that way.'

Surely he could hear the thump, thump of her heart. Surely he knew what he was doing. Never had Catherine felt more vulnerable. 'You have no right to talk to me that way,' she said when at last she could trust herself to speak.

'Why?'

'Because I'm a married woman.'

'And what difference does that make? I'm telling you what I see and feel.'

'You mustn't,' began Catherine, but Bjorg was saying, 'You cannot stop me.'

She turned to look at him, look straight into those blue, blue eyes, felt herself drawn into their depths and knew she wasn't going to save herself. 'Please don't do this to me,' she said, her voice a shade above a whisper.

Bjorg ignored her request. 'You told Gerda that you have no time for a social life in summer,' he said. 'Does that mean you do in winter? Does your husband take you dancing then? I would like to.'

'Don't be silly. You won't be here then.'

'I could be. I can see you in a ball gown, your shoulders bare and diamonds around your neck. You would be the most beautiful woman in the room and every man there would want to take you away from me.'

The picture he painted took Catherine back to Southampton and to the Christmas balls at the hospital: silky, floor-length dresses, paste jewellery, a black-market bottle of perfume shared with fellow nurses and waltzing the night away in the arms of handsome young doctors. It was a far cry from the high-spirited, energetic dancing she had done in the Shetland village halls and she thought she would never get the chance to dance in a ballroom again.

'Would you not like to dance with me?' said Bjorg when Catherine made no reply. Catherine sighed. Oh, yes, of course she would. 'Or would you rather it was your husband who charmed you and danced you away to heaven?'

This was too much. What was he going to say next? 'I think I've had enough of this conversation,' said Catherine. 'Would you please go away?'

Sitting up and folding his legs under him Bjorg reached out and took her hand. 'Have I offended you? Does your husband not speak to you this way? Does he not bring you gifts or treat you like the treasure you must be to him? He should.' Coming closer to her, Bjorg put his arm across her shoulders. She ought to push him from her, but his hand was under her chin and he was turning her face up to his. 'Ahh,' he sighed. 'There are tears in your eyes. Do not cry.'

She was tired, she was weak and he was irresistible. She turned her face into the rough wool of the jumper he was wearing. The smell of a woollen jumper was not new; what was new was the fresh, clean smell of a young man. There was another smell, too, it was of pine and made her think of the pine-clad hills of Norway, his home. It contrasted sharply with the diesel- and oil-splattered overalls Norrie wore. Norrie. Catherine raised a hand and pushed it against Bjorg's chest. 'That's enough,' she said. 'You have to go.'

He looked at her, then, leaning forward, put a soft kiss on her forehead and without speaking got up and walked away.

Putting her head in her hands Catherine wept.

FOURTEEN

THE RITUAL OF going to the meeting house on Sunday was no longer of importance to the residents of Deepdale. Laura was happily spending her days in Lerwick and, for all Catherine knew, was attending a church in the town. Joe and June slept late and didn't care for church at all. Lars and Gerda hadn't inquired after one so no one knew what their intentions were. Jannie didn't know which day of the week it was any more and, since the episode of the fanatic little preacher on her first visit to the meeting house, Catherine had not been since. Oh, she had been required to attend church again, for her first husband's funeral, then that of Mina, his aunt. But that was it and Sunday was treated, as far as possible, as a day of rest.

Norrie had gone to Broonieswick to look over the sheep he kept there and Catherine was busy preparing vegetables for Sunday dinner. In the living room the children were playing Snakes and Ladders. To Robbie it was just a game and for the twins it was fun, but Judith was calculating and wanted to win. 'What's the point of playing,' she would say, 'if you can't win?'

'Put the kettle on, Mam, Dad's home,' said Robbie when a car pulled up outside. But it wasn't Norrie. There was a knock on the door and when Catherine answered it, Norrie's cousin Magnie stood on the doorstep.

'I don't think we want to see you,' she said.

'Now I wonder why,' said Magnie. 'I haven't come to fight or to upset anybody, but I would like the chance to come in and talk to you both.'

'What about?'

'I'll tell you, if you let me come in.'

Catherine had kept him on the step. 'I'm not so sure I ought to,' she said. 'I don't want any trouble. Norrie's not here and if you still are when he comes home, there's likely to be some.'

'Not when he hears what I have to say.'

Catherine, her hand still on the door, didn't move. Although they hadn't received confirmation from the solicitor that the property legally belonged to Norrie, she was sure it did, so why was Magnie here? There was no way he could still get them out.

'You know that we've lost and Norrie has legal ownership of the croft, don't you?' went on Magnie. Catherine gasped. 'Oh, you didn't, well, you do now. So can I come in?'

Still Catherine hesitated, but then she relented. 'I suppose so,' she said, 'but I'm busy so you'll just have to talk to the bairns.'

'Do you want to play a game with us?' asked Judith when Magnie pulled out a chair and sat down. 'Though I warn you, I shall win.'

What does he want now? Why doesn't he leave us alone? Catherine busied herself again with preparations for dinner and gave a sigh of relief when Norrie came through the back door. 'What's he doing here?' he demanded. Glowering at Magnie he said, 'You've got a brass neck to come back again.'

'Now hold on,' said Magnie. 'The place is yours. I've no claim on it and I'm not here to dispute that. What I am here for is to tell you something I don't think you'll know.'

'And what might that be?'

Catherine clasped the towel she was holding to her chest and watched the two men. Animosity was still there. The children stopped their play.

'Would you mind if we did this in a civilized way?' said Magnie.

Norrie glared at his cousin.

'Magnie's already said he's not going to dispute your right to the croft, Norrie,' said Catherine. 'So why don't you sit down?'

'In 1958,' began Magnie, when he and Norrie were seated, 'there was a convention in Geneva over the Continental Shelf. You know what I mean?' Norrie nodded. 'They laid down rules about exploration of what was under the sea bed. They've been drilling for oil all over Scandinavia and I reckon they expect to find it under the North Sea.'

'Oh yes, ha ha, pull the other one,' laughed Norrie. 'Is this is another one of your hare-brained ideas? How do you suppose they're going to get it out?'

'I'm not joking. They will.'

'That's as may be,' said Norrie, 'but it's got nothing to do with me. How do you know about all this anyway? Or do you have shares and they got in touch to let you know?' Norrie laughed again, but all the same he was interested.

'If you'll stop pulling me to pieces and listen, I'll tell you.'

'Better make a cup of tea, Catherine,' said Norrie and to the children, 'you can make yourselves scarce.'

'Come on, boys,' said Robbie. 'We aren't going to get any dinner yet.' While Robbie took the twins outside to play Judith slid off her chair and quietly walked behind her father to sit on a little stool in the corner behind a fireside chair. Catherine was busy in the kitchen and didn't notice.

'How do you get to know what's going on in the North Sea when you're on the other side of the world?' asked Norrie.

'Eyes and ears, boy, but not only that. I keep in touch with Gibby Johnson. He's a great one for poking his nose into what doesn't concern him. But this does.' Here Magnie leaned forward and poked Norrie's knee with his finger. 'Land in Shetland is going to go up in value.'

'What? Don't be daft.'

'When they find oil it's got to come ashore and Shetland's the place.'

'Huh. I think you're talking out of the back of your head.'

'You can think what you like, Norrie Williams, but I had a good offer for the land in this valley – yes, that's why I wanted to get my hands on it and if you're interested, which you should be, I'll pass your name on.'

Catherine put a tray with two mugs of tea and a sugar bowl on the table. 'I can't remember if you take sugar,' she said to Magnie, 'but help yourself.'

Norrie took his mug and stared into it. After a while he raised his head and looked at his cousin. 'How could I sell?' he said. 'I only own half the valley. Daa's croft is left to Robbie and Laura's is to go to Judith. I can't sell over their heads and, come to that … they haven't even got possession yet.'

'It's obvious you're not a business man,' said Magnie. 'If you want to get on in life you don't let a little thing like opposition get in your way. Use your power of persuasion, man. Or do you want to run after sheep all your life and get your hands grubby digging in the soil? You don't have to work round the clock to make a living. Unless that's what you want to do when you could do better. Anyway, it isn't going to happen for a year or two. But you'd better keep your eyes peeled and your ears open so you're ready for it when it does.'

'And if I did sell I suppose you'd want a cut for telling me about it.'

'I'd not say no. Think about it, cuz. You could build yourself a grand new house and get a new car. Even travel the world if you've a mind to. And think about the kids. From what I've seen of them they're a bright lot. You could send them to the best schools and get them a good education.'

'I'll think about it,' said Norrie. 'I suppose you'll be going home now.'

'Day after tomorrow.' Magnie laughed then. 'You do pack a good punch, cuz,' he said. 'I'm glad you didn't come out fighting today.'

'I felt like it when I saw your car.'

Catching up on the news there had been no time for at their last meeting the two talked on. Quiet as a mouse Judith slipped away. None saw her go.

'What did you think of that, then?' said Catherine when Magnie had gone.

'He paints a rosy picture, doesn't he?' said Norrie. 'There must be some truth in what he said, though, or he wouldn't have been so keen to get us out.'

'What would we do if we didn't have to go to work? If we sent the children away to school the house would be empty. I don't think I'd like that.'

'No, neither would I,' said Norrie. 'They'll leave soon enough anyway.' He laughed. 'Can you see the pair of us going on a cruise? Pigs might fly.'

Catherine thought it might be nice not to be so busy, to be able to take life more slowly. But even if what Magnie had predicted did happen it would be some time before it did, and in the immediate future she had a family to feed.

'Come on, Norrie, forget the daydreams. It's time to eat.'

FIFTEEN

WHETHER IT WAS the tonic Neil Lumsden had given her or the odd hours she managed to steal for herself that made Catherine feel better, she didn't know. Maybe it was because the uncertainty of their hold on Kay's house and croft had been lifted. Whatever it was, the bounce had come back into her step and she was eager to get out of doors and working.

Today she was going to pen the ewes and select those that were past their breeding age. It would be foolish to keep an animal that was unable to feed properly, lost condition and failed to breed, so, with Fly at her heels she climbed the hill to the sheep and a job she didn't particularly like.

It had been exceptionally hot and dry as opposed to the mix of weathers that usually made up a Shetland summer and, being such a rarity, it seemed reluctant to change. The sun shone daily, but the distant view was now wrapped in a blue haze and there was a fresh feeling in the air that hinted of colder days to come.

Always ready and willing to work, Fly padded along beside Catherine. When they reached the top of the hill and she stopped to see where the sheep were he scanned the area, too, briefly turned his head to look up at her and then, his eyes on the sheep, stood waiting for her command. When she gave the word he streaked away, a streamlined black and white animal running close to the ground. Catherine watched as he did the outrun, wide enough not to alarm the sheep and send them scattering away, circled behind them to gather them and then drove them towards her. He was twelve years old now, old for a working dog, but he and Catherine had spent so many hours together that he knew as well as she what he had to do. Weaving back and forth behind them, he kept the sheep bunched together and sent them at a trot towards his shepherd and the pens. There were several old ewes in the flock that had been penned many times before. The younger ones followed them and it was not difficult for Catherine to get them all in and shut the gate on them. Fly, panting hard, red tongue lolling, followed Catherine's every move. 'Good boy,' she said as she patted his head. 'Go now and lie down.' He trotted a little way off and, facing the sheep pens, flopped on the ground. His eyes keen, he watched Catherine's every move, ready to spring into action if required.

The job that Catherine was doing was one that was repeated annually and one she had learned to do well through trial and error. How well she remembered the early days when she had struggled to come to terms with the tribulations of keeping sheep, of having to work out of doors, of the heartbreak of sick sheep that died in spite of the care she gave them. She was only too well aware that there was a duty of care and kindness to all animals, but when it came to a commercial flock there was no room for sentiment. People had to be fed and as long as they wanted meat on their plates, someone had to rear animals for slaughter. To be unkind or uncaring in the process would only defeat the object and the farmer or crofter would soon be out of business.

She worked on through the morning and by lunchtime the job was done. The ewes to be kept had been let out of the pen and sent away above the hill fence; the redundant old ones she had driven down to the valley and penned in one of the small parks there. It was time for a break. She went back to her house to find something to eat and drink.

Rested and refreshed Catherine picked up the little portable radio that had been her mother's wedding present to her and took it with her to the barn. She had been meaning to go through the boxes of Kay's stuff that Norrie had dumped there again and, with an hour or two to spare it was as good a time as any.

The sweet smell of the meadow hay that they had made so easily in the fine weather, a pleasing potpourri of grasses and wild flowers, filled the building. Catherine took an armful and made a cushion of it on the floor in front of one of the boxes. She switched on the radio and for a time listened to it as she worked, but as she became more and more engrossed with what she was doing voices and music became nothing more than background noise.

She had brought some bags with her and as she worked she rescued knitting needles and patterns. Judith would maybe appreciate them later on. The wool, which the moths had made a meal of, was past recovery. Of the books she pulled out she saved a few; when she did have an hour or so to spare they would be just the thing to curl up with and read. Pens and pencils, writing paper which had become damp but could be dried, she saved for the boys. There were some loose photographs and others in an album. She saved those, too, to show them to Norrie and see if he could name any of the people on them. The rest of it she bundled into a sack, which would be disposed of on the next bonfire.

She didn't hear Bjorg's footsteps as he walked in and when he touched her on the shoulder she let out a squeal of fright.

'Why do I always have to frighten you?' he said.

'You could have warned me you were coming,' said Catherine as she got to her feet. 'What do you want?' A slow smile spread across Bjorg's face. Seeing it, Catherine felt herself grow hot. 'Go away.'

'I am very attracted to you. I have done nothing but think about you since I saw you on the hill,' said Bjorg. His voice was low and seductive. 'I think you are attracted to me too.'

Catherine took a step back. 'No, I'm not.'

'Yes, but yes. I see it in your eyes.' He moved towards her and again she stepped back, but the box was in the way and she would have fallen over it if he hadn't reached out and caught her, caught her and held her, held her so close that she could feel the hardness of his body, smell the scent of pine on his clothes and knew it was where she wanted to be.

'Why do you tremble?' Bjorg whispered into her hair.

'Because ... because ... this is wrong.'

'But you are not trying to get away.'

Bjorg was so like her dead husband. She closed her eyes, was carried away and imagined that it was he who held her. 'No.' She said the word so softly that Bjorg put his head close to hers. 'So you do care,' he said.

She lifted her head to look at him and before she could speak he kissed her, kissed her long and hard and, melting with the flame that threatened to consume her, she returned his kiss. When it was over she leaned her head against his chest and let her arms wind themselves around his waist. This was what she wanted, had dreamed of and thought was out of reach. It had been like this with Norrie once. What had happened to stop it? It wasn't fair; she deserved to be loved.

Loved? Why not? What did Norrie do in all the hours he was away from her? And anyway it was only a kiss. What harm was there in that?

With one arm gently clasping her, Bjorg slid the other down her back until his hand rested lightly on her buttocks. Tightening his grip he pressed her body close against him. Again the flame rose in her and desire for him made her sigh. Eyes closed, she raised her face to his and met his lips with passion.

When the kiss was over he lifted his head. 'Come,' he said and she, looking into the depths of the blue swirling ocean of his eyes felt herself sinking and went willingly with him as he walked, half carrying her, to a bed in the hay.

His hands were gentle as they caressed her. His lips as he kissed her face and neck were as soft as a butterfly's touch. She thrilled to the feel of his fingertips as he ran them down her bare arms. When he felt for the waist of her trousers and undid the button that held them together she felt the muscles of her stomach tense in anticipation of what was to come. She arched her body against him, sinuous as a cat. Her eyes had been closed, but now, as his lips were kissing her neck her head went back and she opened them – opened them wide.

To her horror, Norrie had thrown a pair of his overalls over one of the rafters, where they now hung. It was as though he was watching her. 'Nooo!' she screamed and, taking advantage of a surprised would-be lover, pushed him off. Guilt, as shocking as a bucket of cold water, killed all passion in her. Snatched back to reality she grabbed at the waist of her trousers and, shutting her ears to Bjorg's plea for her to stay, pulled them up and ran. Sobbing as she went she raced to her house and, slamming the door behind her, shot the bolts home and leaned against it. She stood there, hands pressed to her chest. She was trembling and her heart was thumping like a drum.

How could she have been so stupid? How could she have let him draw her into a situation like that? But she knew, didn't she. She had been as mesmerized as a rabbit confronted by a stoat and if she hadn't looked up and been reminded of Norrie she would have let Bjorg make love to her in the only way possible. Her body tensed at the thought of what might have been. She had wanted it. What was so wrong in that? Too often now Norrie was so full of whisky that he couldn't finish what he started and, unfulfilled, she had to turn away. Why shouldn't she seek a little love elsewhere?

SIXTEEN

FOR SEVERAL DAYS after her encounter with Bjorg, Catherine rarely left the house. She was filled with guilt at what she had let herself be inveigled into, feelings that contrasted sharply with the eagerness with which she had looked for him, her desire to be near him, to look at him and long for his kiss. Her skin rose up in goose bumps as she remembered the gentle touch of his fingers on her arm. The thought of how they had so nearly completed their union made her sigh with remembered desire. The fire of longing still filled her loins.

Unable to settle, she roamed round the house. 'You're beautiful,' he had said. Was she, or was he just coming on to her with his sweet talk? In her bedroom she stared at herself in the mirror. Turning her head from side to side she saw skin unlined and free of blemishes, eyes that were bright, lips full and red and hair that curled in a flattering halo round her face.

Oh, Bjorg, why did you have to come into my life? Why does the thought of you excite me? Everything was fine till you appeared. But was it? Hadn't she become disillusioned with the valley, hadn't the hills been closing in and hadn't Norrie been neglecting her? She wasn't an old wife to be left sitting by the fire; she was thirty-seven and still craved the loving caresses that were her due. If Norrie didn't give them to her what harm was there in looking elsewhere? So why was her conscience holding her back?

'Catherine, are you there?' It was Jannie shouting through the house.

'I'm here, just coming.'

'Oh, there you are,' said Jannie, as Catherine came down from the bedroom. 'I thought maybe you was ill. I hadn't seen you.'

'I had a lot to catch up on indoors,' said Catherine.

'Hast du seen yon folk in Laura's house?'

'Yes. They seem awful nice.'

'I see they have a peerie lass now. And yon other man, the young one, is away. He went on the bus. He'd a braaly big suitcase with him. I'd say he's no coming back.'

Catherine grabbed for a chair. 'When was this?'

'Is du no well, lass? Du's gone white as a sheet.'

'I'm all right,' said Catherine. In a daze she made tea and put out the inevitable plate of bannocks. Why had Bjorg left so suddenly? Did she think he would come and find her to say goodbye? Absurdly, she felt like crying.

'Du makes awful good bannocks,' said Jannie as she spread butter on the one on her plate. 'I didn't think du would, coming fae south.'

'Kay taught me,' said Catherine. 'When did you see the little girl?'

'Yesterday. She's maybe a peerie bit older as your bairn.'

'That's nice; she'll be a friend for Judith,' said Catherine. Although she was dropping into the dialect, Jannie was having one of her more lucid days and didn't seem to be making any sign of leaving. How long was she going to keep up this conversation? Go home, Jannie, go home. I want to get out of the house.

'Daa's going to make me a kishie,' said Jannie. 'He says I have to go and fetch the peat now he has the rheumatics.'

'But you can't do that.'

'That's what I telled him. He can go with the pony cart like he always has.'

Catherine looked at her mother-in-law. Poor Jannie; sense had given way to nonsense and the times when her conversation did make sense were getting fewer and fewer. 'Would you like to take some bannocks home with you?' said Catherine. 'It would save you having to make some.'

'Ay, that I will,' said Jannie. With half a dozen bannocks in a paper bag Jannie thanked her and went home. Catherine shut the door behind her and breathed out with relief. She picked up a light jacket and put it on. Going out of the house she turned towards the sea, the bay and the beach. She wasn't going to the moor even though she knew now that no one would come to find her; the beach was the place to be.

Once there, she sat on one of the large rocks that bordered the sands. The water in the bay lay calm and the soft whisper of little waves, the gentle plop when they fell and the sibilant hiss as they curled, lace-edged, over the sand, calmed her nerves.

She looked out through the headlands at the vast expanse of water stretching far, far away to the horizon. Though she didn't turn round to look at them she felt once again that the hills were moving in on her, that she couldn't cope with all that was changing, that she wanted to get away, had to get away and knew even as the thought was with her that she couldn't. She was tied to the valley as surely as if it had her in chains.

So why did you come to upset me, Bjorg? Why did you rouse a sleeping serpent? Will I see you again? She wiped away the first few tears with the back of her hand and told herself not to be so silly. She wasn't going to weep for something that wasn't hers to have, but the tears did come and eventually were too much for her, so she let them. She hung her head, pulled the devil up out of her soul and opened the flood gates to wash him away. When it was done, she dried her eyes, ran her fingers through her hair and tossed her head. Then she took off her shoes and socks and going to the water welcomed the cold as she paddled in the shallows. It was time to go home.

The twins and Judith were there before her. Judith looked at her. 'Have you been crying, Mam?' she said.

'No,' said Catherine, but knew she hadn't fooled her daughter when the child stood there and fixed candid blue eyes on her. Judith, precocious child, older than her years would have you believe; Judith, who was able to size up situations and people and get the right answer every time. There was Robbie, too, who could fasten his gaze on her until she felt so uncomfortable that she had to turn her head. Thank goodness the twins were so absorbed in each other that they hardly seemed to know what else was going on around them.

September got up to its old tricks and, thinking to fool everybody, came in fine and warm, but as the month progressed its mood changed. It wrinkled its brows and frowned, huffed and puffed then, with the equinox, exploded and vented its full fury in howling gales and rain. But its temper was short lived and, with a rueful smile as if to apologize for its bad behaviour, it quietly gave way to October.

Catherine had experienced many times the bouts of bad weather that came when day and night were of equal lengths. Why that should be she didn't know, but that it was so was a fact. Sometimes September gales presaged bad weather for winter, but at other times October brought a lull, a period of respite in which to harvest the oats and barley and lift the potatoes. The harvest workers in Deepdale had reduced in number; no longer were Mina and Laura, Jannie's sisters, long skirts looped up, there to call on. No longer was Daa there with the pony cart, either. The pony had been retired, given his freedom and now roamed the hill and moor for most of the year, only coming down to the valley for shelter and some extra feed in winter. The cart had been parked outside the barn, tipped backwards and now its shafts pointed wooden fingers at the sky.

Norrie had bought more farm machinery. Though they still had to be picked up by hand there was a spinner to get potatoes out of the ground, so, despite the decimated Deepdale workforce the work still went ahead. Other crofters rotated round their neighbours' potato rigs to help with the lifting and at the end of the day were rewarded with a bag of potatoes, but Deepdale residents worked alone and shared the crop.

There was a reaper binder for the corn, which threw out sheaves already tied. Robbie was enlisted to help his mother put them up in stooks – six sheaves of corn stacked together in pairs – to dry in the field.

Sheep sales were over and the ewes kept for breeding had been put on to better pasture to flush them and get them in good condition ready for tupping – when the rams would be with them for mating. Nothing was ready to harvest yet and Catherine took advantage of the lull in outside work to stay indoors.

As the weeks drifted by she was more and more thankful that Bjorg had gone. Her flirtation with him was never to be repeated and was best forgotten. Despite her determination to forget, though, her thoughts often strayed back to him. Every time she carried hay out to the sheep, the smell of it had her remembering how willingly she had lain down with him. Guilt always brought a flush of colour to her cheeks, a wave of heat through her veins. But he was gone.

It wasn't long before Gerda's little girl, Inga, became Judith's best friend. A year older than Judith, Inga often took the lead in the games they played. They went to school together, spent most of their free time together and put their heads together to tease the twins. Robbie, at nearly thirteen years of age, thought himself too old to play with the young ones and certainly too old to spend time with little girls and gradually he became more and more detached from them. Catherine had made him sit down one day while she told him that no way was she going to let him go to sea and he would have to settle for a different occupation. He had protested but she insisted and, in the face of her opposition, he had to agree.

For Catherine, life gradually settled down into the plodding, predictable routine of every day. She saw her neighbours occasionally, Joe more often than June or Gerda – he still hadn't got work – and sometimes Jannie would arrive smiling and happy and sometimes full of grumbles about Daa. Poor Daa hid away from Jannie in the barn or took himself as far away as he could when her bitter tongue held sway. Catherine looked for him and asked if he was eating properly, was Jannie cooking and if not, was there anything she could do. Daa smiled and thanked her, but said a'thing was fine, he was managing. He had been nothing but kind to her from the start and she would have liked to put her arms round him and give him a hug, but thought it might embarrass him.

SEVENTEEN

IT WAS SO easy to flick a switch and fill the room with light that the dark of winter had lost its intensity. No longer did Catherine have to remember to fill the lamps with oil or make sure there were enough candles and matches. For the little ones electricity had always been there, but Robbie would remember when they had been without it. He could tell them what a performance it had been to organize bath time, stoking the fire till it roared like a furnace, filling pots and pans and kettles then waiting for them to boil. But sitting in the big wash tub in front of the fire was a joy, and preferable by far to having a bath today. Though there was hot water to be had at the turn of a tap and the bath tub didn't have to be brought in from outside, the bathroom was often cold and bath time was something to be got through as quickly as possible.

Lifting her head from the piece of work in her hands – she was sewing a patch on Norrie's overalls – Catherine looked at her children. Robbie, Judith and the twins were playing a game of Snap, which, with the rising excitement of the players, was getting very noisy. She smiled and bent her head to her work again. Modern conveniences were supposed to make life easier, supposed to give the housewife more time for leisure, so what happened? Why was she still so busy?

There was a knock on the door. It opened and June's face appeared round it. 'Can I come in?' she said.

'Of course,' said Catherine. 'What can I do for you?'

'Nothing in particular, I just wanted someone to talk to. Joe's not very good company at the moment. He hates being out of work. He needs a job and he's finding it hard to get one.'

'What did he do before he joined the army?'

'Anything. He hasn't got much in the way of qualifications.'

There was nothing Catherine could do, so she said, 'Well, I expect something will turn up.' She smiled at June and wished she could do better. 'Cup of tea?' she asked and when they were drinking it, 'I know Shetlanders don't make much of Christmas, but do you celebrate it?'

'Since I've been married to Joe I do. He loves it and has to go the whole hog. He's looking forward to snowballs and a snowman now. You can bet when it snows he'll be out there with the kids. I swear he's never grown up.'

'Men never do, do they?' said Catherine. 'It's a bit early to think about it but Christmas is sure to creep up on us – it always does. We make such a fuss, plan for weeks, hide presents from the kids, buy too much food and the whole shebang is over in a couple of days.'

June laughed. 'I know,' she said. 'And we eat too much and drink too much and get irritable. Is it really worth it?'

'We used to have family parties at home,' said Catherine. She had finished her mending and put it away. 'Why don't *we* have one? Gerda, Lars, you and Joe and us. We could join forces; share the cooking and the work.'

'That would be great,' said June.

'We'll have to put our heads together, decide who's going to provide what. I'm sure Gerda would be happy to join in.'

'What are you planning now?' said Norrie coming in through the back door. 'Hello, June. Oh, the council are looking for men to work on the roads. You'd better tell Joe.'

'Really?' June stood and put her coat on. 'Thanks, Norrie, and thanks for the tea, Catherine. We'll talk about the party later.'

'What party's this,' asked Norrie when June had gone.

'We thought we'd have a Christmas party, all of us in the valley.'

'You mean Johansson and June and … we haven't got enough room for all of them. We're pushed for space as it is.'

'We can feed the children first and have our meal after. It'll be easy. And anyway, I won't have to do all the work; June and Gerda will help.'

Norrie shrugged his shoulders. 'Well, if that's what makes you happy.'

'You don't sound very enthusiastic.'

'Should I be?'

'Well, it is Christmas. It only comes once a year and you ought to be involved, if only for your kids. It's something special for them.'

'All right then, you have your party.' Norrie picked up the peat bucket, which was almost empty. 'I'll fill it for you,' he said and went out.

All day Catherine toiled, picking up the potatoes the spinner threw out and as it was Saturday Joe had come to help. Robbie had been enlisted, too, and by late afternoon the job was done. The buckets they gathered the potatoes in were emptied into sacks. Robbie and Joe loaded them onto the trailer and Norrie drove it to the barn. The harvest season was over, the corn having already been cut and stacked into small ricks that Daa called skroos.

In the bathroom Catherine rinsed the dust of the day off her face, scrubbed her hands till all the dirt that had stuck under her fingernails was gone. Under such as could be called nails, she thought, after they had been worn down by grubbing in the soil. She looked at them, at her hands too, hands that had been white and soft when she had been a nurse, but had hardened and become calloused through contact with the wooden handles of spade and tushkar, rake and hoe. If he could see them would Bjorg think she was beautiful now…? No, she mustn't think of him; he had only been playing a game with her. He was gone. The state of her hands was nothing to be ashamed of; they were not so different from those of other croft wives who were expected to work alongside the man they had given themselves to. She picked up a towel and dried them: there was a meal to get, a hungry family to feed.

Peter was irritable and for once he and Allen picked on one another. Norrie was short tempered with them, shouted at them and told them to behave.

'Did you have to do that, Norrie?' said Catherine. 'I think Peter's coming down with a cold. He's been off colour for a couple of days now.'

'He should be in his bed, then.'

'I'll keep him off school tomorrow. Will that satisfy you?'

Norrie's reply was no more than a grunt and supper was a hurried affair. Leaving the dishes in the sink Catherine rushed the little boys into the bath and then to bed. Robbie, sensing that the atmosphere between his parents was not good went to his room while Judith, apparently engrossed in a book, curled herself up in a chair and virtually disappeared from sight.

'I hope you haven't used all the hot water,' said Norrie when Catherine began to wash the dishes. 'I'm playing tonight and I need a bath.'

'There'll be enough, don't fuss.'

'There'd better be a dry towel,' grumbled Norrie as he took himself off.

Catherine clenched her fists. Why was he so grumpy? Don't answer back, you'll make things worse. 'Tell me if there isn't,' she called after him. 'I'll bring you one. But I'm sure there is.' There was. She had finished the dishes and was sitting down when Norrie came down from the bedroom, spruced up and ready to go. He had put a shelf up high on the wall, high enough to be out of reach of little hands, and it was there he kept his fiddle. He reached up and took it down.

'I'll see you later,' he said as he let himself out.

I doubt it, thought Catherine. If you come home at your usual time I shall be fast asleep. It wasn't long ago I wished you out of the house and away from the whisky bottle. Now you're never here and I don't know what you're drinking.

'Mam,' said Judith.

Catherine spun round. 'What are you doing there? You should be in bed.'

'I know, but ... Mam, why do you let Dad treat you the way he does?'

For a moment Catherine stared at her daughter. 'What goes on between your father and me is *nothing* to do with you. Now *get* to bed this instant.'

'But, Mam—'

'Judith.' Catherine raised an arm and pointed at the stairs. *'Go.'*

The child needed no more telling.

When she was gone Catherine took pen and paper out of a drawer and sat down at the table to write to her mother. But before she did she sat and thought about her children. With luck she had at last managed to persuade Robbie to give up thoughts of being a fisherman and the twins were so wrapped up in each other that they gave her no worries. But Judith was something else. She was secretive. She seemed to melt into the background and disappear from sight. And she seemed to know everything that was going on. What was she going to do about it? She sighed, picked up the pen and began to write.

Dear Mum and Dad,

It's been a long time since I wrote last but we have been very busy. The last of the harvest is in so life should get a bit easier now. We are all well. The new people have moved in so we are once again four families in the valley. I told you about our black man, didn't I? Jannie doesn't approve, of course. But she's getting more and more confused so it's not to be wondered at. June and I are planning a Christmas party for all of us. Nothing else exciting has been happening. Norrie has gone off somewhere to play – goodness knows what time he'll be back. Hope you and all the family are well. Write soon. Don't worry about me, I'm very happy.

Love,

Catherine x x x

And if you want to believe that, Mum, you can, because I can't tell you anything different. She folded the piece of paper, slid it into an envelope, sealed, addressed it and stuck on a stamp. Then she picked up a book and went to bed.

EIGHTEEN

NOVEMBER SLID BY in a blur. With Norrie frequently away to play at dances and weddings Catherine often went to her bed early. She had made or bought presents for the children and hidden them away in the bottom of her wardrobe. At the beginning of December she began to prepare for the Christmas party; her job was to make the Christmas cake and some biscuits. It was time to start. Outside work done she took off her boots, hung up her coat and changed out of her working clothes. She got out baking tins then gathered together all the ingredients she would need. The cake would be all the better for having time to mature and the biscuits would keep in an airtight tin. She had just finished mixing the cake and getting it in the oven when Gerda opened the door.

'I see you are busy,' she said. 'Shall I come back another time?'

'No,' said Catherine. 'As long as you don't mind if I keep going. I've just started to make biscuits. What can I do for you?'

'I would like to make a Julebrukk.'

'A *what?*' Catherine stopped mixing ingredients and looked at her friend.

'It's a traditional Norwegian decoration. It's supposed to be the goat that pulled Thor's coach. But I need some straw. Can I get some from you?'

'Yes. Look in the barn and help yourself. I wonder if Joe could do something typically American? I'm English, so I'll have to do roast beef.'

'I would also like to contribute some other decorations, if you don't mind,' said Gerda. 'Do you have room for a Christmas tree? I mean a real one.'

'Well, as long as it's not too big. We've never had a real tree.'

'That's settled, then. Is Norrie happy for you to have the party here? I thought perhaps there might be more room at my place.'

'Oh no, it'll have to be here. We'll feed the little ones first. That's the plan, anyway and I'll be able to put them to bed while we share a few drams.' A delicious aroma was coming from the oven.

'Something smells good, 'said Gerda.

'It's the Christmas cake,' said Catherine, proudly.

When Gerda had gone Catherine picked up a jug of milk and was about to pour some into the biscuit mix when she stopped and put it down. 'Damn,' she muttered. 'What was I thinking of? I should have made the biscuits first. Mmm.' She stood and looked at the mix in the bowl, 'Oh well,' she said. 'You'll have to go in the fridge till the cake's done. I guess it won't do you any harm.'

'Talking to yourself, are you? That's a bad sign. Perhaps it's you I should have come to see and not Jannie.' Neil Lumsden stood in the doorway. 'How are you, Catherine?'

'I'm fine. So have you seen her?'

'Yes. I looked in and told her I was looking for you and asked if you might be there. She didn't know me. She asked if I was coming to live in the valley and said I couldn't because there was no more room. She's not coping, is she?'

'No, but Daa looks after her as well as he can. I feel very sorry for him. I don't know what he'd do if she had to go away.'

'I don't think it's come to that yet, but keep an eye on her and keep me informed. How are things with you?' Lumsden pulled out a chair and sat down. 'How's Norrie? Is he behaving himself?'

'Not much change there. But there's nothing I can do about it.'

'Well, my dear, you're not alone. Drink is a problem – when was it ever not? But what are you up to? I can smell baking.'

'We're planning a Christmas party for all the residents of Deepdale. I've just made the cake.'

'Busy as usual, I see, but how about making me a cup of tea. I could do with one.' Tea made, both sat at the table. As they talked Lumsden looked at Catherine and saw the little worry lines on her face. 'You're still looking rather drawn,' he said. 'Apart from the drinking problem is everything all right?'

'Why shouldn't it be?'

'I don't know, you tell me.'

There was an edge to her voice as Catherine said, 'I'm not ill. The tonic helped and I did sneak away and get some time for myself, like you said. I'm a bit tired, perhaps, and I do get fed up at times.' And who wouldn't, she thought.

'You've had a pretty trying year and I expect coping with all that's happened hasn't helped. And, okay, Norrie's still drinking, but how is he treating you?' Catherine was looking down at her hands, fiddling with her fingers. 'You don't need to answer that,' said Lumsden. 'I expect he's letting you do too much. You've really got to draw the line somewhere. Stand up for yourself.'

Catherine's head came up sharply. 'Oh, I can do that,' she said.

'Yes, I know you can, but I wouldn't mind betting you want to keep the peace so you don't answer him back.'

'That would be right.'

'How often do you go out socially?'

'Apart from shopping, the last time was show day. It's not difficult to find a babysitter these days, but where would I go? Norrie goes to the dances to play, not to dance, and the thought of being a wallflower and spending the evening watching other people have fun does not appeal to me.'

'You've got to get out more,' said Lumsden. 'And that's doctor's orders.'

'All very well for you to say that. Actually, I've been thinking about getting a spare-time job, but there's nothing in the paper. I don't suppose you have anything to offer me?'

'Ah, I'm glad you said that because that's just where I can help. I'm making changes to the surgery and I shall need someone to be my receptionist and also give out medicines. Would you consider it?'

Would she? 'I'd be delighted!' she said. 'Tell me when.'

'It won't be till after Christmas. The workmen are still in the house, but I'll let you know. Thanks for the tea.' Lumsden stood up ready to go. 'It would have been nice to have had a piece of cake to go with it,' he said with a grin.

'I never gave it a thought,' said Catherine.

'I know you didn't, but you'd better give a thought to the one that's baking; it smells like it's done.'

But it wasn't. When Catherine pushed a skewer in it didn't come out clean so she shut the door on it and left it to go on cooking.

A job, Lumsden had offered her a job and it was one that would fit in with all the other things she had to do. Perhaps, just perhaps, the position as health visitor might become vacant again and if it did, she would go for it. Norrie could whistle if he thought he couldn't spare her for four months to train. What a good thing it had been when she had walked into Neil Lumsden's surgery and asked for the job as his cleaner.

The hill frowned darkly and as Catherine looked at it a sudden scud of rain splattered against the glass and drummed on the roof. The children were at school; Norrie, Joe and June at work, Lars too. Where Gerda was she didn't know so apart from Jannie and Daa, she was alone.

What a year it had been; the whole valley had been turned on its head. Well-known faces had gone away, Daa had become a recluse and now only he and Jannie, her one-time sparring partner, were left, and maybe it wouldn't be very long before she was gone too. Nothing stays the same, thought Catherine. She sighed, then, speaking out loud said, 'Come on, now, life goes on and you've got a party to prepare for. Buck up.'

In the living room she opened a box of paper chains and other decorations she had bought and began to put them up. As the room grew more colourful her mood rose. She switched on the radio and sang to the music that was being played. She was standing on a chair pinning up a paper bell when Norrie came home from work.

'You're early, what's happened?' said Catherine.

'I'd had enough. It's a miserable day.'

'I couldn't agree with you more. If you've got nothing important to do, you can help me put these up.'

Norrie didn't need to stand on a chair. The height of the room was such that his outstretched arm reached the ceiling. After a while he said, 'If Gerda's bringing a proper Christmas tree I suppose you won't want Kay's.'

'You must be joking,' said Catherine. 'It wouldn't be Christmas without it.' The branch of driftwood decorated with baubles that had been Norrie's aunt's version of a Christmas tree had taken pride of place in Catherine's house ever since she and Norrie had married. That it should be replaced with another was unthinkable. It would go on being the centre of Christmas as far as she was concerned. 'The kids might prefer a spruce, but I'm not getting rid of Kay's tree.'

'And have you got everything else organized?'

'More or less. I'm really looking forward to it. What about you?'

'I haven't got much choice, have I?'

'Oh, Norrie, don't be such a grouse,' chided Catherine. 'I'm sure Joe will liven things up and you *will* enjoy it, believe me.'

'If you say so,' said Norrie.

'What's happened to you?' said Catherine. 'You used to be such fun. You can't turn into a grumpy old man. I won't let you.'

'I've got a lot more responsibility now,' said Norrie. 'I've got a family to provide for. I've got a job to go to, as well as what I've got to do here and at my other place. Larking about is for the young.'

Disappointment showed in Catherine's voice. 'No it isn't,' she said. 'Older people can have fun as well.' But Norrie was walking away from her and she was talking to his back. Oh, well, have it your way, she thought.

NINETEEN

'OH NOOO,' GROANED NORRIE as the sound of excited shrieks came from the children's bedrooms. 'Why does Christmas Day start so early?'

'Didn't it always?' murmured Catherine. 'At least they stay in their rooms now. Go back to sleep.'

Norrie was soon snoring again, but sleep eluded Catherine and a little while later she slid out of bed and dressed quietly. Slippers in hand, she crept down the stairs to her kitchen where she made a cup of tea before starting work.

The small green tree from Gerda and Lars, now brightly decorated, had been brought in the night before when the children were in bed. 'We never decorate the tree till Christmas Eve,' said Gerda. 'It has to be a surprise for the little ones.' It wasn't a big tree, but in the small room it took up a considerable amount of space. Kay's driftwood tree had been placed across the room from it. In contrast to the spruce and its wealth of trimmings Kay's tree paled in comparison, but pretty and sparkling though the green tree was, for Catherine it didn't have the appeal that Kay's did.

Breakfast time went by unnoticed; their appetites blurred by Christmas stocking sweeties the children ate nothing. Norrie grabbed what he could, made his excuses and went to look at the sheep. Catherine made do with yet another cup of tea. Gerda came to help get dinner under way, extra chairs were brought in and the table covered with a cloth and pretty paper napkins. Coffee was made when Joe and June arrived. When June took off her outdoor things – a woolly hat, a warm coat and boots – she was clad in a dress that revealed a slim, trim, figure. Her legs were encased in nylon stockings, her small feet shod in high-heeled shoes. Catherine looked at her and envied the woman her bloom of youth.

The house, home to two adults and four children, was filling rapidly. Heat from the kitchen, where a joint of beef was roasting, drifted into the living room and added to that of a fire burning brightly in the stove. With Gerda's help, Catherine managed to serve the children's dinner first, and when they were done, gave them a plate of mince pies to share and sent them upstairs to play while the grown-ups sat down to their meal.

Joe took charge and carved the beef when Norrie was late coming in. June and Gerda served vegetables while Catherine cleared away the cooking pots. Lars poured the wine. The adults sat long over their meal; they were relaxed and the atmosphere was convivial. They asked questions of one another and learned a little of their neighbours' lives.

The afternoon drifted by in a haze. Lulled by a good dinner and some bottles of wine, conversation became sporadic and in the heat of the room, eyelids fluttered and threatened to close. Catherine opened doors and windows, let the cold of winter blow through to clear the air and rouse her guests from their lethargy. It had the desired effect. 'It's time we had some music,' said Joe. 'I have an accordion. Shall I get it?'

'Oh yes,' said Catherine. She turned to Norrie, 'Will you play, too?'

Norrie took his fiddle down from the shelf. He and Joe fell in quite naturally with what the other was playing and soon the house was filled with foot-stamping, hand-clapping music. Lars had thanked Catherine for her hospitality, excused himself and gone home. 'He isn't much of a social animal,' explained Gerda, hoping he hadn't caused offence. Judith and Inga had curled up on some cushions in a corner of the room. Both were deep into books. The twins were under the table absorbed in playing with a model farmyard. Robbie had gone to his room.

'It's a pity there isn't room to dance,' said Catherine.

'You'd never be able to do a reel,' laughed June.

'Let's clear a space and try,' said Catherine. 'Mina asked for the crofters reel at our wedding, so we ought to be able to do it here.'

The lights went out, then, and the room was plunged in darkness.

'I can still play,' said Joe, but Norrie put down his fiddle.

Catherine fetched an oil lamp, set it on the table and lit it. 'Goodness knows how long it's going to be off, so boys, you can go to bed.'

'Oh no,' they chorused and, 'Oh yes,' said their mother. Regardless of their protests she made them say goodnight and chivvied them up the stairs.

Norrie was in the kitchen, rinsing glasses for re-use. When Catherine came down again, June, holding a glass in one hand and a teacloth in the other was there, too. Norrie's arm was laid across her shoulders; holding a whisky bottle he leaned forward and looked into her face. June held her hand over the top of her glass as he tilted the bottle towards it.

'You'll have me drunk,' she said.

'I'd like to see dee drunk,' said Norrie, a stupid grin on his face.

Catherine stopped in her tracks. What was he up to? She looked at Joe who was sitting in a chair by the fire. Could he see what Norrie was doing? No, he was supping his own dram and, from where he sat he couldn't see into the kitchen.

'Come now,' said Norrie. 'Du's a bonnie lass, will du no hae a drink?'

Catherine looked at Gerda; saw that she was watching Norrie and from her expression, knew that Gerda was no more amused than she was.

'I'll have one, Norrie,' said Catherine.

June extricated herself from Norrie's arm, hung the teacloth on its hook and walked into the living room.

Norrie looked none too pleased. 'Oh, du's here,' he said.

'Yes. Don't keep the whisky bottle to yourself. Maybe someone else might like another dram.'

'I'll have one,' said Gerda.

Her voice unnaturally bright, Catherine said, 'We haven't cut the cake yet. Would you get me some tea plates, Norrie? You'll have a piece of cake, Gerda? And you, Joe? What about you, June?'

'It's very good,' said June as she bit into her cake. 'You'll have to give me the recipe.' But she didn't look at Catherine.

'Come on, Joe. You'd like some cake, wouldn't you?' Catherine's mouth smiled, but not her eyes.

'Is something wrong?' asked Joe. 'There seems to be an atmosphere.'

An atmosphere! Give me a knife.

'I think we're all getting tired,' said Gerda. 'Too full of food and whisky and I do not know about anyone else, but I am ready for my bed.'

Norrie was pouring whisky into his glass again. Catherine watched, but said nothing. Gerda stood up. 'It's been a grand day,' she said. 'Thank you, Catherine.' Taking her coat from where it hung she put it on and was about to go when Catherine said, 'Where's Inga?'

'She went home when you were putting the boys to bed,' said Gerda. 'And don't forget that you have another child here.' She pointed at Judith who was curled up on her cushion, seemingly fast asleep. 'It has been a long day, but a lovely one. Thank you again. Goodnight.'

'We'd better go, too,' said Joe. Catherine saw them out and received their thanks with a smile on her face, a smile that fell as soon as she shut the door. Norrie was not there when she turned round so she picked up Judith and carried her up to bed.

Back in the living room she banked up the fire so that it would stay in through the night and went to bed herself. In her room she looked down on her sleeping husband. Softly, but with menace, she said, 'I'll deal with you tomorrow.'

TWENTY

CATHERINE WOKE TO the sound of a desolate wind. We're going to have snow, she thought. Norrie had spread-eagled himself across the bed, leaving her very little room. She threw back the covers, slid out her feet and stood up. It was time to get up anyway; there were glasses and dirty dishes spread around the living room and kitchen that she had been too tired to bother with last night. It was time to dispose of the debris of Christmas and make way for other things, for one thing in particular, and she was more than ready for that.

Judith was the first of the children to rise. She was wearing a dressing gown that had been one of her presents when, sleepy-eyed, she joined her mother.

'Hello, Mam,' she said.

'Hello, darling, d'you want some breakfast?'

'Not yet. Where's Da?'

'Still abed.'

Catherine was washing glasses. Judith came to stand beside her. She put an arm round her mother's waist and pressing her head into her side murmured, 'I love you, Mam.'

'And I love you, too, but what's brought this on?'

'Oh, nothing. I'll go and get dressed.' What a funny child Judith was.

Washing up done and surfaces cleared, Catherine put a pot on the cooker to begin making the porridge. Robbie wouldn't surface from sleep for some time and the twins would sleep late, too. But if Norrie didn't get up soon she would go and wake him. She was idly stirring the porridge when he came down the stairs. He didn't acknowledge her until she spoke. 'Good morning,' she said. 'And how are you today?'

'I'm all right,' grunted Norrie.

'And were you also, "all right", last night?'

'What d'you mean?'

'Well, the way you were draped round June I did wonder. And not only were you draped round her, you were behaving like a love-sick loon.'

'Draped round? Love-sick? Don't be silly, Catherine. That was *nothing.*'

'Really! It was a good job Joe didn't see what you were up to or I think you might have regretted your little nothing.' Catherine stopped stirring and looked at Norrie. He was lifting the lid of the teapot to see if it held drinkable tea. 'Other eyes were watching as well as mine,' she said.

Judith had crept down the stairs. She stood on the bottom step where she could listen without being seen.

'I don't know what you're making such a fuss about. Has no man other than me ever put a hand on you?' snapped Norrie. 'I don't make a fuss if you dance with someone, do I?'

'That's different. Dancing is in the open for anyone to see.'

'Oh it is, is it? It wasn't as if I had my arms wrapped round June. Nobody could say that.'

'I could. I saw you.'

Catherine gasped. Norrie spun round. '*What?*'

Judith stepped out of her hiding place. 'I saw you in the kitchen with June.'

'You saw *nothing,*' shouted Norrie. 'I say you saw *nothing.*'

'But—'

'We were getting some clean glasses; there was *nothing else* for you to see.'

'Then why did you kiss her?'

Norrie raised a fist and made to strike his daughter. Maybe he would have if Catherine hadn't brought the porridge spoon down across his arm with all the force she could muster. 'Dare you ever strike a child,' she screamed. 'What sort of man are you?'

'You could have broken my arm,' said Norrie as he rubbed his sore limb.

She was angry. 'And I'd have been glad if it made you keep it to yourself.'

Norrie turned on Judith, snarling, 'Get out of my sight or it'll be the worse for you. You don't know what you've done.'

'Oh, but I do,' said Catherine as Judith fled. 'She wasn't the only one who was watching. Gerda was, too, and I could see the disgust in her eyes.'

Norrie wiped the back of his hand across his mouth, walked away from Catherine then came back. He stood and looked at her for a moment, looked away out of the window, then back to her. 'It wasn't like it sounds,' he said at last. 'If I did overstep the mark you should put it down to the drink.'

'It always comes back to the drink, doesn't it? You hadn't had that much,' said Catherine. 'You can't hold a whisky glass and a fiddle bow in one hand and play at the same time. And as for the *"if"*, there wasn't any *"if"* about it. You are a *stupid* man.'

Norrie held out his hands to her. 'I'm sorry, Catherine.'

'Sorry,' screeched Catherine. 'Not half as sorry as you're going to be. You *ruined* my Christmas. It was all going well till you had to act the fool. You *stupid, stupid* man.' Catherine jabbed at him with her finger, followed him as he backed away. 'Don't you realize if Joe had seen you and lost his temper,' – jab – 'we would have had a fight on our hands? There you were,' – jab – 'getting familiar with his wife,' – jab – 'and the little ones still with us.' Her face flushed with anger and tears of rage very close, Catherine raised her hand and slapped Norrie across the face.

Norrie grabbed her wrist, held it in a pincer like grip. 'So it's all right for you to hit *me* then.'

'You're a grown man, not a child, and it's not only all right, but justified.' Catherine gritted her teeth and glared at her husband.

'I'm telling you, you have nothing to get upset about. It wasn't as though I had her in a dark corner. You would have something to get mad about if I had.'

'That doesn't mean to say you wouldn't have liked to.'

'Catherine!' They stood, almost nose to nose. Norrie still gripped her arm. She, aghast at what she'd just said, stared at him, refused to look away. 'I can't believe you just said that,' said Norrie. He let go of her, more or less throwing her arm back at her. 'Perhaps I will … next time … if I get the chance.'

Rubbing her wrist, sore where Norrie had crushed it in his fist, Catherine screamed, 'Go away. Get out of my sight. I don't want to see you. I don't want you anywhere near me. *Get out*.'

For a moment Norrie stood and looked at her. 'That it should come to this,' he muttered. 'Be careful, Catherine, you're going to regret some of the things you've said.' Then he turned on his heel, snatched open the door, slammed it behind him and was gone.

Drained of emotion Catherine sat down and burst into tears. How could this be happening? Was it her fault? Was she doing something wrong? Or was it the drink? He seemed only too ready to put the blame on it himself. She sniffed noisily, swallowed her tears and reached for her handkerchief. Absorbed in self-pity she didn't hear Judith come in, didn't know she was there till a small arm was put about her shoulders and a pair of soft lips pressed to her cheek.

'You still have us, Mam,' said Judith. 'We'll look after you.'

'What *are* you talking about? I don't need anyone to look after me.'

'Yes, you do.' Judith wound her arms round her mother's neck. 'You've sent my da away and he's gone.'

Catherine gave a wry smile. 'Oh, darling, he won't be gone far. He'll be back. It's just one of those things, an upset. Everybody has them.'

'But he shouldn't make you cry.'

'My dear child, women were born to weep. It would be a wonderful world if that were not so. But it is, and people do silly things and upset others.' Catherine hugged her daughter. 'It's not your problem so don't worry about it.'

She pushed her handkerchief back into her pocket. What did Judith really see? Could she have been mistaken? A kiss was a kiss, but they were not all the same and some had more meaning than others. 'Judith,' she said, 'tell me truthfully. What did you really, truly, see your da do with June?'

'He kissed her.'

'Like … how?'

Judith shrugged her shoulders. Then she puckered up her lips and planted a kiss on her mother's cheek. 'Like that.'

'Oh. Just like that? Not on her mouth?'

'Yes. I mean no. Well, that's a kiss, isn't it? I think the porridge is burnt. I can smell it.'

TWENTY ONE

SNOW FELL SILENTLY all day and night and New Year, beautiful, but unloving, for her heart was made of ice, came in clad in a gown of purest white. Snow went on falling and day by day filled every hollow, covered every roadway. The air became still and frost gripped the land. Traffic stopped moving. Rabbits hid in their burrows. Birds took shelter in bush and barn. The native Shetland sheep pawed the ground to uncover and eat what bit of herbage they could. Pure bred and cross bred sheep were not so clever and food had to be carried to them.

Norrie, unable to go to work, put on his boots and went out to look on their sheep. When he'd done that, armed with a staff to aid a cross country walk, he went to Broonieswick to see to his own. Catherine stayed at home. She was worried about Jannie and Daa, wondered if Jannie was managing to make hot meals, which the old folk surely needed. Leaving Robbie in charge of the little ones she went to see how her in-laws were faring. Their living room was fine and warm, Daa had brought in plenty of peat and the fire was going well. There were no pots on the stove, though, and no smell of cooking or a pot of broth bubbling away. Jannie sat by the fire. She was knitting. Her old hands plied the wool and a sock hung from the needles.

'What are you having for your dinner?' asked Catherine.

'Likely a piece of bread and some cheese,' said Jannie.

'But you need something hot on a day like this.'

'Ay, it's fine and warm in here and we'll have some tea.'

'But that's not enough.'

'It'll do fine.'

Catherine went home, took a piece of mutton and some vegetables and put them into a pot with some broth mix and set them to cook. She would see to it that the old folk had a hot meal; she couldn't eat her own and think of them with only bread and cheese.

The twins sat at the table with colouring books. Judith was reading and Robbie had gone after Norrie. Catherine set up the ironing board and fetched her iron and a basket of clothes that needed ironing.

'Hello, can I come in?' It was Gerda. 'Inga wants to know if Judith could come along to our house. She says she's bored on her own.'

'Can I, Mam?' Judith folded up her book.

'Of course you can,' said her mother. 'Take your slippers with you and don't forget to take your boots off by the door.'

'And how are you, Catherine?' said Gerda. 'No Hogmanay celebrations?'

'After what happened at Christmas? You must be joking.'

'I don't think you should take too much notice of that,' said Gerda. 'When men take drink not many of them can resist a pretty girl. He was only flirting.'

'You don't know all that went on,' said Catherine as she folded a cotton sheet and put it on the pile of clothes beside her.

'Oh.' Gerda looked at Judith who, already booted, was putting on her coat. 'She can stay and have her lunch with us, if you don't mind,' she said.

Judith, woolly hat pulled down over her ears, was at the door. 'Bye, Mam,' she said. As the door slammed behind her Gerda said, 'The atmosphere between you and your man is not too warm, then.'

'About as warm as the weather,' said Catherine.

'Wouldn't it be better to forget about it?'

'Listen, Gerda.' Catherine put down the iron, placed her hands squarely on the ironing board and leaned forward. 'I work round the clock for that man. He goes out while I stay at home. I am *not* going to forgive him for making a fool of me in my own house and in front of others. I will make him suffer and go on suffering till he goes down on his knees and begs forgiveness.'

'I think that's a bit harsh.'

'So you might, but ... oh, I'm not going to talk about it.' Catherine picked up a small shirt and spread it over the board. 'Don't worry, Gerda, I'm quite capable of weathering the storm.'

'I'm sure you are,' said Gerda. 'I'll leave you to your ironing.'

When the snow stopped and roads were cleared the children went back to school. In the mornings Norrie ate his breakfast in silence, put on his coat and without saying goodbye, went out of the house and away to work. Catherine had the house to herself. It was very quiet. Where there had once been laughter and nonsense, conversation had descended to what was only strictly necessary. Hands no longer touched and bodies, when they came close, were held stiff and aloof. Loneliness settled on Catherine like low cloud.

'This is getting ridiculous,' said Norrie when Catherine shied away from him once more. 'I love you and only you. I thought you knew that. Can't we stop this stupid charade we're playing?'

'So you want forgiveness now, do you?'

'Please, Catherine.' Norrie held out a hand, but she shrank away. 'I'd like to think you were ready to give it.'

'But if you love me,' she said, 'why did you kiss someone else?'

'It was a stupid thing to do, I know, and God knows what made me do it, but I'm sorry. How many times do I have to say it?'

She wasn't done with him yet. 'You might say it,' she said. 'But do you mean it? I have yet to hear you apologize properly for making a fool of me.'

Norrie threw up his hands. 'Oh, God, what more can I do?'

'Well, perhaps you could try leaving the whisky bottle alone. And it's time you started behaving like a married man and a father and not go gallivanting off to the dances so often.'

Norrie grabbed her by the shoulders, he felt like shaking her.

When was she going to give up goading him? 'Why?' he demanded. 'Don't you trust me? I only go to play. There's no dancing for me.'

'Well ... um.' A niggling little voice told Catherine she was punishing Norrie for what she'd seen when he had no idea what she had done.

'You don't, do you?' Norrie let her go and turned away. 'That nonsense with June was a one-off. It'll never happen again.'

Catherine couldn't help herself. 'Easy for you to say,' she said and immediately regretted it as Norrie turned on her. 'If that's the way you feel then there's nothing I can do about it,' he snapped. 'Go your own way, Catherine.'

She cringed. It wasn't what she wanted. Didn't he realize she was jealous because she loved him? That she didn't want him to put his arms round another woman or press his lips to anyone else? All she wanted was for him to love her as he used to, to be the way he was when he first courted her and to be hers and hers alone. And now she'd ruined everything. It wasn't Norrie who needed to apologize – it was her.

In the weeks following the row between them the air around Catherine and Norrie was as cold and bleak as a snow-covered moor. There was no sign of a let up and when Norrie came home from work, as soon as he had had his tea he picked up his fiddle and left the house, not coming home till the small hours. Catherine went to bed and, waiting for the sound of his vehicle and the slam of the car door when he came back, lay sleepless. Robbie knew his mother was unhappy, but asked no questions. Judith watched too, but she knew the cause of the unhappiness and instead of running to her grandmother or her friend Inga, spent more time with her mother. As far as the twins were concerned, engrossed in each other as they were, everything was normal.

'Listen, luvvy,' said Catherine when Judith persisted in dogging her footsteps. 'You don't have to stay with me. In fact you're only getting under my feet. Go out and play.'

'But, Mam, you're not happy and I want to help.'

'I know, but it's not your problem.'

'I hate Dada,' said Judith. 'You ought to send him right away.'

'I can't do that. He's your father and he belongs with us.'

'No he doesn't. He made you cry. It's his fault. He's horrible.'

Catherine looked at her daughter. This child of hers was more perceptive than many adults, but she couldn't be allowed to carry the burden of her mother's heartache. 'Now listen to me,' she said. 'As you grow up you'll learn that, even if they love one another, people fall out from time to time. They say stuff they don't really mean and then it's very hard to put things right again.'

'But it wasn't what Dada *said*,' said Judith, 'it was what he did.'

Catherine sighed, turned away from her daughter and sat down. In a stern voice she said, 'You are going to have to put this out of your head. It's my problem and you can't solve it for me. So you see, it's nothing to do with you.'

'But I want things the way they were. I want you to smile and you don't do that now.' The child looked close to tears.

'Judith, my love, you really are not old enough to understand. You have to believe me when I tell you that there is a solution to this, but it's for me and your father to find, not you. Come and have a hug.'

The little girl flew to her mother and, wrapping her arms round her neck, smothered her face with kisses. Laughingly Catherine protested, 'You're not a cat and I don't need a wash.'

'But I have made you smile,' said Judith.

'So you have and I feel better. Now, promise me you'll leave me to get on with things in my own way. Stop worrying; everything will be all right. Put your coat on and go and play with Inga.'

'All right. I love you, Mam.'

'And I love you. Now off you go.'

TWENTY TWO

CATHERINE'S PROBLEM SHOWED no sign of being resolved. Everything was not all right and the weeks drifted by with two people doing a slow dance, calculating the movements of the other, living in the same house, but not together. At least, thought Catherine, with the approach of spring, longer days and perhaps better weather, they would not be in such close proximity. There would not be so many dances at which Norrie was expected to play and he would not be coming home smelling of whisky. Maybe the tension would ease. It had better, because it would only be a few weeks before they would be in the thick of lambing. For a month they would have to work side by side through long hard days and broken nights, for sheep gave no consideration to their human midwives and often chose the small hours to go into labour. Someone had to give. It was important she and Norrie were able to communicate, because after the lambing there were still many months of hard work ahead. I suppose it'll have to be me, thought Catherine.

At first she tried to raise the level of conversation. Even when Norrie merely grunted in reply or made no comment she still tried to get him to talk. His continued lack of response often made her feel like giving up, but the situation could not be allowed to continue so she bit her lip and persisted.

'Are you going to put anything in the show this year?' she asked.

Norrie was reading a farming paper. His reply was non-committal. 'We usually do. Did you think this year was to be an exception?'

'No, of course not, I just wondered what you had in mind.'

'There's plenty of time to think about that. It would be better to wait till after lambing.'

'I … I would have thought you'd look over them now, pick something out to feed up … or ….'

Norrie looked up from the paper, stared at her for a moment then went back to it. 'What are you trying to say, Catherine?'

'I'm trying to make amends.'

'Oh.' The whisky bottle was standing on the table. Norrie unscrewed the top and poured some in a glass. 'Did you get today's paper?'

'Yes, it's here.' Catherine handed him their copy of *The Shetland Times*. He wasn't making it any easier for her, was he? And she was sure he knew how hard it was for her to offer the olive branch. Was he going to make her crawl?

'Norrie? Can't you see I'm trying to make things right between us? I've been too hard on you. I want to say sorry.' The level of her voice dropped. 'But you don't seem to be listening.'

Norrie sat at the table, the newspaper spread out in front of him. He didn't raise his head. 'Oh, I'm listening all right,' he said. 'Tell me more.'

'Well …' Catherine went to stand by him, took hold of her cardigan and wrapped it tight round her, crossed her arms over her chest and hugged herself. 'I think I acted too harshly. I should have given you the benefit of the doubt.'

'But you believe I kissed that young woman. Judith said she saw me. The question is … was she right? Had you thought of that?'

Children don't tell lies and especially not Judith. But could she have been wrong? Could it have been a near miss and intention not carried out?

'I … I … no, I hadn't,' stuttered Catherine. '*Was* she wrong?'

'If I told you she was would you believe me?' Norrie was looking directly at her now and Catherine quailed. She had to think carefully for whatever she said was going to tip the balance.

'You're putting me on the spot. Whoever I say wasn't telling the truth is going to make one of you a liar and I'm not going to do that. I want to put all this behind us. I want to forget it and try to get things back to what they were before.'

'Things weren't that good then, though, were they? You accused me of drinking too much even though you're partial to a tipple yourself.'

He wasn't going to let her off lightly. She could hardly blame him for hadn't she done the same to him? The difference was that he didn't know what *she'd* done. It riled her that he was treating her so casually, though, and she was filled with a desire to throw something at him. But that would only make things worse. She had to stay in control of herself. Taking a deep breath she said, 'I suppose it was much like many other marriages, no worse, but probably a lot better. Please, *can't* we stop this bickering and try to make up?'

'Thought about it, have you?' he said. 'Are you sure it's what you want?'

'Yes.'

'You aren't going to change your mind?'

'No.'

'Does that mean you're going to let it rest then, and not treat me like the woman-chaser you obviously thought I was?'

'Yes.'

Norrie looked at her for a long time and Catherine crossed her fingers and prayed. 'All right, we'll say no more about it.' Folding the paper Norrie stood up. 'It's been a long day, I'm going to bed.'

He didn't wish her goodnight. Catherine watched him go then got up to bank the fire and shut it down till morning. She set the table ready for breakfast then followed him up the stairs.

'Mam, do I still have to do electrics?' asked Robbie. 'Only I've been offered a place on a boat.'

Catherine felt her knees buckle. She grabbed for a chair and sat down. He knew she didn't want him to go to sea and she'd told him by saying that he had to pick another trade. 'Oh, Robbie, you said you wouldn't and you promised me you'd train to be an electrician. You *know* you did. But now you want to break your promise. You're too young.'

'Billy Tulloch's going on his dad's boat and he's the same age as me.'

'Ah, but he's going with someone who knows him. What do you know about whoever it is who's asked you?' Robbie hung his head and didn't answer. 'I see,' said Catherine. 'Is it the owner of the boat I saw you on?'

'Yeh.'

'So how many times have you been out on it … and *when*?'

'Um …' Robbie was chewing his fingers. 'Um …'

It wasn't hard to guess the answer and Catherine began to drum her fingers on the table. 'You've been wagging off school, haven't you? Does risking your life going to sea in a smelly old fishing boat mean so much to you that you have to neglect your education?' Her voice rose in anger as she went on. 'Suppose you don't like it when the sea gets rough and you're caught in a gale? Suppose you have an accident and can't go to sea any more, what are you going to do then?'

'I have been out when it's rough and Mr Sandison says I'm a natural.'

'Oh, he does, does he?' What had Norrie said? *'If you'd set your heart on something would you let anything stop you?'* So why was she trying to stop her son from achieving his heart's desire? 'What sort of boat is it?' she said.

'It's a drifter. They don't let you work with the nets to start with. I'd have to cook for the men first.' Robbie looked at her, hope lighting up his face. 'Please say yes, Mam.'

'I'll have to think about it.'

Robbie grunted with disappointment. 'What's there to think about?'

'I'd want to have a look at the boat first. I couldn't let you go to sea in an old rust bucket. And I'd have to talk to the man who owns it. I'd want to know what sort of man he is before I'd let you work for him. '

'Does that mean....'

'No, it doesn't. Don't push me or I'll say no right now and that doesn't mean I might say yes either. When can I see this vessel?'

'She'll tie up at the weekend. Will you go in on Saturday? Can I come?'

'Well you'd better. I wouldn't know one end of a boat from the other.'

'Oh, Mam.' Not normally demonstrative Robbie threw his arms round his mother and planted a kiss on her cheek.

'Don't get excited, Robbie,' chided Catherine. 'I haven't said yes, only that I'll think about it. There's one thing you haven't thought of, though.'

'What's that?'

'You can make toast and open a tin of beans, but you've never cooked anything else in your life, how do you think you'd manage as a cook? The poor men would starve.'

'I'll have to learn then. Will you teach me?'

'You want to inflict your culinary disasters on the family? We'll see.'

The tension between Norrie and Catherine had eased somewhat and as the weeks passed the atmosphere grew brighter. For the twins nothing changed, but for Judith it had and she stopped following her mother around. Robbie's fourteenth birthday was celebrated with a family tea party at which Jannie put in an appearance. Daa had not come to tea, but had given his grandson a model boat. The lure of the sea drew many Shetland men to it and even those who did not make their living from fishing still had a boat moored in the harbour. Daa understood the boy's longing to be on the water and why Catherine wished he did not. 'You have to let him go, lass,' he said and she told him she had come to that conclusion. Norrie still went off to play at dances, still came home in the early hours and Catherine still lay awake till he crawled into bed beside her.

The month of March came in cold and wet and stayed that way. Catherine listened to the radio and hoped there would be a promise of brighter days. The equinox was still to come and when it did she was not surprised to hear that a gale was forecast.

Norrie checked his fiddle for broken strings. 'Are you going out?' said Catherine. 'It's blowing and raining hard; surely there'll be no dancing tonight.'

'Oh, there will be,' said Norrie. 'They've got cars now and don't have to run through the rain and get soaking wet before they get there.'

'How times change,' said Catherine. 'Don't be late home, or I shall worry.'

'All right, I'll try.' As Norrie went out, the wind snarled around him, grabbed at the door, gusted into the house and set loose papers flying.

Robbie had gone to his room. Judith sat in a chair, knitting. Watching her, Catherine smiled to see the little girl's pink tongue running back and forth across her lips as she concentrated, then being popped back into her mouth when she'd finished a row. Allen and Peter were playing Snap. Catherine picked up a sock from a pile in a basket beside her and began to darn; so many socks and all with holes. As she worked she listened to the wind howling down the chimney and pulling at the fire, heard the clatter of rain on the window. Then the lights went out. Judith groaned, the twins moaned and their mother said, 'I'll light the lamp.'

When the room was illuminated again she said, 'Why don't we all have a game of Snap? Come on, Judith, you can't see properly to knit now.'

'But I want to finish this.'

'You can finish it tomorrow.'

As the evening wore on and electricity stayed off Catherine's attention on the game was pulled away and drawn to the rising sound of the wind. Where it once howled it now screamed; where rain had merely clattered on the window it now beat on it like thrown pebbles. Loose-fitting doors rattled. A bucket that had been left outside went rattling and banging across the flagstones. Gaining in force the gale was hell bent on destruction. If it was wild here, where they were sheltered by hills, what was it like where it was not? The sea would be a fury. Heaven help all those who were on it. Thank goodness Robbie wasn't a fisherman yet.

Suddenly she jumped up. 'That's it, kids, it's time for bed. Pack up the cards.' When they protested she insisted and a little while later she was alone again. The fire roared red as the wind sucked at the chimney. Where was Norrie? He should not be out on a night like this. No one should. Catherine thought of making tea, but turned to the cupboard and the whisky bottle instead. Hoping that the liquor would dull her fears she poured some into a glass and sat down by the stove to wait for him.

Surely the dance had been cancelled. It would be foolish to be out on a night such as this. It would be impossible to walk and hazardous in the extreme to drive a car. Slowly the hours ticked away. From time to time Catherine looked at the clock and the further the hands moved round its face the more worried she became. The dance, if it had taken place, would be over and Norrie should be home. She was filled with unease. She poured more whisky and prayed that the storm would abate. But the gale still raged and taunted her by slackening; breathing softly and teasing her into thinking it was going away, only to intensify again. It thumped and banged around the house, rattled the door like some madman trying to gain access. On and on it went and the hands on the clock passed two and three and Catherine, warmed by the fire and overcome by the whisky she had drunk slumped in the chair and, despite a valiant effort to keep her eyes open, fell asleep.

It was not noise, but silence that woke her. She opened her eyes, sat up and looked round the room. She was cold. She rubbed her arms and shivered. The fire had gone out. The oil in the lamp had run out and the wicks smouldered and stank. By the thin light of dawn she peered at the clock: 7 a.m. She'd been here by the fireside all night and Norrie had not come home. Where was he? What had happened to him? Please, God, let him have spent the night in someone else's house. He would never have left her sleeping in the chair if he'd come home and seen her there, would he? She jumped up and ran up the stairs to their bedroom. The bed was as smooth and un-rumpled as it had been when she'd made it yesterday.

TWENTY THREE

CATHERINE WAS COLD and her muscles stiff. She went to the window and looked out. It was then she saw that the storm had blown itself away. The sea was still raging; it was always slow to calm down. She could hear it crashing and roaring at the cliffs, pouring into the bay in a tidal wave and sucking out again, but the wind was now no more than a breeze.

Where was Norrie? A rush of guilt swept over her. She should have forgiven and forgotten long ago and not let her jealousy cause such a rift between them. A sob caught in her throat. Please, God, don't let someone come to tell me he's dead, she prayed. But it was morning and she had a family to feed. Slowly she went back down the stairs to begin preparing breakfast. She had just taken a packet of oats, poured some into a pot and added water when there was a clatter of footsteps running down the stairs. A voice called, 'Mam, where are you?' It was Robbie. He looked at her. 'You look as though you haven't been to bed all night,' he said.

'Got it in one, I haven't.'

'Why?'

'I was worried about your dad and I thought I'd sit and wait for him to come home,' said Catherine. 'But he hasn't.' It was time to get on with the day. The room was cold, the porridge wasn't made and the children would be late for school if she didn't hurry up. 'Get the fire lit, Robbie, while I make the porridge.'

'Someone's coming, Mam, there's a car outside.'

Catherine dropped the wooden spoon back into the porridge pot and rushed to the door. She threw it open and there on the step about to put a hand on the latch was Norrie, another man beside him. She looked at the plaster on Norrie's arm and at the sling that held it up. 'What *have* you done?' she said.

'I've had an accident,' said Norrie. 'Are you going to let me in?' Catherine stepped back and held the door open. 'This is Andrew,' said Norrie indicating the man behind him. 'He was with me when it happened.'

'Hello, Andrew,' said Catherine, and to Norrie, 'How did it happen? I suppose you were drunk.'

'No, I wasn't,' snapped Norrie. 'There you go; as if this isn't bad enough the first thing you think about is drink. Ha….' he'd spotted the half-empty whisky bottle on the table. 'Pot calling the kettle black, eh?'

'Oh you can mock,' said Catherine. 'I was worried about you. You shouldn't have gone out on such a night and it would seem I was right.'

The electricity was on again and Robbie, taking in the situation, knew that tea would be called for so had put the kettle on and made it. He handed a cup to Norrie and fetched another for Andrew. 'Do you want one, Mam?'

'Not now.' Catherine sat down and looked at her husband. 'And how long do you have to keep the plaster on?'

'You should know, having been a nurse – eight weeks and I shouldn't do any heavy work for a month or two after that.'

'Well of course I knew,' Catherine shook her head and tut-tutted. '*Well done,* Norrie. You *couldn't* have timed it better. That gets you out of lambing and the ploughing.' Worry and exhaustion had worn Catherine's nerves to a frazzle. Who was going to plough and plant the rigs now? 'Oh my God,' she cried as she put a hand to her forehead. 'How the hell am I going to manage?'

'I'm really sorry, Catherine.' Norrie had come to put his free arm round her shoulder. 'I wasn't drunk, I promise you, and it wasn't my fault.'

'I was with him,' said Andrew. 'We were going down Bank Lane, you know it don't you?' Oh yes, she knew the narrow lanes leading up from the main street, more flights of steps than pathway. 'The wind whipped up an empty can; it hit Norrie in the back of his knees and pitched him headfirst down the steps.'

'Thank God he was there, because I was knocked out,' said Norrie.

'Mam,' said Robbie. 'I think the porridge is burning.'

'What's going on?' Judith, followed by Allen and Peter, had come downstairs and now stood just inside the room.

Andrew stood up. 'I'll have to go. I've got to get to work.' He handed some car keys to Catherine. 'The car's parked down by the quay. It'll be all right there till you can get it.'

'Thank you,' said Catherine. 'And thank you for looking out for Norrie.' She went with him to the door and closing it after him, turned and looked at her family. 'Well, kids, your father's going to be out of action for a while so *you'll* have to help me. And I *do* mean help – there's going to be a lot to do.' She looked at Norrie. 'And as for you,' she said. 'You might only have one good hand, but it's going to *have* to work. I can't do it all.'

'Are we going to have any breakfast?' asked Judith.

'I want some,' said Peter, which Allen echoed with, 'And me.'

'Go and get dressed, then, while I see to it,' said Catherine. 'You, Robbie, will have to stay at home and help me.'

When the family had been fed and Judith and the twins were on their way to school, Catherine left Norrie to wash the dishes as well as he could and, taking Robbie with her, went to check on the sheep. Lambs were due any day and the ewes needed extra feed to supplement the poor grazing that was all there was to be had. It would be a while yet before the first flush of new grass. Robbie carried a bag of dry feed on a shoulder and when they reached the waiting sheep he emptied it into troughs that were there for the purpose. Eager to get at it the pregnant ewes jostled round him.

'I'm sorry to have to tell you this, Robbie,' said Catherine, as they watched the sheep feeding, 'but I think it's going to be a while before I can go and look at the boat. I'm going to need you.' At the look of disappointment on Robbie's face she went on, 'Think about it. We've got two hundred sheep to lamb and it's going to take weeks. It wouldn't be so bad if they were all Shetlands, but the pure breeds need watching and the cross breeds aren't much better. And then there's Norrie's lot at Broonieswick. I'm sorry, son, I really am.'

'Can't say I'm not disappointed,' said Robbie. 'But it can't be helped, Mam. At least Dad hadn't been drinking so it really was an accident.'

'If he had, it would have been another rod for his back and there's enough already,' said Catherine. 'But it isn't just the lambing; the rigs have to be ploughed. I haven't got a clue about how to set up a plough. Have you?'

'No. I can drive the tractor, but only to pull the trailer and that's not the same. I've never been shown how to plough.'

'It'll have to be done. We'll have to have a stab at it. As if I haven't got enough to put up with. Bloody Norrie, of all times of year to break his arm he couldn't have chosen a worse one.'

'He's still alive, Mam, and he will get better,' said Robbie.

'Yes, you're right,' said Catherine and put her arm across his shoulders as they walked. 'You are a lovely boy. How could I be so blessed as to have you?'

'That wasn't what you said when I took the twins fishing.'

'You meant well, though.' They were almost home. 'Wonder how your dad's got on. D'you think he's managed to drop any dishes and break them?'

'We'll soon find out.'

Stifling a yawn Catherine opened her door and was about to step out when she saw June Thomson. 'Hello, June,' she said. 'You're almost a stranger. I haven't seen much of you lately.'

'Well, I have been rather busy. Sorry to hear about Norrie.'

'Not as sorry as I am,' said Catherine. 'I must say if he wanted a rest he couldn't have timed it better.'

'It's made a lot of work for you, hasn't it?'

'You could say that. Thank God for Robbie. We're nearly done with the lambing but I'd never have managed without him.'

June appeared to be about to say something, but bit her lip and looked away, then she turned and said, 'Look, I've got to say this; I'm sorry about what happened at Christmas. But don't blame Norrie. If there'd been mistletoe I suppose it wouldn't have mattered, and these things happen … don't they?'

'Who told you I blamed Norrie? Is that why you've been avoiding me?'

'Joe said Norrie told him he was in the doghouse, but didn't say why, and I haven't told Joe. I thought you'd be mad at me and blame me, too.'

Catherine gave a little laugh. 'Well I was, but it takes two and Norrie should have known better. It's water under the bridge now.'

'Thank you.' June smiled. 'Is there anything I can do to help you now?'

'We're managing all right so far. But if there is I'll let you know. Robbie's on his own so I must go and see how he's doing.'

The two women walked a little way together till Catherine turned to go back to the lambing pens. She found Robbie on his knees beside a ewe, a dead lamb lying on the ground. 'What happened?' she said.

'It was coming backwards,' said Robbie. 'So I pulled it out, but it was dead already.' He looked up at his mother. 'Did I do something wrong?'

'No, you did nothing wrong.' She told him how she'd wept over her first dead lamb and how Daa had told her it was something she had to accept. 'That's life,' she said. 'It isn't easy. Is anything else happening?'

There wasn't and with only a few more lambs to be born, the pressure was off. Detailing Norrie to make periodic forays round the lambing pens, to come and call her if her help was needed, Catherine sent Robbie to bed and, exhausted, crawled into bed herself. She slept soundly and rose refreshed and ready to consider her next move. It was time to get back to a more ordered routine. The rigs had to be ploughed, oats sown and potatoes planted. A solid month of being midwife or doctor to the ewes had been comparatively easy – she had done that many times before – but ploughing was something she had never thought she or Robbie might have to do.

Like most boys who grew up on a croft and were expected to do their share of work, Robbie had learnt how to drive the tractor. Until now he had only driven it to carry tools or pull a trailer; he had not hitched anything else to the back of it and had never had to carry out cultivations. Now he was going to have to learn how to plough and sow, and it would have to be done under the watchful and no doubt critical eye of Norrie. It was not going to be easy, for Norrie, whose temper was unpredictable these days, had been getting more and more irritable. Beneath the plaster an exasperating itch had him exploding with rage and reaching for the whisky bottle again. Drinking did not stop the itch or improve his temper and the next few weeks promised to be fraught with problems. It was too much to expect that things would go without a hitch and without doubt, if anything did go wrong, they would have to bear the brunt of his temper.

TWENTY FOUR

'COME ON ROBBIE,' said Catherine. 'I can't stand it any longer. Let's go and have a look at the plough. Do you know how to set it up?'

'I've watched Norrie, but he wouldn't let me touch it.'

'Do you think we ought to get him to help us?'

'I think we ought.'

'I would hope you wouldn't even *think* about setting it up without asking me,' grumbled Norrie when they asked him. The plough had been left outside. 'Give it a good greasing,' said Norrie. 'I did it when I left it, but it'll need more.'

The tractor, an old wartime Fordson, started first time. Robbie backed it up to the plough, lowered the draw bar and eased the tractor back till linkages clicked and Norrie was able to drop in the pin to secure it. He directed Robbie in setting up the plough. 'You have to have the top links twenty-five and a half inches apart,' he said. 'Where's your measure? You can't guess it.'

Catherine stood and listened, twisted her hands together as she wished she could step in and do it all herself. She prayed that Robbie wouldn't lose his patience and answer back when Norrie berated him for his lack of knowledge. At last Norrie was satisfied that all was as it should be. He directed Robbie into position ready to plough the first furrow. 'Now,' he said, 'when you have the plough dropped and cuttin', look straight ahead. Set your eyes on something and never look back. If you do you'll have a crooked furrow.'

A crooked furrow! As long as the ground was turned over, did it matter?

The tractor belched black smoke as Robbie put it in gear and pulled away, lowering the plough into the ground as he did. Cutting into the soil the first ridge of black earth lifted and turned over to cover the turf. Slowly tractor and plough crept up the rig and came to a stop not far from Catherine. When Robbie pulled the lever to lift the plough out of the ground she could see how the roughness of the soil had polished the mouldboard, the curved iron part that turned the soil over, till it was bright and shining. Robbie looked at her and gave a brief smile then turned the tractor into position ready to cut the next furrow.

For a while Catherine stayed to watch, but then left him to it and went indoors. At first the sound of the tractor held her attention. From time to time she heard a shout from Norrie and an answering one from Robbie. All seemed to be going well and she relaxed. Things were going better than she had anticipated. She glanced at the clock; there was enough time for her to look over the sheep before Judith and the little ones came home from school. She had just put on her boots when she heard the tractor splutter to a stop and Norrie roaring obscenities.

'What is it?' she cried as she ran to see what had happened.

'Stupid boy,' yelled Norrie. 'He's broken the sock.'

'The sock! What on earth are you talking about?'

'The sock, the sock, the point on the mouldboard. I haven't got another.'

'It wasn't my fault,' said Robbie. 'I didn't know I was going to hit a rock.'

'You should have been quicker to stop,' shouted Norrie. 'Trust you to mess things up. It's going to take all of three days to get another, longer, if they have to send south for it. It's going to rain and that'll set us back again. We'll be sowing oats when others are harvesting at this rate.'

'Stop shouting, Norrie,' said Catherine. 'If you were ploughing it could have happened to you and all the shouting in the world isn't going to change anything. Tell me what I have to do to get another, what d'you call it, sock?'

'You'll have to take this one to the blacksmith. He'll need to know what one to order, or maybe he can get this one welded up,' grunted Norrie. 'We'll get it off and you can take it to him.'

'*Do* that then.' Catherine, muttering under her breath, turned and walked away. It was no good getting in a rage when something went wrong and heaven knows so far it had been the story of her life. The thing to do was to get on with it. Robbie had started off so well and she had been so pleased for him. Trust Norrie to blame him for something that could have happened to anyone. Everyone knew that Shetland had grown up on solid rock – there was bound to be some just under the surface. Poor Robbie, there had been the suspicion of tears in his eyes when Norrie had shouted at him. If the sock couldn't be repaired it could be replaced, so no lasting damage was done.

'Don't let the fire go out while I'm away, Norrie.'

'Why, where are you going?'

'I promised Robbie I'd go and have a look at the boat he wants to go on. If it looks all right I may have a talk with the owner,' said Catherine. 'I've got some shopping to do and I shall go and see Laura. I don't know what time I'll be back.'

'And what am I supposed to do while you're gone?'

'You can do the exercises they told you to do and take a walk round the sheep. I guess you'll be able to make a cup of tea for yourself, won't you?'

'No need for you to be so sharp,' muttered Norrie as Catherine picked up her car keys. 'It's time I was allowed to go back to work,' and, as the door was closing on her, 'don't be late.'

As she drove past Gerda's house Catherine turned to look across the rigs. The broken plough piece had been welded and there had been no further accidents. Only a couple of days had been lost and as the rain Norrie had said would come had not materialized, it didn't matter. The land had been harrowed and was level and ready for seeding. There was no sign of a crooked furrow. If the earth was turned over to the right depth did it matter if the lines weren't ruler straight? At Broonieswick she looked at the doctor's house. She had put off going back to work and now she wondered if she would ever get another chance.

When she reached Lerwick and had parked the car she walked along to the harbour. Several fishing boats were tied up, some better and more prosperous looking than others. She found *Adventurer*. In the harbour it looked quite big, but what would it be like at sea? Was she right in letting Robbie go? As she stood there wondering a man came out on deck. She called out to him, 'Hi, halloo,' and when the man looked up, 'Would you be Mr Sandison?'

'I am.'

'In that case, I've come to see you. I'm Robbie Jameson's mother.'

'Come aboard.'

'I'd rather not.'

Ross Sandison chuckled as he pulled himself up on to the quay. 'You don't have sea legs like your son, then,' he said.

'No, and never will have.' Catherine took a good look at the man who stood smiling at her. He was wearing a thick jacket and a pair of waterproof trousers. 'For the life of me,' she went on, 'I can't imagine what makes Robbie want to work on a fishing boat. I thought he was going to work with the sheep.'

'He's a natural born seaman, Mrs Jameson. I shall be very pleased if you agree to let him come and work for me.'

'My name is Williams,' said Catherine. 'Robbie's father was drowned in a fishing accident, which is why I don't really want young Robbie to go to sea. I've tried to get him to change his mind, but he's set on it so I've had to give in.'

'Oh, I'm sorry to hear you lost your husband, but like I say, the boy's a born seaman. Not every boy is. He won't be involved in the fishing right away; he'll have to cook for the men first, so he'll be down in the galley, a better place, perhaps, when the sea gets rough.'

'He told me that,' said Catherine. 'He asked me to teach him how to cook.'

'So he isn't likely to poison us then,' Ross Sandison laughed. 'Right then, are you sure you don't want to come on board?'

'No, thank you.'

'Will we go to the café and have a cup of tea, then? I'll be able to tell you what he'll have to do, what the working hours are and how much money he'll get. That's just so you've got the full picture before you say yes or no.'

Half an hour later Catherine shook Ross Sandison by the hand. 'I'll talk it over with my husband and let you know,' she said. 'Thank you for seeing me today.' There was nothing in what Sandison had said that made her decide there was no way she would let her boy work for him. On the contrary she had come to the conclusion he would be a fair man. Saying that she wanted to discuss things with Norrie was just another way of gaining time, because she knew in her heart that she couldn't stand in Robbie's way. It had been a hard decision to make.

She turned towards Commercial Street and the shops. In all the years she had been patronizing the shops in Lerwick she had seen assistants come and go. Some stayed on throughout their working lives and had become familiar to her. She was often greeted with a cheery smile and inquiries after her health and family and though they weren't personal friends they were well enough known to be called friends. Shopping here was always a pleasure. Never did she have to stand and wait for a gossiping girl to serve her as had often happened at home.

When she got to Laura's she was greeted with warmth and affection. 'Du's lookin' tired,' said Laura. 'Is anything wrong?'

'Norrie broke his arm and it's put a lot of work on me and the children,' said Catherine. 'But with a bit of luck he'll soon be back at work. Robbie's been a tower of strength. He ploughed the rigs and we're getting through. He doesn't want to be a crofter, though; he wants to go to sea. Ross Sandison offered him a job so I've just been to see the man and look at his boat.' She gave a sigh. 'I have to let Robbie go. He knows I don't want to, but he's got his heart set on it.'

'Ross Sandison's a fine man,' said Laura. 'He'll look out for the boy. How is Robbie going to get to work? Will he use his bike?'

'That's what I was thinking.'

'I'll have to ask Willie, but maybe he could stay with us and come home on his days off.'

'Oh that would be good.' Catherine stood up refusing an offer of tea. 'The children will be home from school soon and I don't want to leave them with Norrie for too long. He's like a bear with a sore head. I shall be glad when he goes back to work.'

'I wish you'd stay longer,' said Laura as she hugged Catherine. 'I miss you and the valley. Come again soon.'

TWENTY FIVE

'I've had enough of being stuck at home,' said Norrie as Catherine put down her bag and began to take off her coat. 'The arm's all right. I don't care what Lumsden says, I'm going back to work on Monday.'

Pleased that Norrie would soon be back at work and out of her way, but with a sense of guilt at wanting to see him gone, Catherine said, 'You can't, you have to get the plaster off first. You don't want to make it worse and still have to stay home.'

'How can I make it worse? I've been doing things here no trouble. I'd be better at work, I get paid for that. But I'll get the oats sown first. Can't let Robbie mess that up.'

'That's not fair, Norrie, and you know it.' Coat off and hung up Catherine was putting away her shopping. As she put packets and tins in a cupboard she said, 'I don't know how we'd have got that ground ploughed if he hadn't done it. He may not have done the best of jobs, but at least he did it.'

'I could maybe have got someone else.'

'You could have tried, I suppose, but they would all have been too busy with their own work to come and do ours, and then you might *well* have been sowing oats at harvest time.' She shut the cupboard door and put her bags away.

'Mmm.' Norrie nodded his head. 'You're right, of course. He is a good lad. How did you get on with Sandison?'

'I didn't go on the boat – I didn't want to.' Catherine put on her apron and tied its strings. 'I liked him, though, and Laura said he was a good man and that he'd look out for Robbie. She said Robbie could stay with them if Willie agreed so he wouldn't have to bike back and forth in all weathers.'

'That was good of her.'

'Where are the boys and Judith?'

'They're with Joe. The man's a magnet; they can't keep away.'

'He's good fun and they love him. You should get him to join your band.'

'We've already got a piano player.'

Catherine laughed. 'I bet they're not like Joe, though.'

'No. I'll have to think about it. I won't be playing for a while. My fingers have got stiff. I shall have to practice when I get this plaster off. Still, there're plenty of other things to do, so that'll have to wait.'

When Norrie was finally back at work the bulk of jobs to be done on the croft lay with Catherine. Most of the time, between getting children fed and off to school and being there when they came home, she was out of doors. She walked the parks, checked fences, rounded up sheep and with her dog, Fly, moved them to fresh pastures when they had exhausted the ones they were on.

There was no Robbie to help her now; he had started work on the boat and had gone to live with Laura. She missed him. She had wept the first night he did not come home, but telling herself that worry was a waste of time she threw herself into her work. When she wasn't trying to catch up on housework she was hoeing between rows of carrots and turnips. Good weather, warm sunshine and moderate rainfall, meant that the crops were growing well.

Sometimes, when time allowed, she went along to see Jannie and sit with her. The old lady was still busy with her knitting and Catherine wondered why. But Jannie had held knitting pins and wool in her hands since she was a small child so what else would she do? Her old hands flew over the work and garments grew rapidly. Catherine wondered what she was doing with them.

'How much work do you have put by?' she asked one day.

'Some,' said Jannie. 'Mina will be along to take it to the merchant soon.'

'But....' How was she going to say this? 'Um, Mina's not here now.'

'Yea, I ken, but she'll be back soon.'

'I could take it for you if you like.'

'Na, na, du's a good lass but du wouldn't know how to bargain. I'll wait on Mina comin' home.'

So Jannie still wouldn't accept that Mina had died. 'Where's Daa?'

'I dinna ken,' said Jannie.

And it doesn't sound as though you care, thought Catherine. 'I'll go and look for him,' she said. 'I'll come along and see you again soon.'

She found John Jameson in the barn. He was sitting on a stool making a straw basket. His fingers were knotted with rheumatism and his movements were slow. He looked up at her as she came near and she saw how lined and drawn his face had become. Jannie's illness was taking its toll.

'How are you, Daa?' she said.

'The better for seeing you, lass.'

'You look tired. Are you sleeping properly?' Daa didn't answer but turned away and bent down to pick up a handful of straw. 'You're not are you?' said Catherine. 'It's Jannie, isn't it? Does she keep you awake?'

The old man slumped on his stool his head bent, arms hanging loose. 'She says there's folk outside or the cow's run away.' He shook his head. 'I canna stop her, she must get up and go and see, but she'll no put a coat on and I'm afraid she'll catch her death.'

'Oh, Daa, why didn't you tell me this before?'

'I didna want to worry you.'

'I wish you had.' Catherine put an arm round the old man's shoulders. 'You can't carry this alone. You'll just have to let me help you. Are you getting proper meals? Is she managing the cooking?'

'Now and then, we get enough.'

'You must tell me if you don't. If anything bothers you, you will *have* to come and tell me. I would be most upset if you didn't.'

Daa smiled at her and patted her hand. 'I won't forget,' he said.

'Good.' Catherine tightened her arm round him and gave him a squeeze. 'I'll go and see Lumsden. He'll probably give you something to help Jannie sleep and that would make things better for you. Would you be happy with that?'

'Ay,' said Daa. 'Du's a good lass.'

'I'm not that good. I should have been along to see you before this.'

'Du has a lot to do. We dinna expect you to look after us as well.'

Love and compassion for her father-in-law made Catherine want to give him a hug, but he was not a demonstrative man and she hesitated, not wanting to embarrass him. An arm across the shoulder was one thing; a hug was out of the question. 'You're not to think like that,' she said. 'You were good to me when I came here first. I'm only repaying a favour.'

She left him then and walked away. It wasn't Jannie's fault – she couldn't help what was happening to her – but why did old age have to bring such distress to a gentle old man? She didn't wait, but went to the surgery straight away.

'You told me to come and see you if anything changed with Jannie,' she said when she was sitting in Lumsden's consulting room. 'Well, it has. She's getting up in the night and going out of doors. Daa said he can't stop her and we wondered if there is anything you can do.'

'I'll come along and see her,' said the doctor. 'How are things with you? When are you coming back to work?'

'We're not too bad. Robbie's started work on a fishing boat. I had to give in and let him go. I'm not too happy about it, but it's what he wanted to do. And I can't come back – I'd love to – but not yet anyway.'

Neil Lumsden dropped in to see Jannie after surgery that day. Catherine was expecting him and was there to make sure he saw

Daa as well. Daa was given medicine for Jannie with instructions on how to administer it. 'Do you think he'll remember to give it to her?' the doctor asked Catherine when they were outside Jannie's house.

'Oh yes. It's only Jannie who's losing it. And Daa does need a good night's sleep. He won't forget.'

With regular visits to Jannie and Daa added to her other tasks, Catherine's days were busier than ever. The continuing good weather pleased her, for there were no wet coats to haul up on the pulley to dry and she was able to put out a line of washing and not have to watch the skies for rain. The children walked dry shod to school and she didn't have to stop what she was doing to fetch them home.

The last three days of March, the borrowing days according to legend, came and went, each of them fine, sunny and warm. Kay had told Catherine much of the folklore and superstitions of the islands. Of these, the 'borrowing days' were said to forecast the weather to be expected in June, July and August. Kay had said it was thought the days had been borrowed from April to prolong the boisterous days of March. That they truly indicated the weather for the summer months had been borne out several times and she looked forward to being able to discard her woolly jumpers and sometimes wear a cotton dress.

TWENTY SIX

It was towards the end of July when Bjorg reappeared. Catherine and Norrie were hard at work clipping sheep. Norrie sheared and Catherine folded and rolled each fleece as it was handed to her. The day was hot. Norrie had discarded his shirt altogether and Catherine wore the skimpiest of sleeveless blouses. Both of them perspired freely and sweat combined with lanolin from the fleece saturated their clothes. Neither was aware of Bjorg's approach. The raucous bleating of a hundred penned sheep obliterated other sounds and it wasn't until a voice was raised, saying, 'Is there anything I can do to help?' that they stopped to see who it was. 'Tell me what I can do,' said Bjorg.

'Do you really want to?' asked Norrie. He looked Bjorg up and down. 'It'll make a mess of your clothes.'

'They'll wash.'

'Can you handle a sheep?'

'I can try.'

'All right, then,' said Norrie. When Bjorg was in the pen with him he pointed at one of the animals. 'Get that one,' he said. 'You can keep me supplied and save me catching my own.'

Bjorg proved to be adept at catching sheep and in the time lapse, while Norrie sheared and Bjorg stood waiting, he looked at Catherine and smiled. She felt the hot flush of colour as it flooded her face. Why did he have to come back? She turned away and tried to look at anything but him. He still looked at her. She could feel his eyes on her and inevitably hers were drawn back to him. And now she was conscious of how she must look. The thin cotton of her blouse was wet and now clung to her like a second skin. She might as well be naked as clad. The look on Bjorg's face told her he was as aware of it as she was. She closed her eyes and tried to block out the fact that he was there.

'What are you daydreaming about, Catherine?' shouted Norrie. 'Now is not the time to go to sleep.'

She didn't see the heavy fleece Norrie threw at her. 'Sorry,' she said as she grabbed at but missed it and dropped it on the ground.

'Wake up, then.' Norrie stood and watched as Catherine picked bits of debris off the fleece. 'Pay attention to what you're doing or the brokers will dock money for dirty wool.' He glared at her then took the next sheep from Bjorg.

They had been working most of the day and there were not many animals left to shear. With Bjorg's help they were soon done and while Catherine gathered up their lunch bags and checked that she had everything, Norrie loaded the rolls of fleece onto the trailer. He started the tractor and drove away and not able to go down the hill, which was too steep, had to go home another way. This left Catherine alone with Bjorg and she had no option but to walk home with him.

'You are as lovely as ever,' said Bjorg, 'but your man is still working you too hard. Why don't you come away with me?'

'Don't be silly,' said Catherine. Eager to get away from an awkward situation she walked fast.

Bjorg grabbed for her arm, caught her and turned her to face him. 'Why are you running? What are you afraid of?' he said.

'I wasn't running. I have to get home. I've children to see to.'

'And what about me?'

'Let go of me. Leave me alone.'

'I'll never do that. You excite me. I want to possess you.'

Suddenly he gripped her upper arms, bent his head down to kiss her.

'Don't,' she began, but her words were smothered by his mouth on hers. She struggled, but he gripped her tighter and she was powerless against his strength.

Play dead, her mind said, perhaps he'll give up, and she let her body go limp. It was the wrong thing to do for, despite herself, she began to dissolve with desire.

Bjorg looked at her, a triumphant smile on his face. 'You see,' he said. 'You cannot resist any more than I can. We were meant for each other.'

'No,' she said, pushing her hands against him, fighting her feelings as well as him. 'No, this is all wrong. Let me go.'

'Only until the next time.'

'There'll be no next time,' cried Catherine.

'Oh yes, there will.' Bjorg smiled. 'Oh yes, there will,' he said.

'Would you have a couple of hours to spare, Joe?' said Norrie. 'I've got some fences to replace and I could do with an extra pair of hands.'

Joe didn't hesitate to say yes.

June's parents still found it hard to forgive their daughter for marrying a black man and barely tolerated him. When she did get him to go home with her he was ignored and not spoken to. He was outgoing by nature and found their treatment hard to accept, but here in the valley, after the first shock and looks of surprise that greeted his black face he had been treated as one of their own. The children loved him and he never hesitated to spend time with them.

'Time's my own on a Saturday,' he said. 'I'd be delighted to give you a hand. Wait while I get my boots on.'

With Norrie on the tractor and Joe sitting in the trailer along with posts and wire and all the other things needed for fencing, they set off, up out of the valley and away to higher ground. Except for the protected home ground where crops were grown, sheep were once allowed to roam free. But now some of the hill land that was apportioned to crofters was being fenced off and the wanderings of sheep curtailed. It was putting a fence round some of the land that had been apportioned to Norrie and Catherine's croft that Norrie needed help with.

Joe was willing and keen to help and as he and Norrie worked together he asked numerous questions. 'Could anyone be a crofter? Would I be able to?'

Norrie had laughed at that. 'You'd be able to keep nothing but Scottish Blackfaces,' he said and laughed again. 'No, I'm kidding, Joe. I don't know. If you could prove you were going to be able to run a croft as a croft and not just for fun, I don't see why not.'

'So how would I get one?'

'Are you serious?' asked Norrie. He stopped what he was doing and looked at Joe.

'Working for the council's all right,' said Joe. 'But when I was a kid we had a pig, some chickens and a goat and my father grew vegetables. I like animals and June grew up on a croft and we have talked about it.'

'Well,' said Norrie. 'You should write to the Crofters Commission and ask them.' He picked up a handful of staples, which he put in his pocket.

They worked well together, but didn't talk much while they were fastening wire to the fence posts except for comments such as, 'Dinna hammer the staple right home, Joe, or we'll never get it out and we can use it again if we need to,' or, 'Hold the post steady.'

They'd been working for a couple of hours when they stopped for a rest.

'Do you ever take time off?' said Joe.

'There's not much chance of that,' said Norrie. 'The work has to be done and when you've got animals you never know what's going to happen.'

'But sheep don't need that much attention, do they?'

'You'd be surprised. You have to keep their feet trimmed and treat for scald. You have to dose them for worms. Then they get things like orf, which you can catch, too, and God only knows what else. They have to be sheared and then you have to spend night and day with them at lambing time. Got to watch them then or you can lose lamb and mother. If they get sick they don't have much will to live and you can sit up all night with them and the buggers'll die anyway.'

'Oh Lordy,' said Joe. 'Why do you keep them, then?'

'Because they're right for the place and you don't have to milk them twice a day, like cows.'

Joe was silent for a moment or two. 'But you still find time to go off playing at the dances in winter, don't you?'

'Yes.'

'And what about Catherine, does she ever get to go with you?'

Norrie looked at Joe before he replied and Joe guessed he was treading on dangerous ground. 'I must admit that she hasn't since we had the twins.'

'You should take her with you. June or I would look after the little ones for you,' said Joe. 'You'll forgive me for saying this, I hope, but she's still a young woman. She works hard and she needs time off as well as you.'

'Well, I don't go to the dances to enjoy myself,' said Norrie. 'I have to work. I know I love being part of the band, but it is work, after all.'

'Yes, but she would be with you, wouldn't she? And I'm sure they'd let you take her round the floor for a turn or two.'

Norrie said nothing, but stood stroking his beard for a moment. 'You're right, I suppose,' he said at last. 'I'll bear it in mind. Thanks for the offer to baby-sit. Now, shall we get going again?'

TWENTY SEVEN

Anxious to avoid Bjorg, Catherine found plenty to do at home. He wasn't likely to come to find her there and in a few days' time the children would be on holiday and the danger of being caught alone with him would be lessened. But even as she willed herself not to think of him his words, 'You can't resist any more than I can,' kept coming back. She knew he was right and that she had to stay away from him. If she didn't … she tried not to think about what might happen, but turned her thoughts to Norrie, and there she faltered.

She was ironing. She picked up and folded the shirt she had just pressed. Turning her head she looked out of the window. What was happening to her marriage? Was it her fault Norrie had turned to drink? She had always known he was partial to a dram, but he had never taken as much as he did now. It made him irritable. His behaviour was unpredictable and set her on edge. She put the shirt down, picked up another garment and spread it on the ironing board. Norrie was not the same man she had fallen in love with. Did she still love him? Yes, she did. So why had Bjorg's presence so unsettled her? She had no answer to that and began to iron again.

'Mam.' Judith came bursting in. 'Mam, I got a gold star for my knitting.'

'Well done. You'll have to show your granny. What about you, boys?'

'Didna get anything,' said Allen while Peter offered his mother a drawing of a sheep. A silver star was stuck on the piece of paper.

'He's always drawing sheep,' said Allen. 'He can't do anything else.'

'I like sheep,' muttered Peter.

'And what was your piece of knitting, Judith?' asked Catherine.

'I made a baby's bonnet. Can we have a baby? I could knit a shawl for it.'

'We could *not,*' said Catherine. 'And you're not skilled enough to knit anything as big as a shawl.'

Judith uttered a long drawn, 'Aww. But I'm good. Miss said I was.'

'I'm sure you are. Now run along and get changed.'

Catherine put away the iron and the board and spread the ironed clothes on the pulley to air. The children, promising not to go deeper into the water than to paddle in the shallows, went whooping and laughing to play on the beach. Inga, who was a more studious child than Judith, had joined them. Not for her the riotous romps of the boys; she preferred to be with Judith.

It was time to prepare the evening meal, but before she did Catherine made a pot of tea. She sat down to enjoy a cup while the children were out. It would be the last time she could steal a few minutes to herself till after the little ones were in bed, and even then there would be some mending or other to do.

She didn't hear him coming and not until his shadow loomed across the floor did she look up and see him. He lounged, arms crossed, against the door frame. His cotton shirt was unbuttoned and revealed a tantalizing glimpse of the dark mat of hair on his chest. Her eyes followed it down till it disappeared under the waistband of his trousers. He was smiling, his lips quirking as if amused at the look on her face.

'What do you want?' she snapped.

'Oh, please say you are happy to see me, because I am happy to see you.'

'Well, now you've seen me you can go away.' Catherine stood up and was about to take her cup out to the kitchen. She was about to, but stopped. If she did was he cheeky enough to follow her?

'That is not very kind of you,' he said.

'Perhaps not, but unless you've a good reason to be here, I'd rather you left.'

'I can't. I have a message for you.'

A message? It was just another excuse to come and annoy her.

'Do you not want to hear it?' asked Bjorg when she didn't reply.

'I suppose I'd better,' said Catherine.

'Gerda and I would like to take the children out on Saturday. She thought it would be nice to take them all for a picnic. I have been detailed to help and I have come to ask your permission for them to come with us.'

'Where are you going to take them?'

'I am not quite sure, but I think we are going to one of the castles.'

There were only two castles, both ruins. Catherine summoned them up in a mental picture. Good, they would most likely be going to the one on Unst. There was more room for a picnic there than the one in Scalloway. There was also the fun of a couple of ferry crossings and that meant they would all be away for most of the day.

'All right,' she said. 'Thank you very much, that would be nice. Goodbye.'

If she thought he would go she was mistaken. He moved to put his hands in his pockets and as he did his shirt front opened wider, exposing even more of him. Now she could see his body, youthful and strong, and the sight made her gasp. She put a hand up to her mouth and gave a little cough hoping to disguise it, but he knew what he had done and how it was affecting her. He was playing her, teasing her, and she had nothing to fight him with. She was hooked.

'Make me a sandwich and fill a flask,' said Norrie. 'I'm going over to Broonies today. I won't be back till supper time.'

'Are you going to be away all day, then?'

'Yes, you'll have a nice quiet day on your own. No kids, no me; you can put your feet up for a change.'

'I doubt it,' said Catherine.

'Well, make the best of it, then.'

Catherine stood at her door and watched as he drove away. When the sound of his van had died to nothing the valley lay quiet. There was no movement at Jannie's house. Daa was probably in the barn working on the kishie he had promised her and Jannie would be at her knitting again. Lars was a workaholic and probably at work. Gerda had gathered up the children and bundled them, along with toys and baskets of food and drink, into the car. And now she and Bjorg were away with them. She had seen Gerda's car as it was being driven up the hill. June and Joe had both gone out and just for once she was left on her own. 'Make the best of it,' Norrie had said. So what was she going to do?

It was mid-morning and already the sun was high in the sky. With the absence of any whisper of wind its rays were mercilessly hot. Catherine looked towards the bay where the water lay flat as a mill pond, serene and inviting. It looked good enough to swim in. But it would be cold. Catherine sucked in her breath at the thought. She remembered plunging into icy water once before. A quick dip would be fun, though.

Her costume had been tucked away in the bottom drawer of the chest. She pulled it out and searched it for moth holes – they got into everything – but it was intact. She put it on, grabbed a towel from the bathroom and on bare feet made for the beach. Throwing down the towel she ran into the water, cried out as the coldness of it grabbed at her ankles, but on she went till it was well above her knees, then she plunged in. Down she went, came up gasping then struck out in a strong, clean, crawl. She swam to the middle of the bay then turned back to the shore. Reaching the shallows she stood up, shook her head and the water from her hair. Her body, stimulated and invigorated from contact with the cold water, tingled. Boy that was good, she thought as she picked up the towel and draped it round her shoulders. I should do it again. But how many summers were going to be like this one?

Showered and clad in a cotton sundress, Catherine picked up

the portable radio and carried it out to the barn. She was going to sort out the boxes in which Norrie had put Kay's bits and pieces. She had cleared one last year but the others had been smothered in hay and it was only now that she was able to get at them. Taking a hessian sack she folded it to make a kneeling pad and set it on the floor. Lifting the lid of one of the boxes she took it off and made a start.

She had finished one box and was starting on the next when the programme on the radio changed from one of discussion to dance music. She sang along to the words of a quickstep, but when the opening bars of *Moon River* began she got up and, presenting herself to an imaginary partner, began to dance. She loved to dance and it had been so long since Norrie had taken her dancing. The music was slow and sentimental and, dreaming of days back home, she closed her eyes and gave herself up to it.

A hand clasped hers as an arm slid round her waist and pulled her close. 'Do not stop,' whispered Bjorg, as he looked down into her startled face. He held her close and she couldn't have got away if she tried – at least not without a struggle – and she didn't want to do that for her body blended with his and his hand, firm and controlling in the middle of her back, kept them moving in time and in tune.

'Sssh, do not talk,' he said as she drew in a breath to speak. 'You will spoil the moment.' So she didn't and they danced, moving as one. When the music stopped he still held her.

'Why do you creep up on me so quietly and why are you here?' she said. 'Are the children home already?'

'No. I did not go. When all the stuff they wanted to take was in the car, there was not room for me.'

Catherine hung her head. How was she going to get out of this? There was no one to come and rescue her and they had been in the barn when she had almost lost her senses before. But did she want to be rescued? Wasn't she entitled to a little flirtation? For that's all it was, wasn't it? The music started again and he held her so close there was nothing she could do but dance. Nothing she wanted to do but dance, nothing she wanted to do but go on being close to him, go on being wrapped in his arms. Her nose was so close to his chest that she breathed in the smell of him, the musky smell of man. And again the fresh smell of pine, damp earth and pine needles crushed underfoot. It drugged her, made her forget she was a married woman with a family, made her feel young and free and aching and ready for love....

The music stopped and this time he let her go. Sliding his hands down her arms he held her hands in his. While he smiled at her he said, 'Thank you for the pleasure, Madame, we must do this again.' He leaned forward and kissed her cheek and, before she could say anything, turned on his heel and walked away. Speechless, Catherine watched him go.

For several seconds she stood there. Her body throbbed with desire. 'Don't talk, you'll spoil the moment,' he'd said. He knew what he was doing, knew what he'd done to her. Roused her desire then thwarted it, turned it down and rejected it out of hand. What right had he to stir the fire in her then walk away and leave her? No right at all. Anger rose within her.

Kay's bits and pieces still lay on the floor beside the box. They were things she was going to throw away. But so humiliated was Catherine at the way she had been treated that something had to give. She wanted to strike out, wanted to rake her fingernails down Bjorg's face and disfigure it. How could he walk away from her? No doubt he was smiling now, exulting in how he had played her. She moved to pick up a bag to put the rubbish in. But didn't. Venting her rage at being cheated and played for a fool she lashed out, kicked a book to send it crashing against the wall where its rotten pages disintegrated into pieces. Lashed out again to kick a china jug and send that to smash into smithereens; kicked a glass, which shattered in midair and spread its shards over the floor.

'*That's* better,' she said.

TWENTY EIGHT

CATHERINE LOOKED INTO her bathroom mirror. Her cheeks were aflame. She scooped cold water into her cupped hands and splashed it on her face. It wouldn't do to let anyone see her the way she was and there was no telling what time Norrie would be home. But now there was time to fill. She would cook; baking was therapeutic and there were always mouths to feed. She took out baking tins, flour, fat, sugar and raisins, and began. She wouldn't allow herself to think and she threw herself into her task. There was a batch of scones and bannocks and a clutch of little cakes on the table when the first of the wanderers returned.

'We've been to see the castle,' said Judith. 'Did you know it was three hundred years old?'

'We had a picnic on a beach,' said Allen. 'See what I got for you.' He held out a large shell.

'And I got these,' said Peter, his gift a handful of pretty pebbles.

'I hope you all said thank you to Gerda for taking you.'

Later, when the children were in bed, Catherine sat at the table, a threaded needle in her hand, but she was not sewing. She stared out of the window. Norrie had come home and was upstairs having a bath. She knew he was tired, but yet again he was going out to play at a dance somewhere. Was he never going to give it up? No, she supposed not. Not when other men went on playing as long as they could bend an elbow and run a bow across fiddle strings. Not when they could produce music that could make you want to dance or to cry. Not when music ran in a man's blood. And for sure that's what it did. It wasn't an ebb tide that influenced a fiddler, but the lilting tunes that some claimed had been learned in the halls of the trowie men. And who could dispute that?

'Is anything wrong?' asked Norrie.

She hadn't heard him come down or come into the room. She turned and looked at him blankly. 'Wrong?' She shook her head. 'Oh no, should there be? I was a mile away, that's all.'

'What were you thinking of?'

'Mmm.' Catherine shrugged her shoulders. 'Oh, this and that – you know how it is. I'm all right.'

'Are you sure?' said Norrie. 'Only, I've been watching you. You're not yourself. Did you have a good day or did something go wrong?'

'I think it's the weather. It's been so hot. I don't think we've had a summer like this all the time I've been here. When is it going to break? I would welcome some rain.'

'It'll break all right and when it does, it'll rain like hell.'

'Well it can't come soon enough for me.'

'You might regret saying that,' said Norrie. 'So what did you do today?

'Gerda took the children off for a picnic and, now that I can get at them again, I made a start on sorting out Kay's boxes.' And I mustn't forget to clean up the barn floor. 'Where are you going tonight?'

Norrie had taken his fiddle down. He was looking at the strings, seeing if he had any spare ones in case he needed them.

'I shall be in Tingwall. It's a party so I don't expect I shall be late. Don't wait up for me, though, because you never know.' The fiddle back in its case, Norrie put his coat on. 'Joe said he'd come and babysit if you'd like to come with me some time.'

'Me? Come with you? To a dance, you mean?'

'Yes, why not? I think he thought I was neglecting you.' He was dead right there, thought Catherine. 'It'll have to wait till next winter, though,' said Norrie. 'There won't be any more dances now.'

When the door shut behind him Catherine was alone again.

Norrie had asked her if anything was wrong and what had she replied? 'Oh no, should there be?' No, nothing was wrong, nothing happened. I danced with a lusty young man and I didn't want it to stop. I was filled with desire for him and if he'd laid me down I would not have denied him. But that's not what he had in mind today. No. He had made up his mind to make a fool of me and I fell for it like the fool I am. No, nothing happened. I didn't lose my temper. I didn't kick several of Kay's things up against the wall and break them. It should have been him I was kicking. Oh, Norrie, please rescue me before I do something really stupid.

Cutting grass with a scythe was a way of doing it that was long gone. Norrie had acquired several implements to use with the tractor and one of them was a grass cutter. Haymaking was simplified and time spent working in the field cut to a minimum. Everything depended on the weather, though, and all the labour-saving devices in the world could not compete with a rainy season. With weeks of waking to blue skies and hot windless days the dry summer continued into August. One day Norrie hitched the grass cutter to the back of his tractor and set about his task and when he'd finished the meadow was ribbed in neat swathes. 'You can start to turn it tomorrow,' he said to Catherine. 'It looks as though there's going to be no let up in the fine weather. With a bit of luck we'll have the hay in the barn by the weekend.'

'And what are you going to do?'

'I'll be away cutting for Robertson over at Broonieswick.'

There'll be no swimming tomorrow, thought Catherine. There would be nothing but a day working up and down the rows, flicking her pitch fork under the cut grass to flip it over to dry. If she started at mid-morning, when the dew was off, she could have it done by early afternoon. There would be an hour or two then to prepare something for tea before going out to start again. It was going to be another long day.

She had been working steadily along the rows for the best part of an hour when she heard Robbie's voice calling her. She stopped to look and saw him stepping over the swathes towards her.

'Why are you here?' she asked. 'You haven't lost your job, have you?'

'No, we've a couple of days off,' said Robbie. 'The boat is in for repair. I thought I'd come and give you a hand.'

In the time he'd been working on the boat Robbie had filled out and was growing into a fine young man. He had seen what she was doing and had already fetched another pitch fork and, when he'd passed the time of day with her, had helped her finish her row and start on the one beside her. He worked slightly in front of her and Catherine watched him, saw the effortless flick of his wrists, the toss that separated the grass allowing the air to get through and continue the drying process. He worked tirelessly and she had a job to keep up with him. By mid-afternoon it was done and over some refreshment she questioned him about his work. His eyes were bright and his voice keen as he told her and she knew then she had done the right thing by letting him go. He stayed another day and they worked together, turning the hay.

Joe was on holiday and while Judith spent most of her time with Inga or Jannie the two little boys tumbled out of the house and made directly for 'the chocolate man', as they called him. He was teaching them how to play baseball and even though there was a woeful lack of fielders, they had a great time.

All week, Norrie and Catherine worked from dawn till dark raking the hay into rows then into miniature ricks to leave it protected for the night in case the salty sea mist crept in to spoil it. But they were lucky and by the end of the week they were ready to store it in the barn.

'I wish you'd give up some of your contract work, Norrie,' said Catherine when he was once more preparing to go away for the day. 'You work too hard. I practically never see you and you're never here to see the children.'

'I have to earn money while it's there to earn,' he said. 'We've got to put some aside for our old age. You never know when bad times are coming.'

'But, please, Norrie. How long do you think you can keep going like this? My days are full enough. If anything happened to you, I'd never be able to manage. I'd like to spend more time with you, but when you do sit down you've either got the whisky bottle in your hand or you fall asleep.'

'You never stop going on about my drinking, do you?' snapped Norrie. 'I'm telling you, if I drank as much as some people I know you'd *really* have something to complain about. It's a bit late to tell me off about it now. You always knew I was partial to a dram. So let me be.'

How long was this going to go on, until he'd drunk himself silly or developed some awful disease? If only he would see that she needed him; if only he knew she was afraid she would not be strong enough to resist that other charmer; if only he would love her in the way he used to.

TWENTY NINE

With Norrie away for the day and the children with their favourite people, Catherine was the only one at a loose end. She could wash and clean or sit and darn, but she didn't want to. Her family had gone away and left her. Later on they would come home and expect her to be there, smiling and happy with a meal on the table and ready to hear about their day. They rarely asked about hers and it made her feel irritable and restless. Why should she be at the beck and call of all and sundry? They seemed to think that she should make life easy for them. Mam would know where it was. Mam would know what to do. And Norrie would get the whisky bottle out and after a few drams collapse in the chair by the fire and sleep till bedtime. How exciting.

Come October they would be busy with harvest, but just now it was the lull between oats and potatoes and it was up to her to take advantage of it. 'Time for yourself,' Lumsden had said. The kids had had their picnic; now it was time for hers. She would put something to eat and drink in a bag and go up on the hill where it would be cooler. She would go alone and wouldn't come home till she was ready and if their tea was late, well, that would be just too bad.

Into a paper bag she put some oatcakes and a square of cheese. She fetched a flask to fill, but put it down and went to the cupboard where the whisky bottle was kept. Standing beside it was a bottle of wine left over from Christmas. She took it out thinking she would decant some into a smaller bottle, but when she opened it, she changed her mind and, pushing the cork back in, put the bottle into a basket along with the food. She was going to have a lovely, peaceful, selfish day.

She didn't bother to see that the children were all right. She knew they would be looked after until she called to fetch them. When she saw Gerda through her open window she called out to tell her she was taking herself out and could she leave Judith with her till she got back? She knew what the answer would be before she heard it and smiled her thanks. She called on Jannie and found the old lady sitting by the fire with a pan of broth simmering on the hob. For once Jannie was not knitting. 'Mina hasn't called for the work,' she said. 'I canna think what's keeping her.' And Catherine said that if Mina didn't come she would take it for her and Jannie had smiled and said that would be kind of her. Daa was in the barn as usual, a half-finished kishie on the floor in front of him. Catherine sat down on the bench beside him and took one of his hands in hers.

'How are you doing, Daa?' she said.

He turned his head slowly to look at her then turned away. 'I dinna ken what to do with Jannie,' he said.

'There's not much you can do,' said Catherine. 'Humour her when she talks rubbish and see that she eats enough, you too. She still cooks, doesn't she? There was a pot of broth on when I was in just now.'

'Ay, she does that. It's sometimes no awful good, though.'

'We've been busy just lately, but if I can't get along I'll send Judith and you must give her a list of anything you need. Don't forget, now, it's no trouble to shop for you when I get my own things.'

'Ay. Where's du goin now?'

'Norrie's away and the kids are out so I'm going to take some time for myself. I've put a bite of food in my bag and I'm going to have a picnic all by myself up on the hill.'

'Du always did like the hill. It's no snowing today, though, so you'll be quite safe.' Daa smiled at her and she squeezed his hand and left him.

Up out of the valley Catherine stood on the road and looked up at the hill. It wasn't just one hill but one of a continuous chain that stretched from north to south of the island, an undulating chain, each hill a vertebra in Shetland's spine. She didn't want to go by the peat moor so she walked along the road a way before she left it and began to climb.

The terrain of the hill she now stood on was different; great banks of peat sheltered areas of rough grass. They were sun traps. She chose one, spread the blanket she had brought with her and sat down. Lying back she stretched out her legs and spread her arms, then she threw back her head and laughed. She was free. No kids, no grumpy Norrie, no one to bother her other than the birds. She was all by herself.

How many times had she been able to do this? Not many. She could count them on her fingers. With her hands behind her head she gazed at the blue void above her, so big, so wide and so empty. This was bliss and there was nothing to spoil it. A solitary raven drifted into view, ponderous and slow in flight. She had somehow been surprised to find them in Shetland, though she had since found that sheep country was their natural habitat. But now, as slowly as it had come into her line of vision, the big black bird glided away.

Catherine closed her eyes, lay there and drew the soft clean air into her lungs, a whiff of the sea borne on the breeze, the faint damp smell of a boggy patch somewhere near, the dry herbage of the hill and of peat. If only she could do this more often. She raised her arms, ran her fingers through her hair and yawned. God, she was tired. She yawned again, relaxed and dozed. The steady cropping of a sheep somewhere very close made her open her eyes. She sat up suddenly and the startled little hill ewe ran off. Catherine pulled up her knees, rested her elbows on them and held her chin in her hands. She looked at the distant view, at the sparkle of the sun on the sea, at the stretches of uncultivated land and the small enclosures round Broonieswick. People down there were working, busy at some job or other to earn money while she was sitting here alone. How Mina would have disapproved. 'Does du no have a piece of work to be doing?' she would say if she were here. Catherine laughed. She reached for her bag and took the bottle of wine out of it. She pulled the cork, put the bottle to her lips and drank. It was good.

She scanned the view before her. Norrie was down there somewhere. She put the bottle to her mouth and drank again. Mmm, it was nice. The sun had warmed it and brought out the fruity flavours. She could feel it running down through her chest, warm and comforting. She took another small mouthful, ran it round her mouth, tasted it and swallowed. Mmm. Why had she left it in the cupboard all this time? Why had she denied herself the pleasure of an odd glass of wine when she sat there alone in the evenings? Ah, but that would have been going down the road that Norrie was on. She held the bottle in front of her and read the label. It was made from grapes grown in Italy. She thought of hot sunny hillsides and the blue Mediterranean Sea. She laughed. What had Italy got that she hadn't? Here today were the same blue skies, the same blue sea.

On the clear air noises carried a long way. She could hear voices, but not words. She could hear the purr of a tractor, but couldn't see it. Maybe it was Norrie's. She didn't deserve the way he had snapped at her that morning. If she had neglected her tasks he would have something to be grumpy about, but she knew how hard he worked and tried to lighten his load. He wasn't playing fair. Disgruntled, unhappy with the way he was treating her, she scowled. Holding the bottle aloft she shouted, 'You've got to stop being such a grouch, Norrie, you shouldn't be like that. What's happened to you? You're not fun any more; you're a crabby old man. Oh dear. What's happening to us?' Her arm came down and brought the bottle again to her mouth. The wine was red and fruity. She savoured it and rolled it round her mouth, licked her lips, then drank again.

She loved her family, of course she did, but they tied her down. They took away her independence, stole her time with their demands and made her their servant. What twist of fate had brought her to these lonely islands? Love for a man who had concealed the face of what he was bringing her to. And why had she stayed when the opportunity to run home to her mother and a lifestyle she knew had been put before her?

Lumsden had told her to take time for herself and she knew he was right. She was doing it now. She was alone on a hillside enjoying, *'a jug of wine, a loaf of bread—and thou'*. Yes to the wine, oatcakes instead of bread, but no 'thou', definitely no 'thou'. She threw back her head and laughed. 'I am a wicked, abandoned woman,' she said, her speech slurred. She giggled. 'And I'm well on the way to being drunk and I don't care. I am *not* going to go home. They can whistle for their tea – so there.'

'Do you often drink alone?'

Catherine froze; the bottle was halfway to her mouth. She didn't turn round to look. She knew all too well who was standing behind her. 'Go away, Bjorg,' she said. 'Go away.'

'Not a good idea and solitary drinking is not to be recommended.'

'Go away.'

'I am not going to,' said Bjorg as he sat beside her. 'You are being very foolish.' He took the bottle from her and put it to his own mouth. 'Mmm,' he said as he handed it back. 'That's nice.'

'You can have the rest of it, then.' Catherine was angry because it was obvious he had watched where she was going and had followed her. 'Why did you have to come and spoil things for me? I came here because I wanted to get a bit of peace. I'm going home.' She tried to stand, but suddenly the world was spinning and she sat down again with a thump.

Bjorg held the bottle up against the light. 'This bottle is more than half empty,' he said. 'Tell me you have not drunk all that.'

'Must have,' said Catherine. 'It was full.' She closed her eyes. Oh God, what have I done? I'm drunk and I shouldn't be.

'You should eat something,' said Bjorg. He had moved closer to her. 'Did you bring any food with you?'

She nodded. He looked in her bag and took out the oatcakes and cheese. He opened the packet of oatcakes, gave one to her with a slice of cheese. 'Eat,' he said. She moved her jaw slowly, ate then asked for more wine to clear her mouth. 'A sip only,' he said. He put his arm round her to support her, held the bottle for her and when she'd drunk, took it from her and put it down.

'Did you not you know it is not wise to drink on an empty stomach?' he asked.

She looked at him and could only nod. When he smiled and came so close that she could feel his breath on her face, she closed her eyes. It was nice to have his arm around her. She could feel the warmth of him through the thin stuff of the shirt he wore, thrilled to the sensation of his flesh touching hers. The warmth of him, of the sun and of the wine in her belly stole her senses. She knew she should get up and run away, but also knew that she couldn't. And what was more, she didn't want to.

When at last his lips gently brushed against hers she slid an arm round his neck, pulled him close and thrilled to the sensation of his tongue exploring her open mouth. She didn't resist when he slipped his hand inside her blouse and his fingers teased her already erect nipple. Neither did she protest when he laid her gently back upon the blanket.

THIRTY

THE FINE SUNNY weather broke in September. Rain came soft and fine, caressing the hills, sleeking the coats of ponies and cattle. Catherine lifted her face to it and let the coolness soak into her skin. Norrie complained. 'As long as it stays like this it'll be okay,' he said, 'but if we get a downpour it'll flatten the oats and the ears will grow out.'

'Are you ever satisfied, Norrie?' said Catherine.

'It'll no hurt kale,' he said. 'But we don't want to lift potatoes out of mud.'

'It won't *be* like that. You know we usually get a couple of good weeks for the potato harvest.'

'All very well for you to say.'

'Oh, I give up.' Catherine turned on her heel to walk away. 'Are you coming to help me sort out these lambs?'

They were coming to the end of the farming year, the time of gathering in the crops; September was the month when lambs for the butchers' markets were sold; fat lambs were the crop of the sheep flock. Catherine was as good as Norrie at grading a live lamb, but strong healthy animals need strong arms to handle them and, with the number they had to work with, she needed Norrie beside her. Talk between them was reduced to a yea or nay as to whether an animal was fit for market and from time to time Norrie grumbled when Catherine didn't agree with him. But at last it was done and a batch of lambs was penned where the lorry that would come to take them to market could collect them. Catherine would go to see them sold and report back on how much they made – income from the sale of lambs was a major item in their finances.

The rain that had come with the first of the month had stopped and started and come to nothing. But as the end of the month approached, rain clouds, dark and threatening, billowed up. Big, black clouds, ominous in the way they piled one on the other, raced to cover the sky and turn day dark as night. Thunder rumbled and grumbled and lightning flashed. Catherine looked out of her window. There would probably be a sudden downpour, she thought, and prayed that it would pass them by.

The first drop hit with a splat … splat again … and again. Then raindrops pattered against the glass like so many hurrying feet. Faster and faster, noise increasing with the speed. A crowd running – racing. Big heavy drops, violent, smashing down, filling gutters and ditches, buckets and bowls left outside. Then the heavens opened and rain drummed on the roof, loud and deafening. Catherine put her hands over her ears to shut it out. She looked at the clock; the children were in school, thank God, but where was Norrie? She hoped he wasn't out in it.

John Jameson heard the rain, looked out of the barn and saw that the little burn that ran down the hill had swollen into a raging torrent. Brown, peat-stained water leapt over its rocky bed sweeping loose debris before it. Little rocky pools that were usually clear and calm had become boiling cauldrons. Rain sliced vertically into the ground, striking with the viciousness of arrows. It was a cloudburst. It would soon be over. He stood to wait till the downpour eased. When it did he would go indoors – it was time for his dinner.

Suddenly, as quickly as it had started, the hard rain stopped, softened to a drizzle. Stepping out of the barn Daa closed the door. He had only gone a yard or two when a grumbling coming from the hill made him turn to look. What he saw made him freeze. The hill was coming towards him. Great slices of dark fruit cake with a layer of icing on top were sliding down the hill. What nightmare was this? But it wasn't cake, it was slabs of peat with a thin topping of turf, tons of it cut with a giant knife into chunks three or four feet wide and deep, and they were sliding down the hillside, gathering momentum, threatening to overtake and bury him. Fear gripped him. Pain filled his chest and an iron band tightened round it. He clutched at the collar of his shirt, tried to breathe, but couldn't. 'Jannie,' he cried as he turned to run, only to stumble and pitch forward onto his face.

'Yon man is always late for his dinner, puss,' said Jannie. Her cat purred and rubbed itself round her legs as she stood there stirring a pot of broth. 'But he'll no come while it's raining so hard. Likely I'll have to go and fetch him. What was that?' She stopped stirring and, wooden spoon in hand, stood to listen.

A rumble, a roar then the thunder of something crashing into the house made it rattle, the clock on the mantelpiece chime involuntarily and the china urns either side of it tremble. And there was something else, a sound like rocks being thrown at the walls. Who could be doing that? Jannie laid down the spoon and went to the door. The rain had eased. She stepped out to go and see what was happening.

Catherine breathed a sigh of relief when the rain stopped pounding on the roof. Apart from the soft swish of running water in the down pipes and into the drain there was no sound in the house but the ticking clock. She went to the door and opened it, stood there looking at the saturated ground and little rivers of rainwater that had sprung up from nowhere. Then she heard it, the keening wail of someone in distress. It was coming from the other end of the valley. Slipping her feet into rubber boots she grabbed a coat, pulled it on and, closing the door behind her, went to see what was happening.

She walked as she wrapped her coat round her, then looked up and saw. She stopped – gasped. Clapping both hands to her face she groaned. Then she ran. 'Jannie, I'm coming,' she shouted and when she saw Gerda looking out, 'Come with me, quick.' Gerda saw the terror in Catherine's face and lost no time in running after her.

Jannie was on her knees in the mud. Daa lay face-down on the ground and Jannie was pulling at him, trying to get him up. Tears ran down her face as, her voice rising and falling, she howled. It was a cry of desperation and despair and Catherine, hearing it, relived again the time she stood on the cliff, berating the evil sea as she tore her heart out in grief for her dead husband.

'My God,' said Gerda. 'Look at that.' She was not looking at Jannie or Daa but at the wall of peat and grass and mud that was piled up against the side of Jannie's house. Then she looked at the hillside. Where once it had been green, and in August covered with heather, it was now bare rock.

On her knees beside Jannie, Catherine tried to take the woman in her arms and comfort her, but Jannie fought her off. 'He canna lie there,' screamed Jannie. 'Why doesna he git up?' Ignoring Catherine, Jannie went back to pulling at Daa's clothes.

'What can we do, Gerda?' said Catherine. 'How do we get her away from Daa? She can't squat there in the mud.'

And then Joe was there and Norrie was driving down the track.

'Ye Gods,' muttered Joe, his mouth and eyes wide open as he looked at the devastation, then at Daa. 'Someone should go for the doctor.'

'I'll do that,' said Gerda and ran to get her car.

Norrie stopped the tractor and jumped down. 'Is he dead?' he asked.

'Not much doubt about it,' said Catherine. 'What are we going to do?'

'We mustn't move him,' said Norrie. 'But we ought to get her up out of the mud, though I doubt if she'll go. You'd better get something to wrap round her till the doctor gets here.'

Jannie had lifted her hands and was now holding her head and rocking from side to side. The tears had stopped, but she had set up a continuous, high-pitched wail. Catherine fetched blankets to wrap round her. Choked with emotions she knelt beside Jannie and held the blankets to stop her throwing them off.

They were lucky; the doctor was at home and was soon there. In a short while the injection he gave Jannie to calm her had its effect and her wailing became a whimper. The men lifted her to take her inside, promising to bring Daa indoors too if she would go with them.

'She can't stay here,' said Lumsden, when he saw what had happened. 'I'll arrange for her to be taken into the hospital till I can sort out a place for her.' He looked at Catherine whose eyes were bright with tears. 'It's a terrible business. Are you all right? Is there anything I can do for you?'

'Nothing,' said Catherine who did nothing to stop the tears that began to run down her face. 'Daa and Jannie are the last ones who were here when I came first. Now … this is the end.'

'You've got your family.'

'I know, but it's … oh, don't take any notice of me.' She gave a brief smile. 'It'll all come out in the wash, as they say.'

'You are a funny girl. Now then … find some clothes for Jannie and be ready for when they come to fetch her. I'll get off and get things sorted.'

Jannie sat by the fire, her eyes blank. They had not brought Daa in, but she seemed not to have noticed. Her voice was flat and uncaring as she said, 'Who is du?' when Catherine walked in.

'I'm Catherine. Would you like me to make you a cup of tea?'

'I dinna want tea,' said Jannie. Her face was expressionless, her movements slow. 'Where's Mina? Where's Laura?'

'Mina can't come but Laura will be here soon.' Anything to satisfy her. 'I need to get you some clean clothes. Do you keep them here?' Catherine was standing beside a wooden trunk that stood at the end of the box bed.

'Ay,' murmured Jannie.

Catherine lifted the lid and took out some garments. There was not much in the box and as she lifted a skirt something else came with it. It was a piece of cloth. Putting the items of clothing down she took the cloth to refold it and put it back and as she was about to do so something in the bottom of the box caught her eye. She leaned forward the better to see. Baby clothes! Why should there be baby clothes in the bottom of Jannie's box?

'Do you need any help, Catherine?' It was Gerda.

There was no time to look now. 'Not at the moment.'

'What a terrible thing this is. I've never known anything like it.'

'It's happened before, but I never dreamed it could happen here.'

'Why do you think it did? What started it?'

Jannie had closed her eyes and was nodding. She was totally unaware of the women; obviously the sedative Neil Lumsden had given her was making her sleepy. As Catherine put items of Jannie's clothes into a bag she said, 'They call Shetland the "old rock" and that's exactly what it is. You saw where the peat slid off the hill, didn't you? And that it was solid rock underneath? Well, we had a hot summer last year and this one has been even hotter and drier. Peat shrinks when it dries and there's a lot of it here. The surface of the hill had dried and cracked and then, when the rain came, it got underneath and there you are – landslide.'

'How do you know all that?'

'I knew nothing about Shetland when I came here first, so I read everything about it I could lay my hands on. What's going on outside?'

'Norrie and Joe have covered the old man's body and they're staying out there till the undertaker comes.'

'Good, there's nowhere for him to lie here,' said Catherine. 'What a terrible day this is. Poor Daa, he was a lovely man.'

To grey skies and rain Daa was taken away. When they walked Jannie out to the car that was to take her, too, she glanced briefly at the mess of peat piled up against her house and said, 'Someone's going to have a hard job to clear that up.' She seemed to have put the whole dreadful disaster away into the dark recesses of her mind.

When Daa and Jannie were gone, along with the men and vehicles that had been sent to fetch them, Catherine and Norrie went home. Norrie took the whisky bottle from the cupboard, poured himself a dram, looked at Catherine and when she nodded, one for her as well.

'I thought you might need that,' he said.

THIRTY ONE

SEPTEMBER SEEMED DETERMINED to make every day a wet one. Norrie swore when he saw the feathered heads of his oats hanging their heads. 'We'll lose the lot if we have a gale,' he grumbled. 'The sheep'll go hungry.'

'We've got a field of neeps,' said Catherine. 'And kale.'

'Well you'd better keep the geese off them or they'll be gone too.' The migrating geese that stopped off for a rest on their way south had been known to clear a field of swedes in a very short time.

Norrie's worry over saving his crops was not helped by waking each morning to another wet day. It did not improve his temper. Neither did his continued drinking. It had become a habit and Catherine wondered if he really tasted or appreciated the liquor he was pouring down his throat. 'What else is there to do?' he grumbled when she asked him to stop. The more she frowned the more stubborn he became. There was nothing for it but to leave him to it, even though the children noticed, especially Judith.

'You ought to throw the bottle away, Mam,' she said.

'And do you think that would stop him? He'd only buy another and be cross when he knew what we'd done,' her mother replied.

Jannie had been found a place in a care home in Lerwick. Laura had gone to see her and, though it had distressed her when Jannie hadn't recognized her and told her to go away, she said that she would go again. 'I know I've got Willie now,' she said, 'but Jannie's all I have left of family.'

Though the church had been filled with mourners, Daa's funeral had been quiet for there had been no place to bring them back to and none but Catherine and Laura to see to them if there had. It was a sad end to a life. The house had been left as it was. Laura asked Catherine if she'd clear it out; there was nothing she wanted but maybe the clock, which had belonged to their mother.

Donning a coat, hat and boots Catherine went along to Jannie's house to make a start. She opened the door and went in. With no fire in the grate to keep it warm and dry the place smelt musty and damp. In the few days the house had been empty moisture had crept through the wall against which the mud and peat of the hill-side was piled, and the white-washed stones were dark and wet. She walked through to the ben end. It was just the same as the day she had first seen it; the rug was still in front of the fire, the Bible text above it and the chairs on either side of it. But who would want anything of what was there? It was the same in the little room between the but and ben. It was full of boxes and bits and pieces. Catherine closed the door on it.

In the living room she was drawn to the wooden chest. Lifting the lid she crouched beside it. When she lifted out the little woollen garments she found that they had suffered the same fate as Kay's pieces of knitting: moths had riddled them with holes. Were these Robbie's baby clothes? Laying them aside she reached in again. This time she brought out a cotton dress, another, then a bonnet and a jacket. Underneath them was a packet tied with string. Pulling at the knots and opening it she found letters, still in their envelopes, and some photographs. She took them to the table and sat down.

The photographs were of a little girl, not more than about two years old. No one had written on them to give the child a name or to indicate who she was. Catherine turned to the letters. The envelope of one was edged in black as was the piece of paper she pulled out.

My Dear Jannie, she read,
We are so sorry to hear of your loss. Poor wee Jeannie, such a short life, but you have a son now to help ease your sorrow.

So Jannie had lost a daughter and much later on, her son. It all made sense now and Catherine understood that it was no wonder Jannie had resented the wife that had come between her and her son. She had become attached to young Robbie and made him a replacement for his father. Then, when her mind began to play tricks her interest had turned to Judith, a substitute for Jeannie, her own little girl. Poor Jannie! What grief she'd had to bear.

Peeking quickly into the other envelopes Catherine found bills of sale, invoices and a few personal letters, but nothing more of interest. She left them on the table, but put the clothes back in the chest. For the next hour she turned out cupboards and drawers, stuffed old papers into the grate to burn later and threw out mouldy food for the birds. Then she went home.

There was time for a cup of tea before she began to prepare the evening meal. It would have to be fish again, fish and mashed potatoes and parsley sauce. She was sick and tired of fish. Robbie sometimes brought some home and Joe and the twins fished in the bay. Fish seemed to be all they ate nowadays. She thought about beef, a nice juicy steak with onions and mushrooms, peas and baby carrots and her mouth watered as she drooled over the thought. But fish it had to be. She made tea, poured herself a cup and sat down. Now might be a good time to write to her mother.

What am I going to tell them?

Dear Mum,

I'm having an awful time. Norrie's drinking himself to death. An acre of peat slid down the hill, killed Daa and sent Jannie insane. Jannie's in a home now. We've got fish for tea, again – I'm fed up with fish and all I can think of is beef steak. Everything's changed here and I don't like it and I'm homesick.

No, that would never do. She folded up the pad and put it and the pen back in the drawer, drank her tea and went to the kitchen to start cooking.

She took a piece of cod out of the fridge, put it on the slab then began to skin it. She turned her head away from the smell. But it was fresh – it shouldn't smell. Suddenly her mouth filled with a hot liquid and her stomach belched gas. She felt sick and knew she was going to throw up. Hand clasped to her mouth she rushed to the bathroom. On her knees beside the pan she gripped the edge of it and began to sick the contents of her stomach into the pan. Time after time she retched till it was sore but empty. When it was over she sat back on her heels and wiped the sweat from her brow. What had she eaten to make her sick? Nothing. Then why was she sick?

No, oh no! Realization made her groan with despair. She covered her face with her hands and her mind went back to that day on the hill when she hadn't eaten, but drank wine as though it was water, half a bottle of it. That day when Bjorg had followed and found her, charmed her the way he always did and made love to her. No, it hadn't been love, it had been sex, nothing but sex – wild, tempestuous, and gloriously fulfilling sex. She had been powerless to deny him, hadn't wanted to, but, oh, surely he'd taken precautions? She had been too drunk to notice or care and it was much too late to care now. But he must have known what his intentions were, which was why he'd followed her, so surely … and now she knew he hadn't and now she was pregnant. It had to be him. It couldn't have been Norrie for he was either too drunk or too tired to turn to her at night. Of all the bad things that had happened in her life, this had to be the worst.

'Ask Joe and June if they'd help pick up,' said Norrie. 'We'll start to lift the potatoes tomorrow. The forecast for the weekend is fine. Are you all right? You don't look well.'

Catherine gave a weak smile. 'You know how it is,' she said. 'Women's troubles, that's all.' If only you knew, she thought.

'Oh yes,' grunted Norrie. 'That's the answer to everything. When did women not have troubles? Get yourself a tonic or something.'

It would take more than a tonic to shift what was troubling her.

She daren't think about it, daren't even begin to wonder what she was going to do about it. What would Lumsden say? Would he help her in her time of trouble? She rehearsed in her mind what she would say to him and thought how the expression on his face would change. She hated the thought that he would lose all regard for her and knew she couldn't ask him.

Armed with bags to put rubbish in, Catherine went to finish clearing out Jannie's house. The mantelpiece clock and the china urns had gone. Catherine wanted nothing and bundled bric-a-brac and old clothes into bags ready to burn. Norrie said the furniture was only fit to put on the fire and the house was not worth saving. It would cost too much to put right.

Catherine stood in front of the stove and fed it with anything that would burn. While she waited for the fire to burn down she looked at the wooden surround. It was coming away from the wall. From a crack at the back of the shelf peeped a corner of paper. Carefully she picked at it with finger and thumb and eased it out. It was fragile and had obviously been there a long time.

She had it at last, an envelope addressed to his parents in her first husband Robbie's handwriting. Was this the letter that Jannie swore had never arrived? Catherine turned it over. It had not been opened. Why? And how was it that it had not been seen? But the delivery of mail was so casual here. No doors were locked so the postman just opened the door and walked in, left parcels and letters on the table, even on the mantelpiece at times. She had found her mail tucked behind her mantelpiece clock at home more than once. Perhaps this is what he had done here? She slid a finger under the flap and opened it. There, in Robbie's handwriting, were the words telling his mother that he would be coming home and bringing his wife with him. There were the words that had obviously never been read, the words that could have made for a more harmonious introduction to Robbie's family.

What else had slipped down behind the surround? Catherine seized hold of the wood and pulled. It gave a little but would not come right away, but there was room enough to look and there were other envelopes. She pulled them out and opened them. Some contained un-cashed cheques. Too late, too late, and bundling all together, including Robbie's letter, she pushed them into the fire and stirred it with the poker.

THIRTY TWO

BREAKFAST OVER, CATHERINE put on her boots and went to join June and Joe who were on the potato rig talking to Norrie. The day was fine, but the wind, which was not strong, tempered the October sun and did little to spread any warmth so coats were needed.

'Are we ready, then?' said Norrie as he climbed onto the tractor.

'All ready,' chorused the three who would spend the day, backs bent, picking up the potatoes that the spinner threw out.

Fighting the nausea that rose from her stomach every time she bent down, Catherine wondered how she was going to get through the day. June and Joe had embarked on a contest to see who could pick up most potatoes.

'It's not fair,' laughed June. 'Your hands are bigger than mine.'

'But you've got a bigger bucket,' said Joe.

'Then you'll have to pick faster,' said Catherine.

As soon as she could she called a break for tea and ran away indoors to make some. She came back with mugs of it for them and work stopped while they stood to drink it. Joe had gone to look at the tractor and to fire his never-ending volley of questions at Norrie. The desire to have some land and keep animals filled him with enthusiasm.

'Are you all right?' asked June when Catherine gave her a mug of tea. 'Not pregnant are you?'

'Good heavens,' gasped Catherine. 'Whatever gave you that idea?'

'Well, you haven't been looking too good and I've been watching you.'

Trust a woman to notice. Thank God men were less observant. 'No,' said Catherine. 'It's been a really upsetting time. All that kafuffle with the landslide, Jannie losing her senses and Daa's funeral. I haven't been eating properly and I've been getting indigestion … you know how it is.' She smiled at June and hoped the woman believed her. 'And everything in the valley has changed from when I came here first. I'm the only one of the original residents left. It's a sobering thought, because this place is a little world on its own.'

'Perhaps that's what it is, then,' said June. 'I see what you mean about the valley. We're cut off, aren't we? Deepdale's a secret. You have to drive down the track a way before you can see it. And you do work hard. You really ought to look after yourself.'

'I will,' said Catherine. 'Better get on. Norrie's looking daggers at us.'

The rest of the day was better. Catherine's nausea abated and she was able to work normally. Conscious that June still watched her she tried to put some distance between them. The day's work done at last, potatoes were bagged up and the women free to go while Norrie and Joe took the crop to the barn.

With the good weather holding, after inspecting his field of oats, Norrie said he would cut it. Catherine would have to gather up the sheaves and Joe said if they were cutting on Saturday, he would help – June, too.

'It's good of you to offer,' said Norrie. 'But I think Catherine and I could manage, it's not that big a field.'

'No, no,' said Joe. 'We'd like to. Catherine works hard enough as it is.'

'What are you saying?'

'I'm saying nothing,' said Joe. 'Just that we'd like to help, I want to learn and it would be a new experience for me. The more the merrier, eh?'

'Well, if you put it like that.'

While Norrie drove the binder and cut the corn, Catherine showed Joe how to pick up two sheaves, one in each hand, and stack them with their heads together. Two more were stacked next to them and then one at each end. 'It's called a stook,' she said. 'The sheaves stand like that to let the grain in the heads dry. If they were left lying on the ground they would get wet and the ears would begin to sprout and then it would be no good.'

It wasn't hard to learn how to set up stooks and June and Joe soon became proficient. When Norrie had almost finished cutting, Catherine left her neighbours to finish off. She was tired and wanted some tea and to sit down.

She heard the tractor stop and heard Norrie talking to Joe as he helped him and June finish stacking sheaves. Then she heard their voices as they came nearer and heard Norrie thanking Joe for his help. Then he was coming indoors. He was angry. She could see it in his face, in his stance.

'I can't believe you left your neighbours to do your work,' he shouted. 'What right have you got to—'

'Shut up, Norrie.'

'Shut up? What's got into you? Are you ill? You haven't been yourself lately?'

'How good of you to notice.' Catherine was sitting at the table. She had made some tea and her empty cup was on the table in front of her.

'You can cut the sarcasm,' said Norrie. 'Get up and make me some tea. I see you've got some for yourself.'

'Make your own; you know how.'

He stared at her, his mouth open. She rarely answered him back. 'Now *you* listen to me—'

Catherine thumped the table with her fist. '*No.* You listen to me for a change. I'm *fed up* with you, *fed up* with your drinking, *fed up* with always being here to keep things ticking over while you do what you want.' She thumped the table again. 'I've had enough. I'm not your slave, although you seem to think I am.' She paused for breath and he jumped in.

'Nobody's made a slave out of you but yourself. Nobody asked you to take on a flock of sheep in the first place. It was you who wanted to do what Robbie had planned.'

'But I did it, didn't I?'

'Yes, and I admired you for it.'

'Then why are you taking on more and more and expecting me to do the same? You never take me out anywhere. You sit at home and drink and get nasty when I ask you not to. You know I'm not happy about it.'

Knowing that she was speaking the truth, Norrie glared at her. 'Well, you know what you can do, then,' he said.

For a moment Catherine was silent. Then in a soft voice she said, 'Be careful what you wish for, Norrie.' She took a few deep breaths then stood up. 'All right,' and taking her empty cup to the kitchen she went up to the bedroom. Something in her voice, her quiet determination, perhaps, made Norrie follow her. Standing just inside the bedroom door he watched as she changed out of her working clothes then picked up a bag and put a nightdress and underclothes in it.

'What are you doing?' he said.

'I'm packing a bag. Move aside, please, I need to get to the bathroom.'

He followed her there and then down the stairs. Catherine put her coat on and picked up her bags. 'Goodbye, Norrie,' she said.

He jumped forward and seized her by the arms. 'What are you doing? What are you saying?'

'I'm leaving you. That's what you said, wasn't it? "You know what you can do"? Well I'm doing it.'

'You can't, no you can't. What about the kids?'

'They're your children, too. You look after them.'

'What sort of mother are you to leave your little children?'

'And what sort of man are *you* to leave a wife to do the work you should be doing and let her sit alone while you go out?'

'But I'm not going out for … for….' Norrie stuttered to a stop.

'Were you going to say pleasure? Well that's what it must be for I never see any money coming back and I'm not going to stand here and argue with you. I have to go.'

'But … where?'

'If I get a move on I should be able to get tonight's boat.'

He stared at her, unable to believe what she was saying. 'You *mean* it.'

'Yes, I do. I'll go and see if Joe can take me.'

'*Never.* You can't ask him. Don't go, please don't go.'

For a moment, but only for a moment Catherine hesitated. 'No,' she said at last. 'I'm going and if you don't want Joe to take me then you must.'

'No, Catherine, I can't. Please don't ask me to. Don't go, I need you.'

In spite of his pleading she insisted that one way or the other she was going to get on the boat, even if she had to walk all the way, so he drove her to the town. When they stood on the quay he took her hand and held it as though he would never let go. 'Is it any use asking you to change your mind?' he said.

'Not a bit,' she answered.

'Then when are you coming back?'

She pulled her hand from his and, backing away towards the gangway, said, 'I may never.' Then she turned and ran.

THIRTY THREE

NORRIE, WOODEN SPOON in hand, stood at the bottom of the stairs and shouted, 'Come on, hurry up or you're going to be late for school.' From the bedrooms came the sound of raised voices. The twins were squabbling and Judith was taking charge. 'Hurry up,' shouted Norrie and when Judith called back, 'All right, we're coming,' he went back to stand by the cooker and stir a pot of porridge. Judith, followed by Peter and Allen, ran down the stairs.

'Put out the bowls, Judith,' said Norrie. 'The porridge is ready.'

Judith put bowls and spoons on the table as the twins sat down.

'Be careful,' said Norrie as he doled out their breakfast, 'it will be hot.'

Judith sat and looked at what was in the bowl in front of her. Norrie saw that she hadn't picked up her spoon to eat. 'What's wrong with it?' he asked.

'I'm not eating that.'

'You'll eat it or go without. I haven't got time to fuss with you.'

'It's lumpy. Mam always made lovely porridge and we had cream on it.'

'Well, she's not here, is she?'

Judith scowled at her father. 'And whose fault is that?'

'I want my mammy,' cried Peter.

'Shut up,' shouted Norrie, which made the little boy cry louder. 'Shut up and eat your porridge.'

Great fat tears ran down Peter's face. Allen put his arm round his brother.

'It's no good shouting at us,' said Judith. 'And it's no good you expecting us to eat stuff like this. It's only fit for a pig.'

'There's nothing wrong with it. If you were hungry you'd eat it.'

'And I suppose you're going to tell us that the starving people in Africa would be glad of it.'

'Look I'm not your mother —'

'Don't we know it?' said Judith. 'I saw you, and you were horrible to her and not fun anymore like you used to be.'

'Mind your business,' snapped Norrie. 'It's nothing to do with you.'

'Yes it is. She's our mam. You made her cry. I *hate* you.'

Norrie roared. 'Get down and go to school. Any more of that and I'll have to punish you. I'll deal with you when you come home.'

Judith slid from her chair and the two little boys joined her.

Norrie put the porridge pot on the table, sat down and put his head in his hands. How was he ever going to sort this mess out? From upstairs he could hear Judith as she chivvied her brothers into getting ready for school. He watched as they trooped down the stairs and, not speaking, pass through the living room and away. He knew that Judith had taken charge and seen to it that the boys were washed and properly dressed before she led them away to school.

Child that she was, Judith had spoken the truth and he couldn't get away from it. Catherine was gone and it was his fault. How was he going to get her back? He should have listened to Joe, should have realized that others could see what he was doing. But Catherine didn't complain and he'd been too blind to see that, in order to help him, she had been taking on more than was good for her.

'Catherine, are you there?' June knocked on the door and pushed it open. She looked surprised to see Norrie. Her glance took in the porridge pot and the still-full porridge plates. 'Is something wrong, is Catherine ill?'

'No, she's not ill,' said Norrie. 'You might as well know. She's left me.'

'Left you? What about the children?'

Norrie gave a mocking laugh. 'I tried that, but she said they were my children as well as hers so I could look after them and she's left them too.'

'But … how are you going to manage?'

Norrie shook his head. 'If this morning's effort is anything to go by,' he indicated the uneaten porridge, 'not very well.'

'I can't believe it,' said June. She looked round the room and saw that the fire was out. A quick glance into the kitchen showed her a pile of dirty dishes on the draining board. 'You're going to need some help, and it's no use saying you don't, because it's all too plain that you do. I came to pay the rent, so here it is.' She handed him an envelope. 'You'd better get to work. I'll get things organized here. Don't thank me. You and Catherine were kind to us when others looked down their noses at Joe.'

'I wouldn't want to put you to any trouble.'

'Don't say a word; it's no trouble at all.'

Catherine sat in a corner seat on the train. Her eyes ached. Her head ached and there was a pain in her belly. She folded her arms across it and hugged herself. She closed her eyes and leaned her forehead against the cold glass of the window. She wished she could sleep. She thought of her children, imagined their distress when they knew what she'd done. But there was no going back. She could have stayed and let the world think that the baby she was carrying was Norrie's. But he would know it wasn't and what would that have done to him?

Though her body ached with fatigue she was constantly aware of the noise made by the train as it raced south. It rattled and shook and swayed, its wheels clacking over the points. It whooshed through tunnels, snarled at passing trains, hooted and screamed through empty stations. The boat last night had been noisy, too. The sea was rough and the vessel had pitched and tossed and rolled. With no bunks available she had been forced to spend the night on a hard chair, her head on folded arms on a table. She had been cold. She had been afraid. People round her were being sick and she was afraid she would be too. And then the boat had pitched suddenly, had thrown her off balance and against the hard edge of the table, grazing her ribs and pressing hard into her stomach. Then it rolled, the chair slid from under her and she was flung to the floor. Her stomach still hurt and was tender to the touch.

Sleep eventually would not be denied, but it was restless and fraught with dreams: Jannie swimming in to tell her how wicked she was; Bjorg laughing at her and Norrie in tears begging her to come home. She woke with a fright when a soft hand took hers. She opened her eyes and a woman's face swam into view.

'We're running into King's Cross now, my dear.'

'Thank you,' said Catherine. Her head was woozy, she closed her eyes and wanted to go back to sleep.

'Are you all right?'

The hand was on her shoulder now. Catherine opened her eyes again and raised a smile. 'I didn't sleep well last night. I'm tired, but I'm all right.'

'Do you have far to go?'

'I'm going to my parents in Southampton,' said Catherine. 'But I'll be on the train all the way.'

'You take care now,' said the woman. 'Safe onward journey.'

Waiting till the slow shuffle of people carrying bags and suitcases had made their way to the exit and the carriage had emptied, Catherine picked up her bag from where she'd tucked it between her feet and stood up. Suddenly she was sitting down again. Everything was swimming round her. She sat for a moment then slowly pulled herself to her feet. It was better this time, but as she made her way out on to the platform she found handholds to steady herself. On the platform she began to walk. Round her people were moving fast, half walking half running. Why were they all in such a hurry? They milled around her, weaving in and out, sometimes bumping into her, jostling an elbow, nodding a head in apology, but hurrying on all the same.

They were going too fast and were making her giddy. Why did her feet and legs feel as though they didn't belong to her? Why couldn't she control them? Please someone, hold me up? She reached out a hand hoping someone would save her. But they all rushed on while she was falling … and then she was on the ground … lying down. Peace at last. Now she could sleep. She sighed, closed her eyes and gave herself up to the darkness that surrounded her.

Consciousness came slowly. She was lying on her back, arms down by her sides and something was pinning her down. She stretched her fingers, paused then moved them around. It wasn't the hard station platform under her fingertips; it was a soft cotton sheet. And there were voices, muted conversation. She kept her eyes closed and tried to listen to what they were saying. She flared her nostrils and sniffed the air, smelt disinfectants, antiseptics and cleanliness, the smell of a sick room and not dirt and smoke and trains. Cautiously she opened her eyes. A movement beside her made her turn her head. The fresh face of a nurse in a blue dress and snowy white apron and cap smiled down at her. She was in hospital.

'Ah, you're back with us.'

'I can't stay.' Catherine pulled at the sheets and made to throw them off. The nurse stopped her. 'Do you remember being brought here?

'No.'

'What do you remember?'

Catherine closed her eyes. The boat, the train, the hurrying people, falling and the blessed blackness. 'Too much,' she said.

'All right, don't worry about it. But we can't let you go till the doctor's seen you. I'll get you a cup of tea while you wait. Would you like to sit up?'

Propped against some pillows Catherine looked around at the other beds in the ward. As soon as she could she was going to get out. What was Norrie doing? Had he fed the children and if so, what had he given them? And what would Gerda or June think about what she'd done?

The nurse was back again with tea and toast. 'The doctor will be here soon,' she said. The tea was refreshing, the toast more than welcome and Catherine realized that it was more than twenty-four hours since she had last eaten. She put cup and plate back on the bedside locker and snuggled down. Sleep threatened to claim her again so she closed her eyes and gave herself up to it.

The sound of footsteps, squishing softly on the polished floor, roused her. She expected to see the nurse, but a man in a white coat stood and looked at her.

'Good afternoon, Mrs Williams,' he said. 'I'm Dr Mitchell. How are you feeling now?'

'I'm fine and I want to leave,' said Catherine.

'We'd rather you stayed.'

'Why?'

'You're exhausted and there are bruises on your abdomen. What have you been doing?'

As if I'm going to tell you, thought Catherine. 'The usual things,' she said.

'But how did you get the bruises?'

'I don't know, unless it was on the boat. The sea was quite rough.'

'We know that your home is in Shetland. I'm afraid we had to look in your bag to find out who you were. But you were only carrying a small bag, not really the sort of thing to be going on holiday with. Are you in any sort of trouble?'

'I think that would be my business and not yours,' said Catherine.

Dr Mitchell crossed his arms then raised one hand and stroked his chin. 'But if you were, perhaps we could help.'

'I don't need any help.'

'All right, if you insist. But I have some bad news for you. I'm afraid you've lost your baby.'

She stared at him. 'Lost ... my ... baby?' For a moment time stood still, then she was crying, doubled over, head in hands, tears running free. They were not tears of grief, but of relief to have been spared the trauma of an unwanted child that, whichever way she looked at it, would have ruined her life. The nurse put an arm round her to comfort her. 'There there,' she said. 'Don't upset yourself.' Gradually the tears subsided and Catherine wiped her eyes.

'You're still young enough to try again,' said the doctor. 'But your husband will need to be told. Would you like us to get in touch with him?'

'No, oh no,' said Catherine. 'I hadn't told him, he didn't know. I was on my way to visit my parents in Southampton.'

'I see. Well, you will have to stay here till someone can fetch you. We can't let you travel alone, so can you give us a name and number?'

Catherine wrote her father's name, address and phone number on a piece of paper and gave it to him. When he and the nurse had gone she slid back down in the bed, revelled in its comfort and the peace of mind that her miscarriage had given her. Thank you, God, for my deliverance, she prayed, I don't know what I've done to deserve it, but thank you from the bottom of my heart.

THIRTY FOUR

NORRIE HAD COME to the conclusion that there was a lot of work involved in getting a meal. When he'd lived on his own it had surely not been as hard. But then he hadn't had to consider anyone else and a few potatoes and a piece of smoked haddock had been good enough for him. There hadn't been anyone like Judith to criticize and compare his efforts to her mother's.

He was peeling potatoes, but the knife he was using was quite blunt and he thought that the thickness of what he was peeling off put as much potato in the bucket as remained in his hand. He sent up yet another silent prayer for Catherine to return. Every passing day told him he was nothing without her. He stopped to listen to the sound of a motorbike stopping outside. With potato in one hand and knife in the other he walked through the living room to see who it could be.

'Hi Norrie,' said Robbie. He laughed when he saw what Norrie held. 'Ha ha, since when have you been a cook?' But then his expression changed rapidly as he asked, 'Is Mam ill?'

'No, she's not. Come in, boy, and sit yourself down.'

Robbie took off his gloves and scarf, put them down on the bike and followed Norrie indoors. 'So what's going on, then?' he asked.

'You can hate me if you like,' said Norrie, 'because I have to tell you that your mother left me.'

'Left you? Whatever for?'

'We had a row. It was my fault.'

'Where's she gone? Is she coming back?'

'I don't know.'

'What are you going to do about it?'

'I'm looking after the little ones and living in hope. Are you going to stay for tea? Gerda's made us a meat pie and I'm doing the potatoes. The boys will be pleased to see you.'

Robbie did stay and when his young brothers came home from school he sat them on his motorcycle and told them that when they grew up and earned their own money, they would be able to have a motorbike too. Judith declined to sit on it. 'Nasty smelly things,' she said.

'And what makes you so picky?' said Robbie.

'When I grow up I'm going to earn a lot of money and I will have a car, a lovely shiny one with leather seats.'

'Ho, ho,' mocked Robbie. 'You won't be able to do that here.'

'Then I'll go away,' said Judith and added, with a sigh, 'like Mam.'

'Yes. What do you know about that?' said Robbie.

'It's Da's fault,' said Judith. 'He's been drinking a lot and he made Mam cry. And he shouts at us. I don't blame her for going, but I wish she was here.'

'I expect she'll come back,' said Robbie. 'Don't upset yourself, Ju. She loves Da really.'

'I know.' An unexpected smile crept across Judith's face. 'She'd better come back. If it wasn't for Gerda we'd all starve because Da can't cook.'

It was at that moment Norrie called out, 'Tea's ready, come on you lot.' They sat at the table together, Norrie dishing out their food. They were all there – all except Catherine. It was not the same and they ate in silence. When the meal was done Robbie made his excuse to leave. They trooped outside to watch him go. When he got to the top of the track and waved goodbye the twins went back inside while Norrie and Judith stood on the flags outside the door.

It had been a good day and the October sun was setting the western sky aflame. They watched as it sank slowly out of sight, stealing as it did the intensity of colour until all but a golden glow was left.

'Listen, Dada,' said Judith. 'It's the geese.' Above them flew a gaggle of wild geese. They were not high up and their honking and the strong swish of their wing beats were plain to hear. 'Where are they going?'

'Where the weather is kinder and there's more food. They'll come back in spring and go on to Iceland, or wherever they've come from, to breed and rear their young. They always do.'

'Mam's gone south. She's going to come back, isn't she?'

'I sincerely hope so.' You just don't know how much, thought Norrie.

'I hope she doesn't stay away till spring. What are we going to do at Christmas if she does? Who's going to fill the boys' stockings?'

'I don't have to tell you, do I? Father Christmas does that.'

Judith looked up at her father, put up her hand and tugged at his sleeve. 'You don't still believe that, do you?' she said. 'That's for babies.'

Norrie looked down at her. 'And you're not, I suppose.'

'You suppose right,' said Judith at which Norrie turned his head away to hide a smile. 'I shall fly away with the geese one day,' Judith went on.

'And will you stay away or will you come back in spring?'

'I don't know. It depends on what I find. But when I do come back it will be because I'm famous.' Judith was silent for a moment but then, in a pleading tone of voice, said, '*You* want Mam to come back, *don't* you, Da?'

'There's nothing I want more. But I don't think she'll listen to me. Why don't you and the boys write her a letter and tell her how much you miss her?' Norrie suddenly realized he was speaking to his child as though she were an adult. His face creased into a smile at the thought. Why shouldn't he? Judith was an old soul, wise beyond her years.

'Where will we send it?' she said.

'If you send it to your grandmother in Southampton it will find her.'

'All right, let's do it now.'

*

'Catherine, if you move out of that chair,' said Doris Marshall, 'I shall get in touch with Norrie and get him to come and take you home.'

'Oh, don't do that.'

'Well do as you're told then.' Doris put a tray with cups of tea and biscuits down on a side table. 'Here you are,' she said as she handed a cup to Catherine. 'Now, I want to hear the whole story. What made you set out to come here without telling us? And how on earth did you manage to land in hospital?'

'It's a long story.'

'Well, I've got plenty of time and you're not going anywhere, so fire away.'

Catherine told her mother of Norrie's increasing dependence on drink, how it made him bad tempered and irritable and how he'd lost his sense of fun. 'He never stops working,' she said. 'He's taken on contract work and is away most days. He broke his arm in the spring and Robbie had to stay home and plough the rigs.'

'And you were left with everything else to do,' said Doris.

'Yes. It was hard, but I know what to do and Robbie was a great help. The summer was beautiful, but with no rain everything dried up. And then in September there was a cloud burst; rain was torrential and there was a landslide that wiped out Jannie's house. Daa died of a heart attack and Jannie finally lost it. She's in a care home in Lerwick now.'

'You poor dear. Why did you never see fit to tell me any of this?'

'There was nothing you could do.'

'I could have helped.'

'No, Mum, you couldn't.' Catherine turned away to look out of the window. 'And then I got pregnant,' she said. 'And Norrie and I had a mighty row because he said I was shirking my work. I'd had enough by then and I left.' Her eyes were swimming with tears. 'I made him take me to Lerwick and I got on the boat.' Doris said nothing, but pulled her chair round to sit beside Catherine and put her arms round her daughter. 'I collapsed at King's Cross station,' went on Catherine, 'and woke up in hospital. I'd had a miscarriage.'

Uttering soft comforting noises, Doris held Catherine to her as the tears fell. 'Poor darling,' she said when the flood subsided. 'Have you let Norrie know?'

'No,' said Catherine as she dried her eyes. 'He didn't know I was pregnant and there's no need for him to, so I don't want you to tell him.'

'But surely? '

'No, Mum. You are not to tell him. There's nothing to be done so it's just as well he doesn't know.'

'And don't you want him to know you're here?'

'He'll surely know that already. Where else would I go?'

'You'll stay and be pampered then?'

I've no other option, thought Catherine. She had taken enough money to pay for her journey to Southampton, but that was all.

Pampered was the right word when it came to Doris Marshall's care of her daughter. She fended off would-be visitors, sent her to bed early with a beaker of hot milk and woke her in the morning with tea and toast. She sat on the bed and said that as soon as Catherine was fit enough they were going shopping for new clothes. Pretty clothes, something to make Norrie sit up and take notice. 'You do too much for him,' said Doris. 'It's time to be a bit selfish.'

They shopped, they had lunch in a restaurant, they went to the cinema and Catherine's father took them jaunting in the New Forest. And then the letter came, a grubby envelope addressed in childish writing. Catherine took it to her bedroom. There was nothing from Norrie, just a page that had clearly been written by Judith telling her how much they missed her and that please wouldn't she come home,

Daddy can't make porridge – it's all lumpy.

There was a drawing of a sheep, from Peter, of course, a scribbled line from Allen and to finish, half a page of kisses. Swallowing the lump that had risen in her throat she folded the sheet of paper and put it back in the envelope. Then she went downstairs.

'I've got to go home,' she said, 'for the kids and Norrie, but not only for them.'

'What other reason could there be?'

'I can't hear the skylarks.'

'Good heavens! What sort of reason is that?'

'No skylarks sing in the city, Mum. I don't belong here. Shetland's my home; that's why I've got to go.'

Shetland greeted Catherine with dark November skies and rain. She hoped the gloomy greeting wasn't a foretaste of what she would get from Norrie. Would he welcome her? Would he fold her in his arms and forgive her? Disembarking from the boat she took the suitcase her mother had given her to the bus station and left it there till she could board the next bus home. It was too heavy to carry around. She walked into the town; there was time to shop. She didn't suppose that Norrie had done much in the way of cooking so she would buy biscuits and sweeties for Judith and the boys. As she walked along she thought about the wide, glass-fronted stores that lined the busy streets of Southampton. Mentally she compared them with the little shop fronts in Commercial Street that belied the Aladdin's cave that lay behind. Compared, too, the impersonal assistants back in the city, who called her 'madam', with the fresh-faced girls here who knew her and greeted her with, 'Noo den, what can I get dee?' She smiled as she heard the soft Shetland accent and the dialect, much of which she now understood.

'Been away, have you?' said the bus driver as he helped her with her bags. 'Not a good time of year to be on the boat.'

'I'd agree with you there,' said Catherine as she settled into her seat.

The rain had cleared away by the time she stepped down at the top of the valley. She walked a little way until she could see it all, set down the suitcase and looked. Her heart turned over to see the ruin of Jannie's house. The first time she had seen it she had been mortified to find it was not the smart bungalow she had been expecting. There had been many times after that when she had looked at it and hated it for all the bad memories it gave her. But her life had moved on and as she turned the pages of the book its journey was written in, the plot was slowly being revealed to her. There were more chapters to come, though, and she had to live them to know them.

The valley was quiet; nothing moved but a few straggly wet hens and the rams that were spending their bachelor days in a small park. There was no car outside June and Joe's house so presumably they were at work. There was little doubt that Lars would be and Norrie, too. Maybe Gerda was at home and maybe she wasn't. Catherine picked up her case and walked on.

The door to her house was not locked; she opened it, went in, put down the suitcase and her bags of shopping and looked around. The fire was lit and banked down. The place was tidy. There were no books lying around, no toys lurking under the table. She walked into the kitchen, but where she expected to see a pile of dirty dishes, there were none. A couple of saucepans stood on the cooker. She lifted the lid of one and saw carrots, scraped and clean and ready to cook. The second was full of potatoes, peeled and round and white.

She carried her bags up to her bedroom and put them down just inside the door. Again all was clean and tidy. The bed was made and only a pair of Norrie's pyjamas tucked beneath the pillow indicated that anyone slept there. She went into the children's bedrooms and found that their beds were made, too. It was all too clean and tidy. It surely wasn't Norrie who was doing this. Who had he got in her place? Her heart beat a little faster and she was filled with unease. If he'd found someone else what was going to happen to her? She stood and looked at her bags. She should open them and hang up her clothes, but then again she might have to repack them so she left them where they were.

It would be several hours before the children came home, and more before Norrie was there. She couldn't just sit and twiddle her thumbs; she had to do something. She had expected to find an untidy house, a pile of clothes to wash, a store cupboard that needed replenishing and cake and biscuit tins to refill. But it had all been done. Even the fire was alight, dampers closed to keep it in. She was redundant.

But she would make a cup of tea, the cure-all, and plan her next move while she drank it. She could leave; go away as quietly as she had come. But that would solve nothing, would answer no questions. The kettle boiled and she poured boiling water on the tealeaves in a little pot, picked up a spoon and stirred. While she waited for the tea to brew she stood and looked out of the window. It was early afternoon and grey November skies did little to cheer the scene. On the back green a paper bag danced and flirted with the wind. She didn't want to go away; she wanted to see her children, so she had to face whatever Norrie threw at her. She poured tea into a china cup and took it through to the living room.

The mantelpiece clock ticked loud and slow, noisy in an empty room. Catherine looked at it and sighed. Was that all the time was? She drank her tea, took her time savouring it. Her eyes strayed time and again to the clock. How slow the hours were going. She put her elbows on the table and pressed the heels of her hands to her eyes. How could she have been so stupid as to let some man seduce her? Where was her loyalty? Have I already paid the price, she thought, or is there more to pay? She took her cup to the kitchen, washed it and put it away and was hanging up the tea towel when she heard the door open and close.

THIRTY FIVE

SHE STOOD IN the kitchen doorway and saw him. She had been sitting in the gloom of a winter day, hadn't wanted to put on the light and see how someone else had taken her place and had been working in her house. Norrie didn't see her straight away, but when he looked up and at her, his face registered shock. For what seemed an interminable age he said nothing, just stared at her. 'Catherine,' he said at last. 'Is it really you?' He made no move towards her and she was afraid.

'Yes, it's me,' she said.

Still he didn't move, just stood there looking her up and down. She clasped her hands together and sent up a silent prayer. Pray God he's not angry with me for coming home. Dear Lord, does he know what I did?

She was wearing a smart woollen suit and blouse, shoes and stockings, and her hair had been cut and styled, all at her mother's insistence. He had never seen her dressed like this. His first sight of her had been lying on a peat bank, sleeping. And since then it had been working clothes, the trousers and shirts that Jannie had frowned on. Now and then she had worn a cotton dress, but that had not been often.

Say something, Norrie, her mind pleaded. When he didn't she thought he was going to throw her out. He doesn't want me here. He's found someone else who can look after him and the children. Will they want to throw me out, too, for rejecting them? For wasn't that was what she had done? Oh God. What am I going to do? Something was choking her. It was hard to breathe. Say something,

Norrie, for God's sake say something and put me out of my misery.

'Oh … Catherine.' Norrie, arms open wide rushed towards her and crushed her to him. 'Catherine, my peerie yarta, du's home,' he cried as he smothered her face with kisses. 'I've been so afraid you wouldn't come back. What did I do to you? Will you ever forgive me?' The words came tumbling out of his mouth.

'Norrie, oh, Norrie,' said Catherine. 'Please don't break my ribs.'

He held her off a little way. 'Let me look at you,' he said.

'And I wish you wouldn't use words I don't understand.'

'Why, what did I say?' Then he laughed. 'Oh – my peerie yarta – it means my little darling. You are and always will be.' Again he clutched her to him and Catherine, her face buried in his chest felt her emotions and the nerves that had been stretched to breaking point, give way and the tears of relief that she had been welcomed back, flowed free.

'Du doesna have to cry,' said Norrie as he put a finger under her chin and lifted her face to his. 'Du's home.' But there was an unnatural brightness in his own eyes as he looked at her.

'Will you ever forgive me?' said Catherine.

'You don't need to be forgiven,' said Norrie. 'It was my fault. I was too blind to see what I was doing. Come.' He took her hand and led her to the cupboard in which he kept the whisky. 'Look inside.' He opened both doors. 'You won't find any whisky there or anywhere else in the house.' He laughed. 'Judith is your champion. She said it was because I drank too much and I'd forgotten how to laugh that made you leave. It wasn't only that, though, was it? I was too hard on you. Please forgive me. I gave up the drink and now you're home I'll be able to laugh again.'

Catherine slid her arms round his waist and laid her head on his chest. 'Of course I forgive you. But the house is awful clean and nice. I was afraid you'd found someone to take my place and that I wasn't wanted any more.'

'I could never replace you,' said Norrie. 'June came and cleaned and Gerda cooked for us. They were concerned for you. They'll be glad to see you again, but not half as glad as I.'

'But why are you home in the middle of the day?' asked Catherine.

'There's enough to do here. I never realized how much you did. I do now and things have got to change.'

'It was very kind of you to help Norrie look after the children, June.'

'That's what neighbours are for, aren't they?'

'When I walked in I couldn't believe how neat and clean the house was,' said Catherine. 'I was afraid Norrie had found himself another woman. '

'You must be joking,' said June. 'He worships the ground you walk on.'

'Hi, Catherine,' said Gerda. 'I saw June come here so I thought I'd come along and say hello as well. How are you?'

'I'm fine, and very pleased to be home.'

'That's because us Deepdale folk are just one big family,' said June. 'Don't you agree?'

'It wasn't always like that,' said Catherine. 'When I came here I was met with opposition. If it hadn't been for Norrie's auntie, I don't think I would have stayed. The dragons are all gone, but even Jannie didn't deserve to have her house destroyed like that.'

'But that's life,' said June.

'And Daa,' said Catherine. 'Daa was a lovely man.' She gave a little smile. 'He said I was stubborn.' She remembered the way he said it. 'You're right, of course,' she said as she wiped a tear from her face. 'Nothing stays the same.'

Gerda was in the kitchen. 'I'm making a pot of tea,' she said. 'Have you made any bannocks, Catherine?'

Talk turned, then, to Christmas and who would be home and who away. June said that at last, at long last, her family had accepted Joe and that they had been invited to join them on Christmas Day. Lars had time off over the holiday and he, Gerda, and Inga were going home to Norway.

'So that leaves us on our own,' said Catherine. 'It'll be funny to know we're *really* on our own – no one else in the valley at all. That'll be a first.'

A piercing scream rent the air and a cry of, 'Mam.' The twins were in their bedroom. Catherine leapt up. 'Oh, God, what's happened? I'll have to go.' As she ran from the room and up the stairs June called after her, 'We'll wait for you.'

'It was nothing,' said Catherine when she rejoined her friends, 'just a squabble, not the end of the world. Did you find the bannocks?' Gerda had, and the butter too. 'You'll spoil your tea if you eat too many,' said Catherine.

But June said she didn't care and Gerda swore it didn't matter what, or how much she ate, she never put on any weight. So the three of them enjoyed buttered bannocks and each other's company and Catherine thought how lucky she was to have such good friends. Would they like her as much if they really knew why she had run away?

Despite Norrie's obvious delight in having her home again, Catherine's guilt at what she'd done made her tread warily. She was afraid to believe that he had really changed from the drunken man she had left and again become the loving and thoughtful husband he had been. But, no whisky bottle appeared and, though he had been asked, Norrie rarely left the house at night to play at a dance. Instead, he took a lantern, went out to the barn and started making kishies and straw baskets. 'I can sell them on show days,' he said. 'People from town use them for all sorts of things. They won't earn much but every little helps.' So the days went by and turned into weeks, Catherine relaxed and the air of tension between them eased.

November being the time the rams were put with the ewes, Catherine and Norrie were working together to sort young ewes from old and put them in different parks. Towards the end of the month the Cheviot rams were put with the in-by sheep so that their lambs would be born in April and May. The Shetland rams would have to wait till December before they could go to the hill. Though the little native sheep were hardy, the chance of better weather in May meant a better survival rate for lambs born into a hostile environment.

'What do you want for Christmas, Catherine?' asked Norrie when they were on their way home.

'I don't know,' she said. 'Something for the house, perhaps.'

'But that's not for you. How about a new radio? That one your mother gave us is getting a bit ropy.'

'That would be nice. I like the radio.'

'Might even get a television set one day.'

Catherine laughed. 'That'll be the day.'

'Well, stranger things have happened. You know there's talk of drilling for oil in the sea here, don't you?'

'They'll never do that.' They were home. Catherine opened the door and, stepping in, took off her boots. 'I mean, all that depth of water, I can't see it.'

'The sea isn't bottomless, Catherine. In fact in some places it's quite shallow. If they say they're going to do it you can bet they will.'

'I'll believe it when it happens.' Coat off and apron on Catherine was in the kitchen filling the kettle for tea. 'Before you sit down, Norrie, could you get me some potatoes?'

Accompanied by the twins Norrie came back from the barn with a bucket of potatoes. 'You realize,' he said, as he set the bucket on the kitchen floor, 'that next year we are going to have to equip these children with overalls and boots.'

'Why?'

'Because we give them a home to live in, a bed to sleep in, carrots and neeps and tatties to eat and they do nothing to earn them. We're going to have to make them work for their keep.'

'Oh, Dad,' cried Judith. 'You don't mean it.'

'Yes, I do.'

Peter was smiling. 'I want some red overalls.'

'How much are you going to pay us?' asked Allen.

'Now let me see,' said Norrie, as he ran his fingers through his beard. 'I think perhaps….'

'Stop teasing them,' said Catherine.

'Teasing?' laughed Norrie. 'Well, perhaps I am, but I'm afraid, little children, you are going to have to help. Mam and I can't do it all.'

'I'll help,' said Peter.

'I know you will, son. Now, all three of you, I'm going to write a letter to Santa so I'd like you to tell me what you would like for Christmas.'

'Oh, Dad,' said Judith as she threw herself at him and wound her arms round his neck. 'Can I have a piano?'

'A piano! Where do you think we are going to put a piano? There's barely enough room in the house for us. Do you know how big a piano is?'

'Of course I do,' cried Judith. 'Joe's got one, hasn't he? Oh, pleeze.' She had climbed onto his lap and pushed her face so close to his he had to pull back to stop his eyes crossing. 'Pleeeze,' she said. 'Joe says I'm getting really good.' Her fingers were twirling her father's hair then moving down to stroke his beard. 'Pleeeze, Dad,' she wheedled.

'We'll see,' said Norrie. 'Go and help your mother.' He pushed Judith gently to the floor.

'I want a bike,' said Peter.

'So do I,' echoed Allen.

'Two out of three are easy, but … oof … I don't know about the piano. It would never go down the chimney.'

'And neither would a bike,' said Allen.

'Well,' said Norrie. 'We'll have to find another way. Now, boys, you can lay the table.'

THIRTY SIX

ROBBIE CAME HOME for the holiday a couple of days before Christmas. Catherine threw her arms round him and hugged him. Judith looked him up and down before she smiled and said it was nice to see him again. Allen and Peter mobbed him, rained questions on him about what it was like to go to sea. Did he get sick? they asked and did they have fish for dinner every day? They trooped out to admire Robbie's motorbike, wanted to know what was in the parcels he had brought. When he wouldn't tell them, they persuaded him to sit at the living room table and play a game of Snakes and Ladders with them.

Catherine had been drying dishes in the kitchen, and now, tea towel in hand, she stood and looked through to the other room. Her attention was on Robbie. He had grown and was now head and shoulders above her. He was not broad and muscular like Norrie, but lean like his father. No longer could he be called a boy for he was well on the way to manhood. So absorbed was she in drinking him in that when Norrie put his arm round her shoulders, she barely acknowledged him. He smiled and put his mouth close to her ear. 'You'll not forget your Robbie while this one's here, will you?'

'Never,' she said.

'There's no doubt about whose son he is. It's almost as though he were here. Does it upset you?'

'No.' Not like the other one who reminded me, thought Catherine. 'This is little Robbie,' she said. 'He may be like his father in looks, but he's a person in his own right.'

'He's a good lad. You should be proud of him.'

Catherine sighed. 'I am.' She turned her head to look up at Norrie. 'I love him, but I love our children just as much.'

'I know you do.'

'But I still wish Robbie had not gone to sea. I know he loves it, but I'm afraid for him and whenever the weather's rough I worry.'

'There's danger in everything, darlin', and no skipper is going to risk his boat and the lives of his men if the forecast is bad, now is he?'

'No, I guess not.'

'So stop worrying. Fretting won't change anything and you'll just make yourself miserable. Have you got the kettle on? I could do with a drink.'

Catherine's children no longer tolerated the idea of stockings on the bottom of the bed. 'That's for babies,' said Judith, and they no longer came to their mother's bed with their presents. Once Catherine would have had to light candles and share their excitement, now darkness could be banished with the click of a switch. But, stockings or not, she still left little parcels on the bottoms of their beds. 'Would you rather I didn't?' asked Catherine when Judith shook her head and said, 'Oh, Mam.' 'Because I will, if you don't want them,' said Catherine, and Judith had hugged her and said, no she shouldn't stop because she loved finding them.

Christmas Day began with the sound of excited voices and running feet. Catherine smiled. Though there were presents under the tree to be opened later, other things had been left in the living room for them to find and it was there the children were headed now.

How quickly they had grown. She thought that Judith was destined to go a long way. The child was a strong character, one that would fasten on what she wanted to do in life and brush aside anything or anyone that threatened to get in her way. The twins, she was sure, would be the farmers she had wanted Robbie to be; their characters were different but complementary. Peter had a natural ability to work with animals while Allen had the business head. She had tried so hard to stop Robbie from going to sea, but he had set his heart on it and she had had to give in. It was no use trying to plan their lives; they had to find their own way and she hoped she would be able to encourage them in whatever career they decided to take up.

Norrie was stirring beside her. He grunted. 'Are you awake?' he said.

'Yes. Did the stampede wake you, too?'

'Was that what it was?' He put an arm round Catherine and pulled her close. 'We don't have to get up yet, do we?'

'Not if you don't want to.'

'I don't think I could face all that excitement.'

Lying beside him Catherine could feel his warmth. How lucky she was to be loved by this man. How could she have been so foolish to have…. No, she wouldn't think about it. Bjorg and that summer madness were in the past. It was gone, never to be forgotten, but never to be repeated. It was Christmas Day; a day to rejoice that she was here in the bosom of her family. She raised herself and resting on one elbow, bent her head and kissed her husband.

'I love you, Norrie Williams. Happy Christmas.'

Christmas Day dawned with bright clear skies despite the fact that the sun did not climb over the horizon till late. Allen and Peter were out on their bikes as soon as breakfast was over and it was light enough to see. Judith had her wish for a piano partly granted. It was not a full-size instrument that her parents had tried to disguise with wrapping paper, but an electronic keyboard. Her excitement knew no bounds and no amount of persuasion by her mother would make her sit down and eat breakfast. Torn between playing and wanting to go and fetch Joe to hear her, she experimented with the different inbuilt voices of the instrument.

'You have to put that thing up in her bedroom, Norrie,' said Catherine, raising her voice above the noise. 'I shall go mad, otherwise.'

When the keyboard had been set up in Judith's room, nothing more was seen of her that day other than an enforced presence at the table for meals. Robbie had been given leathers to wear when he rode his motorcycle. 'If you ever have a tumble,' Norrie told him, 'I believe they're the best protection to be had.'

The rest of the day passed quietly. After Christmas dinner had been eaten and dishes cleared away, Catherine and Norrie went out to walk round the sheep, as much to take advantage of a fine, crisp day as to check that all was well. When they were on their way home, Norrie tucked Catherine's arm under his. 'We do nothing but work,' he said. 'You never complain and you've never asked for a holiday. You've only gone home a couple of times since you came here. How long ago was that? Twenty years? It's time we did something about it. We could go on holiday together. You could take me south with you, show me how things have changed, because they must have.'

'And what would happen to the sheep?' said Catherine. 'Who'd look after them? You know what they're like for getting into trouble.'

'I've thought about that. Joe's been spending a lot of his spare time with me. He'd do it, and I could tell him who to go to if he needed any help.'

Norrie was offering to take her away, to give her time to be with him. It would be like a honeymoon, a very belated one, but one she'd never had.

'Time goes so quickly,' said Norrie. 'I was thinking that earlier when I was looking at the bairns. It seems no time at all since they were crawling about the floor.' He seemed to be speaking his thoughts aloud. 'Before we know it,' he went on, 'they'll be leaving home.' He stopped and turned to Catherine. 'What are we going to do when we're left on our own? It's no good waiting to do all the things we haven't had time for. We've got to do them now.'

'I'd love to go on holiday with you. How about next year after the harvest, eh? I shall look forward to that,' said Catherine.

*

They stayed up to see the New Year in and as the clock struck midnight Catherine went to the door and opened it. There was no welcoming peal of church bells here as there had been in Southampton. There were no bell towers on Shetland churches and no ring of bells and, even if there had been she would not have been able to hear them; the bluster of the wind and the roar of the sea would have drowned them out.

'What are your wishes for the new year, Norrie?' she asked.

'I always wish for the same thing,' he said. 'That is to be healthy and able to work and provide for my family. What about you?'

'The same as you, but that this year will be better than the last. It's strange knowing that there's no one else home, isn't it? We could be the last two people on earth and we wouldn't know because there's no one here to tell us.'

'I think you've forgotten something,' said Norrie.

'What's that?'

'There are four children asleep in our house. I've no doubt they'd remind us we weren't alone.' Norrie turned to go. 'Are you coming in?'

'No, I'd like to stay a bit longer.'

'Not too long, then, or you'll get cold.'

Catherine wrapped her coat tightly round her and stood looking into the night. A thin crescent moon slid out from behind a cloud only to be obscured again seconds later. The wind that gusted and eddied round the roof top snatched the narrow plume of smoke from the chimney and threw it down to where she stood. The smell of it was so familiar now that she never gave it any heed, but, as it filled her nostrils she remembered the first time she smelled it. When she'd asked Robbie Jameson he had said, 'It's peat reek, smoke, to you.'

There had been so many things she'd had to learn. To remember to fetch enough water for drinking before night settled in because it would be impossible to climb the hill to the spring in the dark. Not to allow the fire to go out but to 'smoor' it at night, heaping ash over the peats to keep them smouldering till morning and to keep the store cupboard full in case of a long spell of bad weather. There were so many things to remember, so many things to do.

She thought about Joe and June and was glad that June's parents had at last decided to accept their daughter's choice of husband. Joe was such an outgoing character, who could not like him? He'd been accepted by the community, too, and was often in demand to play at dances and social evenings; his prowess on the piano was always greeted with rapturous applause. Then there was Gerda and Lars. She was tall and good looking and Catherine wondered if she hadn't been a model at some time. Lars didn't talk much and socialized even less. Looking at him the impression Catherine got was that there was a lot going on in his brain and all of it far and away beyond her. They were good neighbours and had proved to be good friends into the bargain.

Norrie no longer played at the dances. He had given it up at the same time he forsook the whisky bottle. One led to the other, he told Catherine, and both to disaster. It was a young man's game and no longer for the likes of him. She had said nothing, but knowing how much he enjoyed being part of a band and playing his fiddle, she wondered how long he would be able to stay away.

THIRTY SEVEN

THE NEW YEAR was not so new now. January was slipping fast away. The children were back at school. Catherine had sent them off that morning well wrapped up with woolly hats pulled down over their ears and scarves wound round their necks. Norrie had gone to see to the sheep on his croft at Broonieswick and Catherine was about to set off to do the rounds of her own. The day was cold and dry. She put on her boots, shrugged herself into a warm jacket and pulled on a hat. Stepping out of her front door she stood for a moment and scanned the valley floor where her Cheviot ewes were grazing. She stepped out, then, to fetch some feed to put into their troughs. They pushed along behind her as she dribbled oats from a bag. She loved the look of the Cheviots, their hard white heads, sturdy legs and feet. She stood and watched them for a while then took the empty bag back to the barn.

As she went back to the house she looked towards the sea and the sky beyond. Sunrises here were often heartbreakingly beautiful – but not this one.

Skulking below the horizon, the sun poked witches' fingers into the sky, painting it with the ominous rich red of blood. Ragged, slate-grey clouds, bruised mauve and purple and held together against their will by wispy, dark veils, writhed and twisted as if trying to escape. As she watched she saw them melt away then reform, expand, darken and become more threatening as they combined with the violence of the background. She shivered. What did it mean? The old people here had so many sayings for the signs and portents they saw in the skies, the habits of animals, the quarter from which the wind blew. There were so many that she could not remember them all. She had never been told of, or seen, a sky like this before. And then, slowly, the sun clawed its way up out of the sea, a flame-red orb that might have been dragged up from the centre of the earth. Unable to tear her eyes away Catherine watched spell-bound as slowly, very slowly, it rose higher. As it did it put a match to the sky and the sea and set them alight, set them on fire and made them burn with the colour of devouring flames.

At the end of the world the earth will be consumed by fire.

Well, it could easily be starting right now, but then, as the sun climbed higher it cooled, diminished, lost its fierceness. The red wash of the sky paled and, little by little, softened to a rosy glow. As if to apologize the sun reached up to edge the clouds with gold.

All this while, the wind that seemed to think its job was to scour the face of the earth had lain low, but now that the sun had put on its show, had bowed out and retired to the wings, it saw its chance and began to blow. Prelude to what it had in mind for later it blew gently, making no more than ripples on the surface of the water in the bay.

The morning had lost its angry appearance and Catherine, realizing how tense she had become, let her shoulders drop and her body relax. She shook herself, turned and went about her business.

As the day advanced so did the wind. First it flirted with wisps of straw, the wool on a sheep's back and anything that was light and not fastened down. By lunchtime it was playful, but by teatime it played rough and when Norrie came home for his supper, it threw him in through the door.

'I'm thinking it's going to be a rough night,' he said. 'I'll be sorry for all the … animals that are going to be out in it.' A quick glance at Catherine had shown him her worried face and he knew she would be thinking of Robbie. 'Of course,' he went on, 'no right thinking skipper will be at sea on a night like this.'

'It's all right, Norrie. I know what you're saying. Come and have your supper. Allen, run up the stairs and get Judith, will you?'

'Is she still on that keyboard?' asked Norrie. There was really no need to ask, not if he had heard the muted sounds of base notes thumping and the occasional squeak of an immature voice.

'She's never off it. I have to insist she does her homework first or it would never get done. And now she's taken to singing. She knows all the latest songs.'

'Oh well,' said Norrie, 'it gets her out of your way and gives her something to do now that Jannie's gone.'

Allen rattled down the stairs. 'She says she's just coming,' he said. 'What's for supper, Mam? I'm hungry.'

'You can't be hungry; you had some biscuits not long ago. I saw you.'

Norrie laughed. 'You should know better than that, Catherine. You know our kids are always hungry as gannets. Shall I put the radio on? It's nearly time for the news.'

The new radio that Norrie had given to Catherine for Christmas stood on the press. Norrie switched it on and began to tune it in.

'News!' scoffed Catherine. 'All it's ever about is the price of fish or mutton or the cost of —'

'Sssh!' said Norrie. 'Listen.'

… a mayday call. The boat has lost steerage and the Lerwick lifeboat has gone out. The announcer's voice held no emotion. He was in Scotland, he was reading the news and this was just another item that held no significance for him.

Catherine froze. She stood holding a spoonful of potato. '*Lerwick* lifeboat – it must be one of ours.' Dropping the spoon back into the bowl she slumped onto her chair. 'I hope Robbie's not out there. I couldn't bear it if he was.'

'You don't know that it's one of ours,' said Norrie. 'Eat your supper and stop worrying. Where's Judith?' Norrie went to the bottom of the stairs and called to his daughter. 'Get down here right away or there's no supper for you.' At the table he looked at Catherine, then reached out and covered her hand with his. 'Eat up. I'm sure there's nothing to worry about.'

'You're probably right,' said Catherine. But she ate little, talked less and when she'd cleared away the dishes and washed up, said, 'I want to go into Lerwick and find out what's going on. Will you look after the kids?'

'If you're going, so am I,' said Norrie. 'I'm not going to let you go in there on your own. I'll see if June will sit in for us.'

On their way into the town the wind buffeted the car, thumping it and banging it by turns. Sometimes a squall of rain rattled against the windscreen. Norrie cursed the weather. Catherine twisted her hands together and prayed that her son was not on the boat that was in distress. When they parked the car they made their way to the small boat harbour. A small crowd of people was already gathered there. Catherine clutched at the sleeve of a woman and shook it. 'I've got to know,' she said. 'What boat is it? Who's in trouble?'

'I believe it's the *Adventurer*.'

Norrie caught Catherine as she crumpled. 'Bear up,' he said as she clung to him. 'It may not be that bad. We don't know yet.'

The woman put her hand on Catherine's arm. 'I'm sorry,' she said. 'Is someone of yours on it?'

'My son,' said Catherine. 'He's only sixteen.'

'The time to be upset is when they don't come back, not now. Be strong and pray for their safe return.' The woman smiled and patted Catherine's hand.

Norrie held Catherine close and she calmed down. He had said it might not be that bad. But how was it for Robbie? It wouldn't be good if she was a wreck. The woman was right; she had to be strong. Lifting her head, Catherine pulled herself upright. 'Just hold on to me, Norrie,' she said. 'Just hold on.' She turned then to look for the woman she had spoken to. She wasn't there, had moved away and someone else stood in her place. Catherine reached out to her. 'Excuse me,' she said. 'Do you know what's happening?'

'About the boat, you mean? The one the lifeboat's gone out to?' The speaker was an older woman; headscarf pulled over her head and tied tightly under her chin. 'It's not good.'

'What do you mean? How do you know?' Catherine clutched at Norrie's hand and held it tight in both of hers.

'Didn't you hear the maroons?'

Catherine shook her head. 'No.'

'First one puts the lifeboat crew on standby and the second says the boat has been launched. We all pray the third one doesn't go off because that means the coastguard rescue has been called out.'

Not wanting to hear the answer Catherine hesitated for a second or two before saying, 'And did it?'

'It did.' The woman paused. 'There's nothing we can do.'

Was the woman right? How could she know what was going on out there? But she knew about the maroons. She must have waited here before. Ice filled Catherine's veins. The wind snatched her coat and slapped her legs hard, but she didn't feel it. She'd forgotten her gloves and her hands were cold. People milled around her. She stood upright and very still and with every fibre of her being she willed the boat and all hands to be brought safely ashore. A little voice in her head was saying, 'Be strong. You have to wait for as long as it takes.' She turned to Norrie. 'Perhaps you ought to go home and look after the children. I'll stay here. I shall not move till they bring my Robbie back to me.'

'You've got to be joking if you think I'd leave you at a time like this.' Norrie tried to put his arms round her. 'Catherine, my love—'

'No,' she said, pushing him away. 'I've got to be strong.'

'I'm not going home,' said Norrie. 'My place is with you. How could you think I'd leave you? The children are all right and June will understand.'

Catherine put up her hand and touched his cheek. 'It's not your child that's in danger. It's mine, so you don't have to stay.'

'You can't get rid of me like that,' said Norrie. 'You're my wife; whatever ails you ails me too. I'm staying.'

Catherine looked up into that so-familiar face, brown eyes darker than ever in the half-light of the street lamps. 'What did I ever do to deserve you?' she said.

Along with the gathering number of people, all whose attention was focused on the darkness that encompassed the sea, Catherine strained her eyes, eager for the merest glimmer of light that signalled the return of the lifeboat. Her feet and hands were numb and cold was creeping into her body.

'Will you have a cup of soup?'

'What?' Catherine looked up at a woman who carried a tray full of mugs.

'Have something to warm you. Soup. Take one.'

Catherine did. 'Thank you,' she said and held the cup between her hands. Eyes still riveted on the horizon, she sipped the hot, thick, liquid. How slowly time moved. What was happening out there? Surely the boat should be coming home now? It must be hours since they heard the announcement on the radio. Why hadn't she insisted that Robbie stay ashore? Why had she given in and let him go to sea? If she'd kept him at home she wouldn't be standing here wondering if she was going to lose him too. No, don't think like that. Robbie was going to come home. He would be here soon.

THIRTY EIGHT

TIME TICKED SLOWLY away. And still Catherine chastised herself mentally. She had known something like this would happen, hadn't she? She had had a premonition of disaster when Robbie's father said he was going lobster fishing, wouldn't be going far out to sea, and she had told herself it would be all right. But it wasn't. She had the same feeling when young Robbie told her he wanted to be a fisherman and she'd let him go when all the time she knew she shouldn't.

'Look,' cried a voice. 'Look, isn't that a light?'

'Where?' Catherine shielded her eyes with her hand and peered out to sea. A shiver ran through her. Was it the lifeboat? Could it be?

'No, it's gone.' The watchers sighed and gave a collective groan.

An air of expectancy, like an invisible thread, pulled the waiting crowd together. They, like Catherine, would wait for as long as it took and for some of them it was probably not the first time. There was low murmur of voices as some comforted and reassured others. Catherine was breathing hard and trembling. She covered her mouth with her hand and from behind it whispered, 'Oh, please, please, God, bring them home safe.'

'Look,' cried a voice. 'Is *that* a light? Is *that* the lifeboat?'

For an agonizing few minutes while the pinpoint of light danced up and down, appeared and disappeared, the crowd was silent. Gradually it became clearer and recognizable as being on a boat. Then it was coming into view, the orange hull of the Lerwick lifeboat.

A man's voice, loud and strong, shouted, 'Yes. There it is, it's the lifeboat and she's towing the *Adventurer*.'

'Oh, praise be,' said another voice. 'God willing, all are safe.'

Tears sprang to Catherine's eyes; she dashed them away with the back of her hand. The crowd surged, Catherine too, the long wait forgotten. She had let go of Norrie and was going forward to greet her son.

The watchers on the quay beside the small boat harbour had been joined by others. Men from the Seamen's Mission were there, coastguards too, and an ambulance was parked close by. Catherine had been so intent on straining her eyes to watch for the return of the lifeboat that she had been unaware of their presence. All eyes were on the boat now. The closer it came, the more distinct it was. The *Adventurer* was behind her. Out of the rougher water the lifeboat moved slowly. It crept at a snail's pace into the harbour. Men who had been waiting with coiled ropes on the deck of the fishing boat, threw them to the quayside where other men caught them and made the ship fast. With no power to control it, it was up to the men to make the boat secure. 'Somebody must be hurt,' said a voice as men from the ambulance went aboard.

There was an agonizing wait, then, before the crew disembarked. Some were draped in blankets while some walked upright and strong, but the strain of what they'd been through showed on their faces. The people who had gathered on the quay held back in respect for the trauma they had suffered, for these were men who put their lives at risk every time they went to sea.

Trembling now, clutching Norrie's hand, Catherine bit her nails as she searched the face of each crewman. There should be six. She counted four. Robbie and the skipper were not among them. The skipper would be last off, anyway, but where was Robbie? What had happened to him? Was he hurt? Was that why the ambulance men had gone aboard? A figure with an arm in a sling, a blanket round his shoulders and accompanied by one of the ambulance men was stepping onto the quay.

'Robbie, oh, Robbie,' cried Catherine as she ran to meet him.

'You're hurt.' As he turned to look at her, she saw the ashen colour of his face.

'We're taking him to the hospital,' said the man beside him. 'Likely you could call them later.'

'Yes, of course.' Catherine turned to Robbie. 'You're home – thank God for that.' She stood and watched him being led away. Suddenly, 'No, no, I can't let him go. I've got to go to the hospital. I have to speak to him.'

'No,' said Norrie, grabbing her in an attempt to stop her. 'Let him rest; you can see him tomorrow.'

But Catherine had thrown him off and was chasing after Robbie. Then she was getting into the ambulance, the doors were being closed and it was being driven away.

Norrie had gone to the hospital to fetch Robbie home, and now Catherine was fussing about him, plumping the cushions in the chair by the fire. 'Come and sit here, Robbie,' she said. 'Would you like a cup of tea? Do you want something to eat?'

'I've had me dinner, Mam.'

The twins crowded round him. 'What was it like, Robbie?' asked Allen. 'Was the sea horrible and rough?'

Judith tapped the plaster on Robbie's arm. 'How did you break this?' she asked.

'I got thrown across the galley,' said Robbie. 'The boat was out of control. We were side on to the waves and there was nothing anyone could do.'

Catherine was aghast. She held her face in her hands. 'Weren't you terrified?' she said.

'Not at first, we all thought we'd get going again, but when Mr Sandison had to radio for help I didn't feel so good. I was afraid we were going to get driven onto the rocks. We were that close by the time the lifeboat reached us.'

'Thank God you weren't,' said Norrie. 'Now kids, off you go and let your mother have time with Robbie. You can have him to yourselves later.'

'Will you come and see our farm?' said Peter.

'I can play something for you,' said Judith. 'I can sing, too. I'm a singer.'

'I know you can play,' said Robbie. 'You drove us nuts with it at Christmas, don't you remember?'

'Ah, but I can play better now. And Joe says I've got a good voice. I'm going to be a popstar.' Judith was edging away towards the stairs.

'And is that how you're going to make the money to buy that posh car you said you were going to have?'

'That would be right,' said Judith. 'I'm going to be famous. Come on.'

'Away you go,' said Robbie. 'I'll be up in a minute or two.'

Norrie was shaking his head. 'What a madam that one is. I hope it doesn't get her into trouble.' He laughed. 'She's as stubborn as her mother.'

'I'm not stubborn,' said Catherine. 'If you want something you've got to go for it. It won't just drop in your lap.' She shrugged her shoulders. 'Go away with you, Norrie.' She turned to her son. 'Now, tell me truly what it was like. Has it made you think twice about going to sea again or will you still want to go back to it?'

'I don't know, Mam. No good denying it, I was afraid. And I thought about you, all of you. But the fishing is good. Mr Sandison says it's better than he's ever known. There's money to be made. It would be silly to leave.'

'Oh, darling.' Catherine reached out and took Robbie's free hand in hers. 'I shouldn't have asked. Forget it. We'll talk about it again when you're ready.'

'Robbie.' Judith called down the stairs. 'Robbie, hurry up.'

'You'll have to go or she'll give you no peace,' said Catherine when Robbie made no move to get up.

'She can wait a minute,' he said. 'I just have to say that I'm sorry for causing you all this worry.'

'The trouble with the boat wasn't your fault. I admit I was

worried, but you're here; let's be thankful for that. Now go, or she'll be down here to get you.'

Norrie had been in the kitchen making tea and, when Robbie had climbed the stairs to listen to Judith, he handed a cup to Catherine. 'All's well that ends well, don't you think?' he said.

'I don't know,' said Catherine. 'It's not too bad this time, but what if it happens again? He might not be so lucky. I begin to understand what those women must have gone through when their men went to sea in open boats. They didn't have any lifeboats then.'

'I'd be willing to bet that Robbie will think twice before he goes back,' said Norrie.

'Do you really think so?'

'I'm not saying he won't want to be involved in some way, but not fishing.'

'If he does want to go back, I'm not going to stop him,' said Catherine. 'It has to be his decision.' From upstairs came the steady beat of the base rhythm of a pop song and the clear voice of Judith. Catherine inclined her head to listen. 'I wonder what he thinks of that?' she said.

'No doubt he'll tell us,' said Norrie.

'I wonder what the other two are going to get up to,' said Catherine. 'Do you think they'll give us any worries?'

'More than likely.' He leaned forward, put his hand on Catherine's shoulder and pulled her forward to kiss her. At that moment Judith came into the room. She was on her way to see Inga and relate the drama of Robbie's rescue.

'What are you doing, Mam?' she said, curling her lip as she did. 'Ugh.' Then she was out of the door and gone.

There was a twinkle in Norrie's eye when he said, 'She's ten years old and it won't be long before she's a teenager. What's she going to be like then?'

Catherine laughed. 'It'll be boys and make-up and raging hormones and she'll treat us as though we came out of the Ark.'

'And then it'll be the boys' turn.'

'Oh my,' said Catherine, throwing up her hands. 'Pimples and spots and voices that come from their boots or off the top of their heads.'

There was a big grin on Norrie's face. 'Are you ready for that?'

'Bring it on,' said Catherine and clung to Norrie as they laughed.

Though Catherine prayed that Robbie wouldn't go back to sea after that dreadful night, he had surprised her at how keen he was to get back on board. Ever since then she refused to listen to the news, didn't want to know if he was at sea when a gale was blowing and the sea murderous. There was nothing she could do and she would be told soon enough if the boat was in trouble again.

The years slipped quietly by and gradually Catherine's burden of guilt at what she had done grew lighter and life once again resumed its predictable pattern. Norrie kept his promise to leave the whisky alone and, apart from a dram or two at Christmas, didn't touch it. The children were fast becoming adults. It was 1968 and Robbie had celebrated his twenty-first birthday. Judith, at fifteen, was much in demand as a singer at concerts and socials. She still played her keyboard, but her singing voice had improved so much that it had taken precedence. The twins were totally involved with croft work and it pleased Catherine to know that they were keen to follow on where she would one day leave off.

June and Joe still lived in Catherine's old house, though Joe still wanted his own house and croft. He spent much of his free time with Norrie to the point that Norrie would shake his head and say, 'I don't think I can stand it much longer; he never stops asking questions. I might do something rash one day and sell him the Broonieswick croft just to get him out of my hair.' And Catherine would reply, 'Perhaps that's not such a bad idea.'

Lars and Gerda bought a house in Lerwick where Lars had been offered permanent employment; he had previously been on a fixed, temporary contract. The valley was changing and would continue to do so, for nothing stays the same.

*

'Something smells nice. What are you cooking, Mam?' asked Robbie, who was home for the day.

'Just mince and tatties, nothing exciting,' said Catherine.

'Nobody makes mince and tatties like you do,' Robbie smiled. 'Where's Norrie?'

'Goodness knows. How are things with you? Are you still happy on the boat?'

'Yes. I like being on deck; there's a lot to see out there. It's not just water and not only fishing boats, either.'

'Why? What else is there besides them and the ferries?' Catherine laughed. 'You haven't been seeing mermaids, have you?'

'No, Mam. This is serious. Some of the boats are survey vessels. Not only that; there are drilling platforms as well. They're already drilling for oil.'

'What?' Catherine stopped stirring the mince and, wooden spoon in hand, turned to look at Robbie. 'But there's been nothing about it in the papers.'

'Likely they want to keep it a secret. But wait till they strike oil, then it'll be on TV, radio and all over the papers.'

'What's that?' said Norrie as, on stocking-clad feet – he had taken his boots off by the door – he joined them.

'Robbie was telling me that they've started drilling for oil,' said Catherine. 'There are rigs out there already.'

'It had to come, didn't it? Is the kettle on?'

Mince and tatties left on a low heat, Catherine, Norrie and Robbie sat down to drink tea.

'I can't believe what's happening. What's it going to do to us?' said Catherine. 'How is it going to affect Shetland? I don't know if I like it.'

'It'll make a lot of work. There'll be jobs and good money for everybody and there won't be enough people in Shetland to do it,' said Norrie. 'They'll have to bring in folk from outside.'

'The harbour's awful busy,' said Robbie. 'I've never seen so many boats there. And my mate John Burgess, down the south end, says the airport's buzzin' and there's talk of a new terminal being built.'

'You know what's going to happen, don't you?' said Catherine. 'All those clever clogs, the business men in sharp suits, will be coming here. Shetland folk will have to wake up or they'll get seen off right and left.'

Norrie laughed. 'Don't be so sure about that,' he said. 'We've got enough folk here with their heads screwed on the right way.'

'Perhaps you have, but the Shetlanders I know seem to be too trusting. I wouldn't like to see them taken for a ride.'

'Don't worry, they won't. In fact the shoe might be on the other foot. '

'I've heard tell they're going to develop Broonie's Taing,' said Robbie. 'Somebody said they thought it was for servicing supply vessels.'

'Well, that won't work,' said Norrie. 'Hasn't anyone told them what the tides are like? And anyway, I doubt if the water's deep enough.'

Catherine gave a sardonic little laugh. 'You know very well that the so-called experts never take any notice of local knowledge and experience.'

For a while no one spoke. Catherine gazed out of the window. 'Well,' she said, 'sitting here thinking about it isn't going to change anything or stop what might happen. How about you go and find the boys, Robbie, and I'll dish up.'

'They'll be paying good money,' said Norrie when Robbie had gone. 'There are going to be spin-offs. It's like Magnie said, the oil will have to come ashore, which means they'll have to build a place for it. But that'll be a major job and it won't be done in five minutes.'

As she dished up their food Catherine banged a spoonful of potato down on a plate. 'I don't want to talk about it. You know what it'll be; the rich will get richer and the ordinary people will get walked over. It happens every time.'

'No, it'll be the making of the place,' said Norrie.